THE
TRANSLATOR

THE
TRANSLATOR

NINA SCHUYLER

PEGASUS BOOKS
NEW YORK LONDON

THE TRANSLATOR

Pegasus Books LLC
80 Broad Street, 5th Floor
New York, NY 10004

Copyright © 2013 by Nina Schuyler

First Pegasus Books edition July 2013

Interior design by Maria Fernandez

Library of Congress Cataloging-in-Publication Data is available.

ISBN: 978-1-60598-470-4

10 9 8 7 6 5 4 3 2 1

Printed in the United States of America
Distributed by W. W. Norton & Company

For Peter, Fynn and Yohann.

THE
TRANSLATOR

Chapter One

STANDING IN THE KITCHEN MUNCHING *on pickled cucumbers, watching a stray dog pee in his yard, Jiro hears something crash into the garage door. The entire house trembles as if it is about to fall off its foundation.*

He runs down the hall and yanks open the door. The electric garage door is broken, boards desperately clinging to the frame. Fragments of glass shimmer on the cement carport. The black Honda's engine is still sputtering, spilling gassy blue smoke from the exhaust pipe. And there is his wife, sitting rigidly in the driver's seat at a forward tilt, staring straight ahead as if she's pondering whether to plow into the wall.

He rushes over to the car window and pounds on it. "Are you all right? What happened? Can you move? Open the window!"

Aiko doesn't turn her head. Her white-knuckled hands grip the wheel. He looks at her fingernails, which he's seen hundreds of times, but still he's startled that they are so severely bitten, exposing raw pink skin. There is a moment of eerie silence, as if one world has shattered and another has yet to rise up in its place. Jiro can't think what to do. Pull her out of the car? Call an ambulance? Her doctor? Her self-inflicted paralysis leaches into him and turns him into stone.

Last night in bed she told him again that her heart was punctured and her life was slowly dripping out of her. "What do you want me to do?" he said, not bothering to hide his frustration. Hasn't she been talking like this for a year now? "Tell me and I'll do it. I'll do it right now." Even he could hear the anger and helplessness in his voice.

As if coming out of a fog, Jiro realizes the door is unlocked. He opens it, turns off the engine, pockets the keys. She doesn't appear to be physically harmed; and that's the problem, he thinks. The harm is tucked deep inside. She's seen dozens of doctors who've given so many different diagnoses, yet her hurt remains nameless.

Hanne sets down Kobayashi's novel. The book did well in Japan, in part because Kobayashi revealed in an interview that his main character, Jiro, was inspired by the famous Noh actor, Moto Okuro. So intrigued, so fascinated was he by this remarkable man that Kobayashi began the book right after he met Okuro. "Moto cured five years of writer's block," Kobayashi told the magazine. "If he reads my book—and what an honor if he did—I hope he sees it as an homage to him."

The name Moto Okuro meant nothing to Hanne, and she doesn't know much about the ancient Japanese theater art of Noh, except that masks are used for different characters, and the characters speak in a stilted, almost unintelligible language. There's music to contend with, and, almost like a Greek play, a chorus.

Unfocused anger Jiro may have, but not in the American way of yelling or stomping around the house, spewing vitriolics. Jiro means second son. Kobayashi would have done much better if he'd named him Isamu, which means courage. Jiro is a man of courage and enduring restraint who has been patient and loving and thoughtful and kind throughout this ordeal. Yes, ordeal. His wife begins to fade away for an inexplicable reason, and Jiro is left to salvage what he can of the marriage, of her. His anger would be quiet. Nearly invisible, but no less real.

Ittai nani o shite hoshii-n dai? What do you want me to do? Kobayashi dropped the verb, *desu*, which, if he used it, would have suggested a polite tone. Jiro is frustrated, at wit's end.

Last night, Hanne dreamed Jiro whispered this same question to her, though his tone was not one of frustration, but seduction. For months now, she's been dreaming about Jiro, erotic dreams, dreams of kisses stolen behind doors, of bare feet rubbed beneath tables, of tangled bedsheets and limbs. She can even conjure up his smell, or what she thinks it would be. Underneath his deodorant a slightly earthy smell, which she likes. That she's fallen a little bit in love with him is no surprise. She's spent months and months with him and when she wakes can't wait for their daily sessions.

Another fragment from last night's dream floats up to the surface of her mind. Jiro's voice wasn't just a sound nestled near her ear. It was all around her, as if his voice had become warm water and she was immersed in it. She also remembers water sloshing. And a porcelain bathtub. Steam. A man—Jiro?—was washing her feet, gently soaping each toe. Or was it David? No, she distinctly remembers the man speaking Japanese. And it wasn't Hiro; she'd recognize her deceased husband's voice. Besides, the dreams of Hiro always involve her taking care of him. In the beginning, Jiro's hands made her skin tingle, her body melt. But the longer

She'd have to read Kobayashi's *Trojan Horse Trips* herself first, on her own terms, she told the publisher. Only if she understood the main character would she be able to successfully translate the book into English. At her enormous blackboard, custom-made to take up one entire wall, she begins to write a sentence in Japanese.

Iradachi, the Japanese word for frustration. Of course you are frustrated, Jiro, thinks Hanne. You've brought your wife from one doctor to another, and more than a year later there is no sign of improvement, no answers. You are in the same place you were three, five months ago. And what has become of your life? Turned into something unrecognizable, you no longer know who you are.

She then writes *Yariba no nai ikidoori,* meaning an unfocused anger. But also *yaru se nai kimochi,* a helpless feeling, or a feeling of no way to clear one's mind. A neat column of chalk characters fills the far side of the board.

She pauses, baffled. How can Jiro be experiencing an unfocused anger and a helpless feeling? And just a moment ago he was frustrated. It doesn't make sense.

Whatever Kobayashi meant, she's on her own here. Over the eleven months she's been working on his novel, Kobayashi has responded to only a few of her e-mails and always with a curt— "Too busy." "Figure it out." "On another project." Though, after the publisher sent him the first three translated chapters, he found ample time to quibble that she had cut his crucial repetitive words and phrases. But what does he know about translating Japanese, which prefers to keep someone guessing with its verb at the end of a sentence, into English, with its own linguistic quirks? Between the two languages, there are far too many nuances to name. After that charged exchange, based on Hanne's counsel, the publisher decided to hold off sending him anything until the entire manuscript was done.

3

thirty-three-year-old lawyer, he lives in New York City with his wife and two beautiful daughters.

"How is everyone?" says Hanne.

"Everyone's fine," he says, "just fine."

She hears a remoteness in his voice. Everything is not fine, but, for whatever reason, he's not prepared to talk about it yet. It's her job to fill in the empty space until he's ready. She tells him about the novel she's translating from an up-and-coming Japanese author who is about to make his grand entrance into the American publishing world. She is, of course, assuring his entrance is grand. Working day and night, she loves it in the odd way when something consumes you. As she talks, Hanne wonders if the trouble is Anne. Seven years of marriage, that's usually when a couple hits rough waters, when she and Hiro began to drift. She asks about her granddaughters, Sasha and Irene.

Sasha, the seven-year-old, reminds Hanne of her daughter when she was that age, with her raven hair, her slanted Japanese eyes, her nostrils shaped like teardrops. It's been six years since she's seen or heard from her daughter, Brigitte. Where is she now? Married? A young mother? Living in a city? The country? A veterinarian? A businesswoman? It's mind-boggling how little she knows about her daughter.

Hanne imagines Tomas's serious face, his lips tightening into two thin wires, brooding over the best way to phrase what he wants to tell her. He was always a careful, orderly boy, all his toys in separate cardboard boxes, which he neatly labeled, "cars," "trains," and a Christmas file begun in January where he stored his desires. Now Tomas is considered a success. If Hiro could see his son now. Tomas, who, as she understands it, can argue his way out of anything. Their son is tall; his height is his main inheritance from Hanne's German-Dutch side of the family; most everything else comes from his Japanese father.

"Anne wants to take the kids to the Monterey aquarium," says Tomas. "Maybe we'll fly out and meet you there." That seems to get him going, because now he tells her that work is going well. "Hey! I even got to use my Japanese last week," he says. The law firm had a group of Japanese businessmen in the office. "I was pretty bad, but they were impressed."

"I'll bet." Growing up, Hanne had exposed Tomas and Brigitte to five languages, emphasizing Japanese, since that was their father's first language. Tomas battled each and every one of them, as if they were awful, bitter medicine. But Brigitte, she gobbled them up like little candies.

Among a big box of toys for Christmas for her granddaughters, Hanne slipped in a children's book, *The Tower of Babel*. A blatant attempt to expand their puddle of a world not through religion, but language. Anne has explained more than once that they just don't see the need to raise polyglots. There are so many things to learn about the world, and English, after all, is the lingua franca in the global economy. Before she quit her job to become a full-time mother, Anne had been a biologist, doing significant research on cell division or some such thing. Hanne suspects Anne views language as a silly endeavor—subjective fluff that could never carry the same cachet as the firm objectivity of science.

Tomas is talking about his new case that revolves around the word "reasonableness." Did the plaintiffs act reasonably?

Hanne steps into the living room. One entire wall is made of glass overlooking the city. The daylight is at such an angle that she sees her reflection in the big window. Each year she seems to become heir to more of the countenance of her German mother— her dark blond hair and pale, pale skin, her big green eyes that hold an intensity not found in photos of Hanne's younger self. A paring down to an essence that she wishes she could stop. All these years, and she can still conjure her mother's commanding voice—"*Halt die Ohren steif!*" Keep your ears stiff! Her father, a translator for the Italian and Dutch governments, had been transferred again, so she can't remember where this memory comes from because every year, a new country, a new house, new school, new students, most of the girls cocooned in their girl worlds and the entry door firmly shut. Hanne had come home from school in tears. Everyone hated her. The girls made fun of her blue socks. "There will be no complaining in this household," said her mother. "That is not the way of this family. We bear our burdens quietly." And Hanne knew what her mother was going to say next, how hardship was living in rubble in war-torn Berlin. Buildings reduced to charred skeletons and the stink of death everywhere, drunk Russian soldiers careening down the streets, stealing, destroying, raping. For two months until the Allies arrived, Hanne's mother and her Oma hid in the basement of an apartment to escape the Soviet soldiers. "We ate rats, so this hardship you speak of is nothing. A speck of dust."

Then in a quieter conspiratorial tone, "You're a creature out of the ordinary, my dear," said her mother. "More evolved than most, and, I'm afraid, little understood because of it." She told Hanne that with each new language, Hanne became, quite magically, larger and grander than before. And now with seven languages, her mother smiled brightly, "you've become grandest of all. How can any of those silly girls understand you?"

Now Hanne says to her son, "Interesting. What is reasonable behavior?" She stifles a yawn. Her eyelids are heavy, dry. She is exhausted from her self-imposed work schedule. But once she begins work today, she knows she'll tap into energy she didn't even realize she had and will probably work until midnight again, unless she calls David. After spending so many hours in her mind, David reminds her she has a body. A fifty-three-year old body, she tells him, a body that still has hot flashes, though she no longer has to carry a kerchief to mop her face. A kind man, he always corrects her—a beautiful body, a desirable body, a body he wants to make love to. She runs her hand along her gray V-neck sweater and tucks a loose strand of hair back into her chignon.

Tomas is still talking about his case, and now he's resorted to legal jargon and case citations. A cloud covers the weak sun, darkening the room. Across the street on the front porch of an old Victorian stands a tall, wiry man in a fire-engine-red coat and black pants. His hair is a mop of wild black curls, he's too flamboyantly dressed to belong in this neighborhood. He's holding a dozen or so brightly colored flowers and dropping them one by one—peonies? Mums?—deliberately, precisely onto the sidewalk below. Hanne imagines him standing on a bridge, tossing the flowers into a river below. Is he celebrating something? Commemorating a death?

Tomas sighs, probably realizing his mother's mind is somewhere else, and abruptly shifts gears. "I got some news about Brigitte."

"Oh?" She tries to sound nonchalant.

"I got a call she was taken to a hospital. That's all I know. Could be nothing. Could be something."

The image of a feverish Brigitte comes to mind. Bright red cheeks, so lethargic, her lips chapped and cracking. She must have been six, maybe seven, and for days and days she was burning up with fever. Hanne set everything aside, stretched out beside Brigitte on the couch, and read to her or watched movies. Time sloughed away like an unnecessary skin, as Hanne tended to her, putting the cup of ice water to her lips, offering her saltines, scratching her back to lull her to fitful sleep.

Tomas wakes her from her reverie. "When I know more, I'll call you." He pauses, then adds "If she allows it."

"If she allows it," repeats Hanne, her voice heavy with cynicism.

He sighs again. "You know how it goes. I figured I could tell you this because someone else called me, not her."

Brigitte continues to have sporadic contact with Tomas, as long as he doesn't reveal their conversations to Hanne. Tomas says he has to go. He'll discuss taking the trip to Monterey with Anne and be in touch.

After Hanne hangs up, she stares at the lone tree across the street, waving its spindly branches in the air as if trying to grab hold of something. So thin, so fragile, it looks at any moment like it might topple over. She steps into the kitchen, makes coffee, and eats half a piece of toast to try and settle her stomach. The best thing to do is to lose herself in something demanding. Something hard. Something that requires all of her.

She heads to her office, turns on Chopin's Preludes Opus 28, and sits at her desk. Her mother's desk, the only piece of furniture Hanne kept. Though why she did is baffling because when she looks at it, she sees her mother's long, straight back. Her mother always sat facing a window. In Switzerland, a window that looked out at the garden of flowers. In Turkey, a window that looked out at a fig tree; in Norway, one overlooking the icy ocean; in Cairo, a farmer's market. Always another place, another window. A litany of windows. Hanne sees herself standing in the doorway, staring at her mother's rigid back, imagining the bumps of her vertebrae perfectly aligned, like a message written in Braille that she'd never understand, no matter how hard she tried.

Always her father was away at work or traveling, and then, when Hanne was ten, he was gone for good. So it would be her mother she'd tell, though she can't remember what she was waiting to say. Whatever it was, it would never be uttered because her mother whipped around, her perpetual look of disappointment fully displayed: "Don't interrupt me!"

What was the Muse whispering to her that was so important? Not great works of literature, or even mediocre ones. Would that have made it easier? She was poring over corporate documents. French, Swiss, German, anyone who would pay, her mother orchestrating the grand movement of goods, translating French to German, German to English, her Muse murmuring the languages of commerce, of moneymaking. At some point, her mother installed a lock for the door because, she said, "I need utter and complete silence, without even the itch of a thought that I could be disturbed." The entire house enshrouded in silence, Hanne waiting for the Muse of commerce to shut up.

There is no more waiting for her mother, who died twenty years ago and has taken her place alongside her parents in a cemetery in Kiel. Just as her father, who remains a shadowy presence in her memory, had assumed his place with his family members in a cemetery in Delft years before. Where Hanne will end up is easily solved; she'll not lie beside either one of them, but be cremated. But death isn't looming—she has too many obligations—what is looming is her deadline.

She re-opens Kobayashi's novel.

The next day, Jiro wakes. The house feels bigger, relieved of heaviness and gloom. There is no need to reach over and touch his fingers to her neck to find a pulse. No need to run downstairs to see if she's plunged a knife into her heart. Or overdosed on pills or stepped outside and thrown herself in front of a car. He read somewhere that each culture has its preferred way of committing suicide. His wife, however, considered all ways. But now he can luxuriate in a pool of calmness and ease his way into the day.

Sunlight streams in through the bedroom window and he becomes aware of vast acreage in his mind that is wonderfully uninhabited. Where just yesterday it was populated by worry, anxiety, and vigilance, there is now a small country of nothingness. He wasn't even conscious of how much of his mind was devoted to, no, obsessed with her well-being. He feels a funny little smile on his face. He is, finally, a free man.

Then Kobayashi writes, *Heya ga uzuiteiru.* The room is throbbing.

Throbbing with what? *Uzuku* is normally used for something negative—throbbing wounds or aching. But how can that be? He is not physically injured, he suffers no bodily pain. Figuratively, too, he suffers no aches or pains. In fact, Jiro has just regained a huge swath of his mind. A free man is what he just called himself. He is rid of shame and guilt, as much as a human can be. After many months, he's done everything possible to save his wife, and with that comes the knowledge that he can do nothing more. What you've done is brave and admirable, she murmurs to Jiro. So you can't be throbbing with pain, either physically or emotionally, can you? And the next sentence supports that: *He picks up his violin and begins to play.*

Hanne can't remember the last time he played his violin of his own free will. In the past year, he's been so depleted that he barely makes it to symphony rehearsals. So this playing of the violin must signal the re-entrance of joy into Jiro's life. Or is he playing a lament to finally shutting the door on Aiko?

She translates the line: *The room seems to throb.* But she makes a note to come back to this section because she's not entirely satisfied with how it reads.

After he finishes playing, he eats a quick breakfast and heads to his car. He'll be early to rehearsal. When was the last time that happened? Perhaps Fumio will be there and they can practice together. Or Chikako, the flutist. Chikako, tall and lanky, with the sexy mole at the corner of her upper lip.

Chopin's lyrical precision winds its way into Hanne's consciousness. For a moment she closes her eyes and listens. How can anything be so beautiful? This, she reminds herself, is what her translation should rise to. It must sing the human condition.

She works steadily, carefully. Translation is an art, she's said countless times, requiring all the skill of a writer and then some, because the story, written in one language, one as different as Japanese, must be made as meaningful in another language. It is no small undertaking: each human language maps the world differently. Each language fosters a different way of thinking. She's always told herself that in between her paid translation projects, she'll begin work on something of her own. In the past few years, she's toyed with the idea of writing something about the ninth-century Japanese poet Ono no Komachi. At first she had thought she'd translate Komachi's poems from Japanese to English, but too many people already have come before her: all her poems have been unearthed and translated. She is, in fact, relieved. What she really wants to write is a play. She is enamored not only of the written but also the spoken word, and a play, her play, will allow her to work in both forms. Besides, the spoken word affects her differently than the written. Days after seeing a play, lines from the performance still bounce around in her head. It's as if her brain recorded the play and watches it again and again.

Indeed Chikako is there. They talk. Jiro tells her what happened, and she displays the requisite amount of sympathy, assuring him he did the right thing. For years she watched her mother care for her grandmother and by the end of her life, her mother was bone tired. The prolonging of one life drastically depleted the other. Symphony rehearsal goes extremely well and Jiro is congratulated by his fellow violinists for mastering so quickly a difficult section.

Then Kobayashi writes: *Jiro wa isoide uchi e kaeri, toko ni tsuku.* He hurries home and goes to bed. He is not fleeing or running away from anything. Jiro is not shirking responsibilities. He is weary from an eventful day. She translates it: *He heads home and goes to bed.*

But then she stumbles: *He weeps uncontrollably.*

Hanne looks up as if a stranger has just entered the room. Even in the darkest moments of caring for his wife, as her condition deteriorated, Jiro displayed the fine qualities of composure and restraint. It's out of character. And it isn't at all believable. After a long string of dismal months, he finally and most deservedly had an extraordinary day. Why cry now?

For a solid year, ever since Aiko confined herself to the darkened house, limiting herself to the bed or the overstuffed armchair, occasionally shuffling through the house, he has shopped for groceries, picked up the dry-cleaning, cleaned, and, when he could, left the symphony early to cook dinner, though she rarely ate more than a couple of bites. Thank god they didn't have children, thinks Hanne, or he'd have had to assume the child-rearing as well. Upon the advice of one of her doctors, who said she suffered from a weak kidney, Jiro spent money he didn't have on a vacation to Hawaii, hoping a change of scenery might help. Her trip in the car was the result of three weeks of coaxing by her newest doctor—let her drive and perhaps she will gain her konjo, or willpower.

She translates: *He weeps uncontrollably, feeling a serenity he didn't know he was missing.*

For several minutes she stares at what she's written. Does it feel right? *Is* it right? So much of this is intuition and insight gained through living a life. There is the life of words and there is the life of the translator—her life. She paces her study, running the sentence through her mind again. It is right. He's earned his freedom and this peace. He no longer has to be in such tight control. The catharsis of weeping is part of his new freedom. She moves to the next section. *Jiro calls Aiko's doctor to find out how she's doing. The doctor says not to worry, she's in good hands. They even have her eating three meals a day. In a week, she'll look so much better. After the call, Jiro plays a piece by Antonio Bazzini, one of his favorite composers. He plays it over and over until he is infused with delight. When he's done, he feels like celebrating. He calls Chikako and asks her out to dinner.*

Hanne translates a chapter at the restaurant, where Jiro has a wonderful time. They make plans to see each other again. On Friday night, he goes to Fumio's party, knowing she'll be there. He spots Chikako across the room and feels his hand move as if it might find its way across the expanse and explore her spine. She is talking to a man who has a sly smile and startlingly shiny shoes. Occasionally she glances over at Jiro, as if to measure the lust in his eyes. His eyes fix on her, the body that is unknown to him but feels so necessary.

Then Hanne comes to a long section that occurs nearly a year later. There are scenes of weeping, staring at random objects, talk of a lost, lonely soul wandering the earth alone. Kobayashi didn't use a subject or personal pronouns. That's not unusual in Japanese, but it doesn't help her. And the verbs don't lend much direction either—standard form and sometimes informal in present tense. It could be anyone, anyone but Jiro. Because in the next chapter he and Chikako are a steady couple. He can't stop thinking about Chikako's heart-shaped face, her easy smile, how quick she is to laugh.

Maybe Kobayashi has moved into Aiko's point of view. There is the image of a sterile stretch of corridor. That has to be a hospital,

decides Hanne. But does that make sense? The doctor has repeat-
edly assured Jiro that Aiko is doing better. But is she? Who can
this mystery narrator be? And who is muttering "Don't go," like
a mindless mantra? Maybe Jiro's music. Maybe Kobayashi took a
risk and personified it, let it roam from hospital room to hospital
room like a ghost.

Hanne had noticed this problem when she read the novel the
first time, but she thought Kobayashi would be available to clarify.
Kobayashi's last missive was months ago: "I'm not the translator,
you are!" written in Japanese. What should she do? She just can't
see Jiro carrying on like this. It's too emotional. Too melodramatic.
She looks out her study window at the brick siding of the building
next door. A small alley separates the two apartment buildings,
and during the day only a bit of light funnels through. She puts
this dreary section in Aiko's point of view.

She keeps working, writing words on the board, erasing them,
rearranging them. When she glances at the clock, she sees it's
nearly midnight. She has forgotten to call David. Will he forgive
her? Tomorrow, she'll do it tomorrow. Besides, working until she
is exhausted is one of the few ways she manages her insomnia. She
has her faults, but discipline is not one of them.

She realizes her stomach is still upset. She heads down the
hallway and stops in the living room. Her big window offers her
a sweeping view of the Golden Gate Bridge. For a moment, the
dense winter fog has cleared. The black swath of sky provides the
perfect backdrop for the red-orange of the bridge. She stands at
the window, watching the red taillights of the cars as they speed
across to the other side. It's been years since she's hiked the head-
lands. Not that she's yearning to go. She has plenty to do here,
and besides, she's hiked those trails enough times. She already
knows what's over there.

Chapter Two

AT THE UNIVERSITY, HANNE FINDS David in his office grading papers.

"There you are. I've been impatiently waiting for you to reemerge," he says, smiling.

She kisses him on the cheek.

They head to Café Grandissimo, their usual spot across from Colbert University. He's finished teaching for the day, and she doesn't have to be in the classroom until Friday. The last chapters of the translation have been sent to the publisher, who'll send the manuscript to Kobayashi, who lives in Tokyo. The translation required a Herculean effort sustained over twelve months to transform the novel into something worth publishing. Before seeking out David, she called Tomas and left a message that she finally had sent off the beast. Good riddance. She hoped to never see the likes of Kobayashi again. She was being ironic, of course. She loved every minute of it. After months of being steeped in it, she can't get Jiro out of her mind. She keeps thinking she's going to run into him on the street, at a restaurant, anywhere.

In the coffee shop, a couple of students wave at David. He teaches composition and Classical Greek; she, Japanese. He loves it and the students reciprocate, showering him each semester with outstanding evaluations. She, on the other hand, is lukewarm. Most of her students sign up for Japanese because of their interest in manga and anime, and they couldn't care less about learning the standard form of Japanese. Though she started out enthusiastic, Hanne now sees the job as just another source of income because her first love, translation, is hardly lucrative.

David sits beside her and holds her hand. Ever since his divorce two years ago, they've had a casual relationship. It's an arrangement that suits them both, since David has three children, two of whom are in middle school, and he's stretched in all directions.

"So is the world ready for Hanne Schubert?" he says, smiling.

She's explained that Kobayashi is positioned by the publisher as the new Japanese writer with worldwide appeal. And the publication in English of *Trojan Horse Trips* is his big debut. In the world of translation, this is Hanne's big break. It will, most likely, lead to accolades and a slew of work, so much that she'll have to turn projects down. After twenty-five years of translating, with the publication of Kobayashi's book she finally will reach the lofty heights of her profession. To say she's been waiting for this for a long time is an understatement. While staring at the menu, she turns the fantasy over again in her mind.

The waitress brings them two coffees. The shop is efficient and Hanne approves, though she wishes it was farther from school, away from the students who keep interrupting, saying hello to

David and fawning all over him, and tossing only a cursory nod to her, as if she's someone who must be recognized solely because of her proximity to him.

"I've something for you." He reaches into his pocket and pulls out a small box. A gift to mark this moment, he says. "Few people become recognized masters of their field."

A turquoise bracelet that, when she tries it on, hangs too loosely around her wrist. "It's lovely."

"I can have it properly fitted."

"No. It's perfect," she says. "I love it."

She's always amazed when someone gives her a gift. She never expects it, and so the present, whatever it is, gives off a glow. And the gift-giver? She immediately assigns him the attribute of generosity. She's always been attracted to David, his extensive vocabulary, which he uses to make the ordinary shimmer. Having grown up in London, David is proof that the English educational system is superior to the American, at least when it comes to language. It also helps that he has a handsome face, with dark liquid eyes and long lashes, and chestnut hair cut short. There's something tidy and clean about him, an attention to detail that she finds necessary as one ages.

"So, what will you do with your newly earned freedom?" he says.

She tells him she's been invited to Japan to speak at a conference about language and translation. She turned it down, though, because she doesn't really enjoy traveling anymore. And before she's buried under a mountain of new translation projects, she wants to try her hand at writing. For years she's wanted to write about Ono no Komachi, the premier poet of her time. "Maybe a play. I'm interested in her early days in the court when she was wooed by every man."

"Sounds like the perfect time."

She smiles. "With all this free time, how about we go away? This weekend?"

"I wish I could." There's the older boy's baseball practice and the younger one's soccer, and a spaghetti fundraiser. On and on. "Why don't we steal an hour away," he says, "right now."

This is another reason she appreciates him. She's not by nature an impulsive woman, but sometimes he manages to coax it out in her. For these occasions she gets to believe that there may be more to her than what she already knows, that her life isn't going to be a humdrum steady beat of what's come before. And for that, she is grateful.

By now they know to head to her apartment, not his. Though he's a fastidious dresser, he has no standards when it comes to housekeeping. When she's there, she can't resist washing the stack of dirty dishes in the sink, wiping down the counters, picking up clothes, and anything else she can find until he grabs her and tells her to stop, my dear, please stop.

In her apartment, he stands in her living room. "I love it up here. It's like you're on top of the world. Not bombarded by images and sounds and people. Only the grandeur of that stunning bridge."

She bought it twelve years ago, after her husband moved out of their two-story house and down to Stanford. For convenience, they told each other, but Hanne worried it was more than that. It's a big apartment, three bedrooms, two bathrooms, a study, with plenty of space for her and Brigitte, who was thirteen at the time, and for Tomas when he visited from college.

She offers him a glass of white wine.

He opens his eyes wide in mock surprise. "In the afternoon, my love?"

21

She leads the way into the bedroom. A man slightly older than her, he knows how to make love to a woman; a man who is receptive and who also initiates, a man who knows what she wants. And if he doesn't, if for some reason Hanne feels more blunt and fiery, as she does this afternoon, they have enough history that she can tell him.

"You have confined yourself for too long," he says, stroking her bare thigh and kissing her all over again. "And I'm the lucky beneficiary."

She smiles. He wasn't the sole beneficiary. In her imagination, she made love to Jiro. She didn't intentionally invite him into the bedroom, but if he insisted on a second time, she wouldn't say no. Of course she knows he's a character in a book. Still she marvels at how real he's become for her. Her loyal companion.

"Can you stay for an early supper?" she says.

The usual sigh. The oldest must be picked up from school and then driven to ballet. The youngest needs help with a project for school. "Another time?"

"Yes."

He's a good father, attentive, present in their lives. She'd like to see more of him, but she won't put any demands on him. Not if it takes away from being a father to his children.

In her study, she begins to clean. Into the recycling go her tall towers of paper—the first draft of the translation of Kobayashi's novel, handwritten on lined paper. The second draft, done on the computer. The third, done to smooth out the transitions and choppy sentences that clunk. The fourth, to fiddle some more with the difficult passages. The tall towers of paper, like a city unto itself, are gone, as if a tornado had swept in and now a wide stretch of polished oak blinks at her, waiting. As always, she keeps the final draft, setting it on the floor beside her desk. Though, really, the story is so tightly woven into her being, she doesn't need to look at it to remember it. She runs her hands over the desk's smooth empty surface. She has found no other way to be in the world, only the movement of words from one language to another. She knows most people don't even think about translation, and when they bother to, they don't assign it much value: a mechanical process, substituting one word for another, a monkey could do it; worse, a computer. She's tired of defending it, of explaining that even though she's tethered to an already-assembled drama, her role is akin to being an author.

Well, now she's ready to make her own drama. She pulls out her notes on Ono no Komachi. During Japan's Heian era, 794–1185, in the aristocratic culture of the Heian court, art stood center stage. An unusual time made more so because women, not men, were considered the masters of poetry. Every significant experience was accompanied by a poem, and Ono no Komachi, who lived in the palace in the capital city of Heian-kyo—present-day Kyoto, was one of the best, writing magnificently about love and the transient nature of life, sending poetic jewels to her lovers to coax, excite, or cool passion.

She has no interest in delving into Komachi's august years. Besides, someone has already done that. She found a Noh play written about the poet. A Buddhist priest takes his young poetry students to a rural area to visit an old woman who is thought to know the secret art of poetry. In this play, Komachi is an old hag, hiding her face under a straw hat. Eventually she reveals that she was once the famous poet who resided behind the imperial palace walls. The final act is the night of Tanabata, the festival celebrating love and poetry. One of the priest's students performs a ritual dance. Touched by the event, Komachi, in her feeble state, rises and begins to dance on stage.

Her play will be about romance and sexual intrigue. There will be five acts, and it will open at a teahouse. A magnificent old teahouse within walking distance of the imperial palace. She picks up her pen and writes: low-ceilinged, nestled among bamboo, the low tables, tatami mats, the thick green broth, *matcha*, in a cup so big it must be held with both hands. She is opening with a scene in which Ono no Komachi sends away one lover so as to begin the seduction of another. During the tea ceremony, she slips a poem beneath the new man's cup. *Like ripples in the water, I want to caress you.*

She looks at what she's written so far, but tells herself not to judge it. It's not fair to face inspection so soon. Just enjoy this making of something from nothing; this soaking in words; this remaking of the world. But she can feel a part of her assess what she's done and call it not bad. Not bad at all.

Of course it can't be all romance, sex, and seduction. Someone must get hurt and it will be Ono no Komachi. Looming is her great fall. The final act will be her expulsion from the court. No one ever learned why, exactly, she was thrown out, so Hanne will have to make it up. Literary license.

Something shatters outside. She looks up. Her gaze lands on her blackboard. It's still jam-packed with Japanese sentences from Kobayashi's novel. She grabs an eraser and begins to wipe it clean, chalk dust floating in the air, making her cough. She's about to erase the last bit of it, but stops. That line that bothered her, she fretted over it, rewrote and rewrote. *What you once loved lies there, inert, sucked of all its juices because you forgot it.*

She stares at the sentences. It was supposedly Jiro's interior monologue, lamenting that he had sent his wife away, and, as

Hanne saw it, chastising himself far too harshly. She didn't want to include it. Haven't you gone through enough, dear Jiro? But it stayed in the novel as it was, despite her personal objections.

The next day, Hanne has been working all morning, but the play is going nowhere. She can't seem to enter the mindset of a twenty-year-old beauty. There are festivals, ceremonies, parties with their gossip, and a new lover who secretly slipped a poem into Komachi's obi. And now she must compose the right response. Should she further ignite his passion? Prolong the courtship? Or snub him outright? Hanne yawns. Really, she doesn't care what Komachi decides. It's just frivolous escapism. She pushes aside her notebook and opens a book of Komachi's poetry.

Hana no iro faturi ni keri na itadura ni
Hanne translates: *Color of the flower has already faded away.*
Or she could translate it: *Cherry blossoms pale after long rain.*
Or, *The flowers withered/ Their color faded away.*
Or, *Flowers fading. In the long rain of regret.*
She moves on to the next verse, then the next. When she sets her notebook aside, she glances at the final version of the Kobayashi translation. She wishes she had just received it and was only now beginning. She opens it to a random page: *Aiko liked to soak in the tub for hours. Jiro told her he sometimes stood at the door and listened. When she stirred, he could hear the water slosh against the porcelain, and it reminded him of their sunny days by the sea. He went on, describing the lull of the waves, the heat of the white sand, and how she said the sun warmed her cold bones. What he didn't say is that he'd been listening with a certain rising panic, waiting for the water to splash so he knew she was still among the living.*

What a good man, Jiro, thinks Hanne. And how exhausting, those hours of vigilance, attentiveness, and care. She sighs. There's nothing more to be done. Kobayashi is probably reading it right now. It's only a matter of time before he signs off and the book is published. She sighs again. She's in that amorphous in-between time, in between major projects. Yes, she wanted to write her own drama, but her original vision isn't right. Maybe a walk will stir up a new story.

Hanne grabs her heavy coat and a scarf. Outside, she's assaulted by noise—screeches, horns, engines, sirens—and people and taxis and cars and more people. Forms whiz by. All morning she's been in an isolation tank with scant sensory stimulation—and now a barrage. Suddenly a loud, prolonged sound of the emergency warning system test for earthquakes charges the air—which means it is Tuesday noon.

She's never out at this hour. On the days she teaches Japanese, she's in the classroom. On the days she doesn't teach, she rises early and goes for a long walk, then hurries home and gets to work. As she heads down the sidewalk, Hanne sees herself, a woman in a blue swing coat, her eyes watering, the rims pinkish red from the constant cold wind. In the distance is the white dome of City Hall. She didn't intend to head this way, the opposite direction of the Golden Gate Bridge, but it's been years since she's been inside, where she and Hiro were married. A civil ceremony, one is conducted every half hour. It wasn't the least bit romantic, but it was cheap and quick, and they didn't need anything more because they dwelled in a bubble of passion.

They met during her last semester of graduate school at Columbia. She was studying at the library, and at some point she looked up and saw a Japanese man sitting across from her, the desk light dancing in his thick glasses. His round face, the stubble encircling his soft, gentle lips. His eyes were playful, full of delight. He dressed well, with a blue-and-white striped suit coat, a white shirt, and no tie. That first electric charge when their hands brushed, reaching for the same book, the title of which she can't recall. "Sumimasen," he said. She told him in his language that she, too, was sorry, but not that sorry. It was completely out of character, and she was about to apologize again, earnestly, but his face lit up with the most glorious smile, a smile just for her.

He was a chemist, in the United States on a full scholarship. He also spoke fluent French and loved Japanese literature and poetry.

"I can help you with your Japanese," he said, reaching over and touching her hair. That first gesture, so full of impulsive desire.

They ended up at a hotel that first night. But he wasn't wealthy and neither was she, and they both had dorm rooms and room-mates, so their spot became the library basement, beneath the stairwell, a hidden storage room. No sign on the door, the room was musty and stuffed with discarded old chairs and tables covered in white sheets. At the level of the sidewalk, a dirty window let in murky light. They could hear footsteps above them and muffled voices, as if the world existed above their heads and they'd sunk, with all the other forgotten things, underwater.

Though the door locked from the inside, they couldn't be sure no one possessed a key, so they rarely exchanged words, rarely made a sound. There was that, the thrill of possibly getting caught. But also him, his hunger for her, the way he tasted her. And more surprising, her hunger for him. She didn't know she had that inside, a consuming craving that once sated needed only moments to reignite. As the hour of their meeting approached, her entire body quivered with anticipation, as if every cell yearned for his body.

Two lives, for months she led two lives, a studious, driven student, and in the dingy storage room, stretched out on the table, his hands and mouth electrifying her, she became something she'd never been before.

Those early months of the courtship, he fervently pursued her, writing her a steady stream of haiku. She'd reach into her drawer and find one. Or open the refrigerator or a cupboard. Once she found one in her shoe. For the longest time, she carried one in her purse, *Water in the brook/No chill in the soft spring air/ Time to wet our feet*, along with a pair of his thin black socks. She loved him, and even if that love eventually faded, it never disappeared completely. Brigitte was wrong when she accused Hanne of never loving him, not loving anyone.

Now she climbs the stairs to the second floor, where they were married. It's as she remembered. Sunlight streams in through the large windows, onto the white marble floors, and the light bounces up, illuminating the white walls and ceiling. If such a thing as heaven exists, she thinks it should be like this—so light, so airy, except for the muffled sound of a man shouting, bringing her quickly back to earth. She opens a big wooden door and there he is, a short, squat man shaped like a bowling ball, bellowing into a microphone. Though she'd prefer a quieter place, rows of wooden pews are nearly empty, inviting her to rest her sore feet.

In the front of the room, eleven men and women sit in a half circle, each with his or her own microphone, waiting for the squat man to end his tirade. City officials of some kind. She doesn't follow local politics, nor does she intend to now. She has a bench to herself, she's only one of a handful of people in the audience. Three appear homeless, with reddened, weathered skin, torn clothing, and rumpled bags of belongings beside them. One is stretched out on the bench, sleeping, his boots unlaced, his socks covered in dirt. Another sits, his chin on his chest, eyes closed. He could be twenty, he could be sixty.

Within minutes she picks up the thrust of the man's argument. He's engaged in a debate about whether to pass a resolution urging the city to condemn the actions of Norway, which killed four whales, despite a global moratorium and protests. Apparently, the outer fat of the minke whale is a delicacy in Japan, where it is eaten raw.

It seems there's no getting away from Japan, and it's a short leap in her mind from Japan to Jiro. He liked to imagine what music would go best with whatever was going on. She remembers him saying *Every situation, every person has a melody playing, even if you can't hear it.*

"If we pass this, we're jeopardizing our city's reputation of tolerance," says a pock-faced official.

"If we sit here and do nothing, we are condoning it," argues another. "Each member of the Board of Supervisors knows we are a city that takes a stand. And this is an easy one: we are not a city that supports killing whales."

She closes her eyes. It isn't long before the city officials become nothing but voices, voices that have vacated their mortal bodies and now swirl in the ether. On and on about the resolution, dead whales, live whales, dollars lost, dollars gained. She no longer feels her body with its aching legs and a thudding heart from the climb up the stairs. She is just a disembodied and blissfully emptied mind. Suspended in this slumberous state, she lets herself enjoy a voice that must have roots in England with its soft "ah," and rich vocabulary; to hear "labile" in a public forum, who would have thought!

Something tickles her hand. She opens her eyes. A young woman in a pin-striped suit is handing her an agenda. They are only on item two and there are twenty-four items on the list. Street repair, menu labeling at chain restaurants, road closures, a resolution urging people not to buy eggs produced by caged hens. Everything must be debated, dissected, interpreted.

She buttons her coat and steps into the hallway, where a throng of people, a hundred or more, have gathered, and they all seem to be heading in the same direction as she, toward the marble staircase down to the lobby. Where did all these people come from? There's no defining characteristic—young, old, she hears Mandarin, English, Cantonese, French, Thai, and someone with an Australian accent—perhaps a tour of the building? Or another meeting just adjourned? She's never liked crowds and considers waiting for the great mass to descend ahead of her. But she's had enough and wants to head home. Perhaps now she'll find some spark in her young Komachi.

She enters the flock. People are ahead of her, beside her, behind her, pressing in, the space between her and another almost non-existent. The crowd is dense, streaming along, taking her with it. She feels claustrophobic, the air is suffocating and hot, the same air everyone else is breathing, inhaling, exhaling. If she could, she'd back up and remove herself from this mob. She remembers that Jiro hated crowds, too. It was one reason he didn't visit his wife in the hospital as often as he planned; it took four different subways, all of them jammed with people. And now that line that bothered her comes back. *What you once loved lies there, inert, sucked of all its juices because you forgot it.* He didn't forget her. That wasn't it at all, despite what his lack of visiting and new love affair might have indicated. How could Kobayashi have written that? It seems an instance, one among many, in which the author didn't really know his character. Authorial intrusion, she thinks it's called. She's imagining Jiro jammed in one of the Japanese subways, bodies pressed against him, elbows digging into his ribs, as she takes another step down the stairs, but her foot finds no purchase. Only air.

And now she is falling. A young woman turns, her eyes wide, mouth open, "Oh!" someone cries out, and the sound echoes off the walls. A pink shirt flits by, a shiny black purse, other heads turn, a pair of brown sandals, gray gum stuck on a stair, *Catch yourself*, one arm in front of her, her hand, she recognizes her long fingers. It's the only thing in front of her, how can that be? And people parting like the Red Sea, clearing the way for her to crash cleanly and fully. Yes, let the middle-aged fall. It's her hand that breaks the fall, and her forehead, as it slams into the white marble edge of a step.

Could this be it? Surrounded by gawking strangers, her corpse at the bottom of public stairs on public display? Her life doesn't pass in front of her, instead, she's firmly grounded in this moment, the shrieking, shouting, the hardness of the marble steps smashing into her arms, her hips, her nose, the taste of blood—she's still tethered to this life—and now she recalls a warm summer afternoon in the community pool, Hiro looking at her, smiling, as if he'd never seen anything so beautiful, with both children clinging to her shapely mother body, still heavy from pregnancy, her son's arms wrapped around her neck, and she's breathing his sugary breath, and her infant daughter in her arms, babbling something softly, patting the water, smiling at Hanne, her big toothless grin. A perfect moment. She wishes she could stay in this memory forever.

Hanne is stretched out on her back. Faces hover in a circle above her. A boy with big blue eyes. A woman whose front teeth rest on her lower lip. An old Chinese woman wearing all gray, her face expressionless, as if she's seen this before, and much worse. Suddenly a man's face zooms toward her. Beads of sweat on his upper lip. Dark sideburns. Dark nose hairs. His eyes are close-set, unnervingly so. "Don't move," he says, his breath reeking of garlic and cigarette smoke.

An imperative. She tries to sit up, and when she can't, attempts to understand why she's on the floor. This is not where she should be. She knows that. What is she doing here? "She's bleeding . . . hurt. A woman." But nothing hurts. Liquid streams from her nose, down her cheek, pools into her ear. The circle of faces still above her. But she can't right herself. The world is tilting. The man with sideburns is squatting beside her. What does he want? He's saying something to her. Telling her something, his horrible breath assaulting her. *Get back.* She can't get her mouth to shout, *Move back!* She hunts for that perfect moment again, the water, her children when they were young, Hiro, but it is gone.

Chapter Three

WHEN HANNE FIRST OPENED THE door to the new apartment, Brigitte had stood there, glued to the carpet in the dimly lit hallway. Hanne stepped inside and opened the blinds. She liked this apartment, a space with so much light and so high up, as if she were living in a cloud. And it was convenient, within walking distance of Brigitte's middle school. When Brigitte finally crossed the threshold, she wandered around and around, as if she was lost in an enormous department store and couldn't find the exit. Boxes were everywhere, nothing unpacked, the furniture huddled in the center of the rooms, waiting to be assigned its rightful place. Brigitte's footsteps echoed in the emptiness.

On her fourth lap through the apartment, she stood in the living room, her face crestfallen, and gestured to the wall of window. "The people down there don't even look real."

Hanne got to work, unpacking a box of books. Their old house had been snatched up the first week on the market. Though they weren't legally separated, Hiro was firmly and happily ensconced in his new apartment, a bike ride away from Stanford. Tomas was away at college, and now Hanne and Brigitte must forge something else.

"It feels like a hotel. And it's cold here." Wrapping her arms around herself, Brigitte said she missed their old house with its big green lawn, the porch swing where she liked to read, the old-fashioned stove, the garden in back, the banister staircase—

"We have to make it a home," said Hanne.

Brigitte's long black hair hung like two gloomy curtains on either side of her face. "It won't ever feel right."

"You'll get used to it," said Hanne, thinking of all the places that as a girl she'd had to call home.

"Why can't I live with Dad?"

Hanne could feel herself becoming impatient. Hiro had said he expected to be too busy with his research to have Brigitte live with him. He'd see Brigitte on weekends and every other Wednesday night for supper. He was on the verge of a major discovery, something that would shake the world of chemistry. For years he'd worked to reach this point.

"And after I do that, you'll fall in love with me again," he said, half kidding, but his eyes looked tired.

It wasn't as simple as that. No explosive event, no hair-tearing affair or sudden falling off a cliff out of love, the end was more insidious. By the time Hanne noticed the huge gap between them, it had calcified into something other than a marriage.

In the beginning, he worked all the time, a brilliant dreamer caught in the dream of a Nobel Prize. Wasn't that what his professors whispered to him during graduate school? You're on to something, Hiro. Keep at it. His research had something to do with protein degradation.

She, too; she wasn't so naïve as to assign all blame to him. She was caught up in her own dream. In this way, they were very much alike, driven, ambitious, pushing themselves. Before children came along, there was time at the end of the day to find each other again. But the practical took over, with carpools and cooking and cleaning and laundry and carpools and cooking and cleaning and laundry, and when she bothered to look up, he wasn't there, or only half there, a mist of himself. From that distance, he lost his brilliant sheen for her; as did she for him, she supposes. The absentminded yes or no, trailing off into nothing, their sentences becoming as minimal as their marriage. It was no one's fault; it was both their faults.

"You know, your grandmother and your great-grandmother had to endure—" Hanne said to Brigitte.

"I know. I know."

For months and months in Brigitte's room, there was nothing but a bed and desk, not even a rug on the hardwood floor. She refused to hang anything on the walls. Her bedroom at the old house had contained bits and pieces of the world that, for some reason, caught her eye. On their hikes, Brigitte would pick up pinecones and bits of eggshells and branches shaped like letters, a K, a T, smooth rocks, a papery fragment of a wasp's nest, a red cellophane candy wrapper. But Brigitte had thrown it all away when they moved and her room remained painfully bare. And her window was always partly open, so on cold days her room was freezing.

So many times Hanne stood at the doorway of her cold bedroom, staring at the blankness, restraining herself from hanging something—anything on the walls. Or she'd wake on a Saturday, thinking she'd take Brigitte shopping. Let her pick out things—anything. But so many times she'd wake to find Brigitte gone. Out for a walk, she'd say when she returned late afternoon. She liked to walk the city to get a sense of things. Or she rode the bus to watch people or the sunrise at Ocean Beach. The light is different at the beach, Brigitte would say. She wanted to be able to look at the horizon, to feel the expanse of the world. They'd argue about it; a young girl out alone, you're not safe, Hanne scolded. But it never did any good. Never stopped Brigitte.

A year later on a warm Saturday afternoon, Hanne drove down to Stanford to deliver Hiro a box of his dusty books. She was hoping to have a serious talk about their marriage. Was there any chance at patching it back together? She missed him. He'd been the great love of her life. She kept turning to tell him something, consult with him, seek his counsel and was startled he wasn't there. He knew her best. Hardest were the nights, to sleep without his steady, patient breathing. But there would be no talk. She found him dead on his kitchen floor. He'd been chopping an onion when he had a heart attack.

"He never should have moved out," cried Brigitte. "If he was living with us, we would have found him and saved him."

Who knew if that was true? When Hanne found him, the coroner said he'd been dead at least twelve hours.

Brigitte had been struggling in school, and was soon failing nearly every subject. The news didn't come from Brigitte, who had turned herself into a private world of one. The principal called. He recommended counseling or therapy. And how would Hanne pay for that? Hiro might have been brilliant at chemistry, but he was lousy with finances. And Hanne wasn't much better. If Brigitte's grades didn't improve, the principal was afraid he'd have to expel her. Might drugs be involved? Had Hanne seen any signs?

Signs? With Hiro gone, Hanne had taken on more work to pay the bills, including Tomas's and Brigitte's tuitions. She supposed Brigitte complained of being tired all the time. In the morning, it was hard to get her out of bed for school. When she finally did rise, she pulled on whatever clothes were lying on the floor. She rarely brushed her hair, and her skin took on a waxy look, probably from not being washed enough. But the signs Hanne saw were the dark pouches under her own eyes, the sag to her cheeks, her dull, lifeless skin. Working all the time, when she came home, she barely had enough energy to eat before she fell asleep. Only to wake up and do the whole thing over the next day. Driving to work one morning, Hanne fell asleep at the wheel, ran off the road and plunged into a ditch. Luckily she didn't hit anyone. She escaped with only a cut to her forehead from the steering wheel.

One afternoon she came home from work early to find music blaring, and Brigitte draped around an older boy. They were swaying in the living room, and Brigitte was wearing one of Hanne's thin, strapless party dresses, a plunge in the front, revealing only the possibility of womanliness. In bare feet, her toenails painted blue, her not-yet-woman body was pressed against that young man, a sly look in his eye and a flare to his jaw. He looked sixteen, dressed in raggedy blue jeans, his hair gelled and standing straight up, like an electric fence.

Hanne watched him finger a curl in Brigitte's hair, before sauntering out the door.

It seemed it was only a couple months later, and there was another young man, this one slightly older, already a smoky creature. Hanne could see on his old jeans pocket the faded outline of a pack of cigarettes. That time Brigitte stormed out with him. She came back the next day, her clothes smelling of cigarette smoke

37

and alcohol, a tattoo on her left arm of Munch's *Der Schrei Der Natur*, The Scream of Nature.

Brigitte stood there, hands on her hips. "Why are you looking at me like that? It's all meaningless. I've heard you say that before. Don't deny it."

Hanne saw another tattoo on the tender inside of her daughter's wrist: *I wonder why it hurts to live.*

With her grueling work schedule, Hanne could only do so much for her daughter. Hanne located a boarding school, the Dover Academy, in Connecticut. It specialized in languages and had a rigid discipline policy: no alcohol, no drugs, the administration conducted periodic room checks and random urine tests and provided counseling. Homework done on time, lights out by 10:00 P.M. It was the right thing for Hanne to do. Brigitte was very bright, but she needed help, much more than Hanne could give her, to guide her through this rough patch. Hanne used the money from the sale of Hiro's apartment, took out a second mortgage, and paid the first year's tuition. What she'd do after that, she didn't know. It didn't matter. She'd save her daughter somehow.

To pay for the steep fees, Hanne took on more work. She landed a prominent job translating a new Japanese author. Her translation was highly praised, which led to more work. She taught ten Japanese language classes a week. She buried herself in work.

Brigitte eventually settled in at the school, and Hanne didn't receive any calls of complaints, no threats of expulsion. When Thanksgiving arrived, Brigitte said she wanted to go home with one of her new friends. Her friend lived an hour away.

Hanne was pleased her daughter had so quickly made a friend. "Well, then Christmas," said Hanne.

When Christmas arrived, Brigitte said she wanted to stay for the winter interim session. Ice skating, skiing, and Mandarin.

Hanne didn't even have to pay. Brigitte had applied for a scholarship and got it. You're considered a parent suffering from financial hardship, she told Hanne. Hanne sensed it would make no difference if she protested. Brigitte wasn't coming home.

Hanne flew to Connecticut for a visit in January, but school was in session, so she barely got to see Brigitte. And when she took Brigitte out to dinner, Brigitte invited two other girls to accompany her. Hanne's questions were answered with one-word responses or silence. At dinner, the three girls ordered the most expensive thing on the menu—lobster—and spent the rest of the evening whispering and giggling to each other, as if Hanne did not exist. When Hanne touched her arm, Brigitte moved it away. At least Brigitte seemed happy otherwise, if not with her.

During the summer, Brigitte told her she got a job at the summer camp at her school teaching basic Mandarin and Japanese. Later Hanne found out this wasn't true. She worked in the cafeteria serving food and had acquired a boyfriend. Hanne eventually stopped asking Brigitte to come to San Francisco for her holidays.

Then it seemed Brigitte was off to Dartmouth. Her third year, she took a leave of absence, supposedly to do volunteer work, building homes for Eastern Europeans. The next thing she heard, Brigitte had left the organization, dropped out of school, and joined some religious group.

Brigitte made contact with Tomas and told him where she was. At the time, Brigitte hadn't invoked her demand for confidentiality. That was to come later. After dragging the information out of Tomas, Hanne flew to France, then drove to Cologne, to an old monastery owned by a group sometimes called the Higher Beings, other times Higher Thought. Hanne came on the pretext of delivering boxes full of Brigitte's things.

"Brigitte doesn't care about objects," said a dumpy woman in a flowered dress who helped run the spiritual group. "They hold no meaning for her. Things," the woman said, not bothering to conceal her disdain, "are not of any concern to her. Or to us."

As for seeing her daughter, that was impossible; Brigitte, who'd changed her name to Nivedita, was on retreat. For how long? Possibly years.

Chapter Four

"READY FOR A LITTLE RIDE?" A different man, this one cleanly shaven, with breath of peppermint, crouches beside her.

The question seems profound. A ride? To where? How to answer? Words are flying around in Hanne's head. *Iie, Nan desu ka? Abscheulich, wutend sein, informaste a los vecinos? Roto. La maleta esta cerrada y no la puedo abrir.*

A thick hand slides beneath her head, back, legs, something hard against her spine. It seems no answer is required, she is moving sideways, effortlessly, traveling fast, and now she's sinking onto something downy soft. Thankfully, the circle of gawkers vanishes. Flat on her back, she stares at the ceiling, a world of white swirls, like cloud sculptures, no, not sculptures, not at all, a word, a word fixes upon her. She makes out the letter "H," then "O," "W," slowly it comes to her. "However" written in puffy letters

41

on the ceiling. What does it mean? But then the letters scatter and it's again nothing but meaningless swirls of mist.

"Hang on."

Another imperative, this one comes with a lilt and she relaxes into it. She's moving, not sideways, but up, soaring above the ground, as if flying. But what if she falls again? Despite the new rush of panic, there's nothing she can do about it. She's tumbled into a place where she has no agency. She can't move a muscle, trigger a nerve ending, or spark a synapse to make a decision and then carry it out. In this new place, everything just occurs. She's certain something bad will happen; but hasn't it already?

Someone's warm breath is near her ear. The scent of peppermint. Peppermint Man is nearby. A splash of cold air strikes her face, her lungs, the squeal of a car tire, shrieks, laughter, a man's voice shouting something about broken. "A broken window!" Everything about her body seems to have departed, except her hearing, which has become excruciatingly acute. Noises are loud, deafening. She wants to press her hands to her ears, but she has no sense of her hands. Or her legs or feet or any part of her body. Where is her body? She can't lift her head to see it. Though she still has thoughts—her hearing and her thinking remain, as if her mind has been severed from her body. If that's the result of what's happened (what *has* happened?), well, what good has her body been, anyway? A vessel intent on aging, demanding pills to quell anxiety and insomnia, pills to level out cholesterol and high blood pressure, eventually rushing to its demise. More liquid streams down her face.

Hundreds of clouds overhead, the cold wind must have torn the sky apart. If she could move her mouth—*Where? Doko? Donde? Wohin?* A grinding, then another, a pause before she places it— rusty doors opening, the light is dimming, the gray disappears.

White overhead. She stops moving. Bam, bam, two doors shutting, the outside world muffled. Her mind is working so slowly, as if each thought, each word must pass through a solid wall. She knows where she is, but can't think of the word. Peppermint Man climbs in with her, smiling. A chipped front tooth. She hears someone else enter, huff, the sound of springs squeaking, the slam of a door. What is the name of the thing she's in?

A siren blares. Something bad has happened. To her! She remembers the circle of faces, the boy's eyes, people ogling. The warm liquid on her face.

Peppermint Man stands and pulls a dark blue blanket from the shelf. He wraps it around her, carefully tucking it around her shoulders, the sides of her, her feet. His skin is tan, the kind of tan young people wear, and he's bare-armed, revealing strapping muscles. Probably a job requirement, along with the bright smile. "You doing all right?" he says.

Okay, I think. She does not know if she said these words out loud.

There's an ease about him, about her situation. What *is* her situation? She's beginning to feel the first stirrings of a horrible headache right above her eyes. The bridge of her nose aches. Her eyelids feel heavy, her lower lip trembles and droops. He opens a cabinet, unwraps a cloth, and wipes her face. "Clean you up a bit. How about it?" His voice is low but riding alongside, that light inflection, as if none of this is truly happening—the blood on the cloth, a lot of blood. From her? When she closes her eyes, he grabs her forearm. "Oh, no you don't. No sleeping on my watch."

He wraps a cloth sleeve around her arm and pumps it up. The red needle on the dial jags higher. Somewhere in her brain, she knows the name of the device he's using, knows what he's doing.

The needle falls, stutters, falls again. He rips the sleeve off, writes something down, then snaps off the overhead light. "All done."

Indeed, something is done, and to the dull drone of the car—is it a car?—she sinks into murkiness, her eyelids hovering half-mast. That lullaby, she tries to conjure it up, the one her mother used to lull her to sleep, but just as it rises, other words swoop in: *'Twas brillig, and the slithy toves/Did gyre and gimble in the wabe;/ All mimsy were the borogoves,/And the mome raths outgrabe.* She memorized *Jabberwocky* when she was a girl and went around her small town—where did they live?—repeating it to the confusion of everyone. Calls from neighbors, "Has your daughter gone mad?" *Beware the Jabberwock, my son!*

From somewhere far away, she hears someone talking. The tan man says something, but the words enter her brain like drips. "Why don't you—" but she loses the rest. The place where they lived, she remembers old buildings, blackish green moss on white, bone-white, church bells chiming, a funny echo afterward. Switzerland. They lived in Switzerland. *The jaws that bite, the claws that catch!/Beware the Jubjub bird, and shun/ The frumious Bandersnatch!*

For a while her parents thought it endearing, even clever. She took the poem and developed a new language, something with its own logic, inserting a consonant or a vowel where one was least expected. An almost-word. She spoke what she secretly called The Language of Jabberwock—all the time, refusing to utter any other language. Her teachers sent her home from school, "an incorrigible child." Worried, her parents enlisted the help of a Viennese shrink, who declared her sane, a clever, mischievous girl who carried things too far, such as this riddle-making havoc. If she didn't want to age her parents prematurely, she'd better straighten up and act like a proper young girl.

For the first time, she notices two small windows. They give her a view of what's outside, what she's leaving behind. She has to squint—the world outside is too bright—an endless stream of cars, people on the sidewalk, the white dome of City Hall. She closes her eyes. *He left it dead, and with its head/He went galumphing back.*

"What's your name?"

A voice floats around her. An accent, a missing "r" in "your." From New York? Almost a "wa," "youwa." A gray-haired man in a white coat stands beside her bed. Red broken veins cover his cheeks, and his wire-framed glasses, the lenses thick and strong, make his intense gray eyes larger than normal. Peppermint Man had not taken her home. From somewhere comes *byohin*, then *Krankenhaus*, a cascade of words, ending in "hospital." The last time she'd found herself in a hospital was with Brigitte, getting her stomach pumped.

The man in the white coat and glasses leans closer. He has a bulbous nose, like a clown. Is he a clown? But why is he in the hospital too? None of this makes sense, yet she can't stop her mind from wondering.

"Do you understand the question?" he says.

She nods. Her name. What is? *Namae wa nan desu ka?* She understands perfectly, but she can't make her mouth move, nor can she recall her name. He repeats the question, louder, more firmly, as if her hearing is impaired or her mental capacity—and it is, yes? A panic seizes her, turning the question into a crucible that must be answered. What . . . her name . . . is? *Namae wa?* She frantically searches through the corridors of her brain, opening doors, slamming them shut. Where is?

"Can you tell me your address?"

She's still searching for her name!

"Phone number?"

The clown is waiting, not smiling. Unwanted words swirl around her head, pineapple, helium, quail, harpoon, fie fie fie, rooster, sock, Prussian blue, toad, then, *chiisai, hyaku, karai, sarada, akai, Puedes salir de casa un poco mas tarde, Gaze, hauchfein, versteinern, wiederherstellen, doyatte kaisha ni ikimasu ka?*—as if she had opened too many doors and now everything is flying around, a nonsensical mess, shoes on top of a toad, the rooster with a harpoon, and the ringing of fie fie fie. But her name? Where? Buried underneath the pineapple? Or the harpoon stomping around like a one-legged pirate—fie, fie, fie! She used to say this as a child when she was angry. Fie! Her name, where?

A woman magically appears beside the clown. Arms folded, she's in the same white coat, the same solemn face. Her hair is coppery gold and pulled back in a bun, revealing a broad forehead. Her plump lips move, she's speaking to the man. Slowly, how slowly her brain works. What . . . her brain . . . to . . . happened? Doctors. Doctors are. If she could get her mouth to form words, she'd say, *What . . . to me . . . happened? Incomprehensible.*

The doctors wait, write something on a notepad, then whisk away. For a long time, she is alone. How long has she been here? A flowery pink curtain stretches across the room. A TV blares. But there is no TV. It's not a TV, but moaning, a man is moaning. "Call 911!" he shouts. Over and over. "911 911 911!" A refrain, like a Greek play, the only tragedy to be sung. A cosmic joke on her! Her love of words ridiculed by the endless loop of numbers. What might come next? A recitation of prime numbers? A stream of calculus? She must stop. He's probably in a great deal of pain. Someone must help him.

A nurse with a band-aid on her chin suddenly appears at her bedside. Help that man, Hanne wants to say. The nurse is young, not a day over twenty. "I draw blood."

An accent. Romanian? A prick and she watches, almost as if it's someone else's blood rapidly filling the vial. Dark red, rich. A beautiful color. Inside her, this beautiful rich red. Another vial. Another. Five, six, how many vials? She wants to protest, "Too much!" The nurse disappears, six vials of blood gone. It feels like five minutes later when another nurse with tight white curls comes in and says she must draw blood. But! There must be a panicked look in her eyes for the older nurse explains matter-of-factly, "We can't find them. Misplaced or mislabeled."

The nurse finishes, changes the band-aid on Hanne's forehead, her nose, and disappears in her soft shoes. A sliver of silence strolls in, but the man in a nearby room snatches it away, shouting "911!" A belly laugh echoes in a hallway, garbled words float into her room. She drifts, as if in a dream. Maybe it's not a circus, but a dream. The 911 shouter, the belly laughter, the whir of an engine, the buzz of an electric light. Anything, anything at all could happen. And now here materializes a man in a powder-blue uniform. He's huge, his face is the size of a cannonball. He lifts her onto a gurney as if she were a leaf.

In her version of events, they are sending her home—she has failed to provide sufficient answers, so out she goes. She can't tell them name, phone number, address, so they cannot or will not accommodate. Whatever role they had for her in their circus, they must give it to someone else. She wants to cry, "Please give me another chance." Though why she feels this, she doesn't know because she'd actually like to go home.

He rolls her into a small silver room that smells of disinfectant. He pushes a button and they start to descend, finally stopping with a shudder and a rattle. The doors magically open and spit her into a dreary corridor.

"I'll go see if they're ready for you," he says. "Wait right here."

She looks at her hands resting on the blanket. Her long fingers seem perfectly designed for a piano, and perhaps they could play; she's never tried. No piano lessons or violin during her childhood; no ballet or dance. Only musty libraries and museums, her bedroom, plenty of time spent in dark places. When her father left them, not for another woman, but for work, a position in China, mother took a full-time job. Hanne was sent away to live with her Oma. For the best, said her mother. A small, bitter, old woman, Oma dressed head to toe in widow's black. She had a long dour face, and her breath smelled like garlic and onions and pickled herring. She lived in a small town, Brunsbüttel, in a drafty old house on the North Sea, where she'd grown up as a child. She spent her hours plotting myriad ways to defeat the Russians. Her mind was still firmly planted in the aftermath of World War II, certain the Russians would return to rape and pillage some more. She'd taught herself Russian to prepare and made Hanne learn too. "They are a cold, cruel people, Hanne," she said. "This time I will negotiate our freedom. You must speak the language to get what you want."

Every day Oma cleaned the floors. "Out!" she ordered Hanne. And Hanne stood in the snow for hours, shivering, knees knocking, cursing her Oma and her mother for sending her here, as she waited for the floors to dry. If she spilled her milk or didn't clean her plate, she was locked in the cellar, dark as black ink, with the rats scratching. If she cried, if Oma heard even a whimper, if she pleaded with Oma to let her out, she was kept down there longer. So Hanne discovered that if she held her breath, taking only shallow sips of dank air, the tears stopped. Despite the bleak childhood, Hanne now has a deep longing for her mother, even her Oma. For someone to take care of her. Mama! She hears the cry in her head.

When she realizes there's no one around, she closes her eyes and imagines Hiro has come back to life. Just as he reaches for her, his ghostly hand disappears. And now it is Jiro. He is writing scores of music, wearing a scowl, his eyes blazing. When he sees her, his expression instantly changes into something milder, kinder. To be looked at like that, soft, lovingly. He puts his hand on her forehead. "What can I get you?" he says. "Have you had breakfast? You must eat something." She smiles, tears running down her cheeks.

She's moving again. She opens her eyes and watches herself being rolled into a white room with a large white tube in the center. A young woman comes over, smiling, showing squat white teeth. She begins to talk fast, a waterfall of words cascading from her red lipstick lips, pouring over Hanne. She tries to hold on to something, to stop herself from hurtling over the fall of words, "picture," "brain," "scan," "rattling," "pounding."

She's slid into the tube, surrounded on all sides by white and utter quiet. Here she will be buried, she thinks. In a soundless white tube, no one present, no gathering, no ceremony of solemn words. It's what she's always known: underneath everything, the thoughts, the situations, there is nothing. The entire stretch of life is a wild distraction from this nothingness. There's no white light at the end of a tunnel, no God or Gods, just a white tube. After she's placed in the tube, she imagines it will be inserted into a cannon that will shoot her into outer space, where her dead body, cocooned in the white tube, will orbit the earth forever, for why should she take up any more room on the planet? What use is she?

Suddenly she is surrounded by pounding. A perfectly designed punishment, given her keen hearing. And why must she suffer this way? There is no reason. And just as quickly, the pounding stops. She hears herself breathing. Rapidly. Panting. As soon as she thinks the torture is over, the pounding begins again. Stops. Again. Again.

"Hanne Schubert."

The four syllables float above her, then slowly fall, like raindrops. Their texture feels familiar, both mellifluous and hard. A puff of air, a hush, a full-voiced stop. Her mind runs over and over the sounds, finding them immensely pleasurable. She's always believed words to be music and her name, she thinks now, is evidence of that.

The gray-haired doctor says the ambulance driver had had enough smarts to pick up her purse. And what luck, inside they found her driver's license and an address book. Her name is Hanne Schubert. "We've contacted your son. He'll be here later today."

She has been named, words bonded to the subject. She has a name. She's half listening—"head trauma, left frontal lobe," busy running the four syllables of her name through her mind, like stroking smooth silk. "Confusion, impaired motor functions, aphasia, all quite normal. Your brain is likely swollen." Han ne Shu bert. "—watch for intracranial hemorrhaging, but so far, a scan—as a precaution," Han ne "—inserting a small tube—a fifteen-minute procedure." A name, a beautiful name. "—relieve the pressure by removing spinal fluid." Her eyes are watery, she is weeping. Hanne. "As the brain finds its normal shape—faculties return, most likely." Something about pain medication, a speech language pathologist. Her mother had had the good sense not to christen her with a name hurtful to the ear. Like her mother's name, Dorca. Hanne Schubert. Han ne. Her mother had met a Swedish woman by the name of Hanne, a woman full of poise, intelligence, charm, and something else. A quick smile? No, Dorca wouldn't care about that. From the chaotic clutter of her mind comes this memory; her name has a meaning. "Grace," unmerited divine assistance. If there is a God, she thinks, now would be a fine time to make an appearance and bring to fruition the full meaning of her name.

For the first time, the doctor smiles. A dimple in his right cheek. In his earlier years, before he witnessed over and over the tragedy of the human body, he must have been quite handsome. He rests his hand on her shoulder. "There, there, it'll be all right, Hanne Schubert."

Thank you. She may or may not have said that out loud. But she says it again. Thank you.

It's late when her son rushes into her room. Prior to his arrival, she remembers being rolled into a bright white room and out again. The doctor came and went, telling her they had relieved some of the pressure. "So now we're in the wait-and-see mode," he said.

Tomas's face is white as paper, and with the lines of worry on his forehead, around his tired eyes, he's aged ten years. What is she doing to her son? He pulls up a chair and takes her hand in his. "Mom, what can I get you? What do you need?" His voice sounds like hard shoes racing over cobblestones. When was the last time she walked on cobblestones? Prague? She can't remember. You cannot rush on cobblestones.

She senses that someone else is in the room. Brigitte? She thinks she smells Brigitte's hair, or what used to be the scent of her shampoo—lavender. An image comes to her: Hanne on her knees in the bathroom, soaping Brigitte's long black hair with shampoo, Brigitte's face tilted to the ceiling so the suds didn't run into her eyes. She must have been eight or nine. She'd have spent a good hour in the tub reading, her whole body submerged, just the orb of her face and the hand holding the book exposed. Now Hanne tries to sit up to see, inching her back on the soft pillow, carefully.

She hears not a woman's voice, but a man's. The man is speaking Polish. Not just one man. Now a woman. Have they been here the entire time? The room smells of barbecue chicken.

Tomas takes up his position as guardian and inquisitor of those who dare approach. He can stay as long as she likes, he tells her. All his work has been assigned to other attorneys. Anne and the kids are coming in a couple days. He thought it might raise her spirits to see her grandchildren.

He pauses. "Do you understand?"

She nods, looking at the knife crease of his trousers, and he squeezes her limp hand.

When a nurse comes into the room, he leaps out of his chair. "Is everything being done for her?"

The nurse with puffy eyelids assures him she is receiving the best care.

He leans over Hanne, as if he's preparing to kiss her cheek. "Why is she black and blue around her eyes? Those big scoops of color."

The nurse explains it's from her broken nose.

When she leaves, Tomas sits again and adjusts her blankets. The TV blares from the other side of the room. The room erupts in awful canned laughter. A grunt from behind the curtain, the Polish woman's voice, angry, loud. The man answers in turn, louder. Now that Tomas is here, she's listening more closely, as if she, too, has just entered the room. She realizes the Poles have been here the entire time; she just blocked them out by lumping them together with the dreadful drone of the TV. Tomas's jaw flares. "How can you stand this?" he says.

He charges out of the room.

How can she stand this? The same way you stand anything that isn't under your dominion to change—you accept it and move on.

But does she really accept any of this? No! She feels a fresh wave of fury. The couple behind the curtain is arguing. Tomas returns stern-faced with a new nurse in tow, who isn't smiling. Tomas gathers her few belongings from the narrow closet. A hefty man appears with a gurney. A private room, her son tells her. He's paying for it, whatever it costs, he doesn't care. She wishes she could hug him and say "Thank you. Thank you. God bless you."

"Don't cry, Mom," he says, wiping her face with a tissue.

She's moved to the south wing and the new room is four times as large, with shiny wood floors, big windows, a view of the city, white and gold lights twinkling, as if showing off for her. The other side of the hospital, from where she just came, is an impoverished country, on the verge of anarchy and revolution. Here, there's beauty and peace and a stunning view. Even marigolds on a table by the window. And a private bathroom.

In the morning, another MRI is taken. The result reveals less swelling. "We should see improvement soon," says the doctor.

We. As if somehow they're in this together. The doctor is up and about, and here she lies like a rotting log, speechless. She knows she's in a gloomy mood. He's doing all he can for her; she must not yield to her dark feelings. *Patience. This will change. It will have to change.* Jiro's words, she recognizes them, spoken right before his wife crashed into the garage, right before his life did, indeed, change.

She reminds herself that there has been improvement. She can now move her hands and legs. And here is her son bringing her orange juice, blueberries, and a newspaper. But the words on the front page keep moving on top of each other, then floating around, blurry, as if they are caught in a heat wave. How will she work again? More than anything she wants her old life back. She pushes the paper away. With a shaky hand she writes *Please call school. Tell them what happened.* Unless there is a minor miracle, she won't be out of here in two days to teach her classes. She thinks about having him call David, but decides against it. When she can speak again, she'll contact him.

Late afternoon, the speech pathologist arrives. She's a lardy woman who takes huge sips of air, as if she's just run up a flight of stairs. "Oh, you've got the best room in the house," she says, pulling up a chair beside Hanne's bed, and now Hanne can see the dark mustache above her upper lip. She says she's going to get Hanne's "old brain clicking again." "Isn't that a good idea?" she says, patting Hanne's arm.

Hanne nods. Her natural inclination is to be a good student.

Tomas steps out to get a late lunch so the two of them can get to work. They'll go through a series of little exercises, says the woman. She'll say a phrase and Hanne will finish it. "We'll play a little game together. Doesn't that sound fun?"

"The early bird—"

Hanne opens her mouth, but nothing comes out.

The woman waits.

"—gets the worm." The woman shifts in her chair. "Short but—"

Even if she could move her tongue to move, she's not sure she could utter these clichés. Dead words beating their lifeless wings.

"Sweet. A bird in the hand—is worth two in the bush."

The woman scoots her large behind on the chair. "A friend in need—"

Hanne closes her eyes and breathes deeply.

"—is a friend indeed. Rob Peter—and pay Paul. Beggars—can't be choosers."

She's just trying to do her job, Hanne tells herself. She picks up her pen and paper: "I'm sorry."

The woman sighs and goes on. As the clichés pile up, she no longer waits for Hanne to respond.

"All right. Enough. We'll try again tomorrow." Her tone is cheery, upbeat, but her eyes suggest otherwise.

Anne arrives with the girls, bringing purple lilacs that send forth a lovely scent that fills her palatial room. Hanne nods, hoping they see her appreciation, her gratitude for their visit. She tries to smile, but feels only one side of her mouth twist upward.

Sasha looks at her wide-eyed. "Mom! What's wrong with Grandma?"

Hanne is reminded of the fairy tale: And what big eyes you have. What a big nose, big ears. Anne, glowing with youthful health, says in her cool, collected voice, "Grandma had an accident. We discussed this on the plane." A cut on her forehead, her nose broken, a jostle and bump on her brain.

Sasha tentatively comes over and strokes Hanne's arm, while Irene, happy to be out of the hold of her mother's arms, explores the room, pulling on the cord of the shades, raising them as high as they can go. A bright light fills the room, clinging to Hanne's white sheets. For a moment, Hanne can't see. Anne comes over beside Sasha, casting a great shadow, slicing the bed in half. With a hand on her daughter's head, Anne explains what happens to the brain when it hits the hard shell of the skull. She uses all the correct terminology—everything has a specific name, a name fashioned from Latin roots—even drawing a diagram on the sheet, with her finger, of the frontal lobe. Like a science experiment, thinks Hanne.

When the brain lesson is over, Sasha looks at Hanne. "Hi, Grandma." Her voice is shy, barely audible.

"Grandma can't speak," says Anne. "You can talk to her, though."

She turns to her mother. "What do I say?"

Anything, thinks Hanne. Anything at all. I'd listen to you until the end of time.

The shades slam down, darkening the room.

"Tell her about the science museum we went to yesterday."

Of course, thinks Hanne, more science. Irene runs out the door, and Anne dashes after her. As Sasha strokes the dark hairs of Hanne's arm, she talks about dinosaur bones and sharks, dead beetles and dead squid. No, she made a mistake, alive squid with their tentacles swimming in a glass case. She reaches into her backpack and pulls out a brochure. NEW YORK SCIENCE, she begins to read the fine print.

So bright, thinks Hanne. Just like Brigitte, who, at the age of two, spoke complete intelligible sentences. And without anyone's counsel, began to sound out words, as if she would not be denied access to the world of language. It was pure Brigitte, naturally gifted and gravitating toward sounds and words and sentences. Of course Hanne was delighted. Wasn't this every parent's secret dream? To give birth to a wonder? A child prodigy who might rise to unheard-of heights? That her gift was language delighted Hanne even more. Cut from the same cloth as I, thought Hanne. And something meaningful that they could share.

"Listen to her," Hanne whispered to Hiro as Brigitte read the stop sign. Brigitte was in the back in her car seat and they were driving to Brigitte's music class, which wasn't far from their home in San

Francisco on Noriega Street, a house perpetually wrapped in cold fog. "Do you hear her? She's reading. At age two."

Brigitte kept saying "stop" as if it were a live thing that must be rolled around in her mouth to be kept alive.

"Did you read that early?" said Hanne.

"Hmm. No." Hiro was his usual restrained self. "She's just being herself."

"Which is remarkable. Tomas wasn't reading until age five."

"Hanne, don't compare. They will each have their strengths and weaknesses."

He was right, of course, but she couldn't help herself. Brigitte's language ability was just one of many differences. Unlike Tomas, who came out with an elongated head because of an agonizing labor, Brigitte was a beautiful baby. Her perfectly shaped head courtesy of a Caesarean, her symmetrical sparkling eyes, her tuft of black hair, like a dark rain cloud. Tomas liked the playpen, so he could stand up and throw blocks at the wall; he was independent and strong-willed, always wanting to do things for himself. But Brigitte would swing for hours, as long as Hanne was in view. When she could walk, Brigitte trailed Hanne around the house, up and down the stairs, to the basement and into the kitchen. When suppertime came, Hanne gave Brigitte a chore—folding the napkins or stirring the pudding—so she could stay near. If Brigitte took pleasure in Hanne's company, Hanne reciprocated. Hanne cooked and sang to her in different languages. German made Brigitte's eyes widen; French made her smile. Japanese she imitated, saying kokonoko. Nine. At night when she'd cry out, a small whimper, it was Hanne Brigitte wanted, not her father.

A baby girl, unexpected, but certainly wanted. There was an eight-year gap between the two children. With Tomas, Hanne had split herself into two, working and mothering, each role never fully committed to, and therefore, in her mind, never done well. With Brigitte, Hanne wanted only one role and to perform it to perfection. She would give her daughter the world. Hiro was an assistant professor at Stanford in the chemistry department, and though there wasn't a lot of money, it was enough. They'd make the sacrifices.

Hanne signed Brigitte up for French. And when French proved a breeze, Hanne added German and Japanese. All by the age of six. To be fair, she enrolled Tomas, but he despised the lessons and by age fifteen had dropped out of everything except Japanese. Brigitte loved to practice with Hanne. "Do I sound good, Mama? Do I? Are you proud of me?"

"Beautiful, my love," said Hanne. "You sound like music. Tell me about your day in French."

Now Sasha is reading about penguins. Wonderful, thinks Hanne, anything to transport her away from here. She is ravenous for life. Keep talking, tell me anything, anything at all, and I'll follow along gladly, willingly, forever grateful. Penguins and penguins mating, mommy told her, making babies, and a blue poisonous frog. Sasha pulls from her pocket a long necklace of colorful glass beads, and raises it to show Hanne, but the knot must be nonexistent because the beads slide off and bounce across the floor. Sasha scrambles, chasing them all over the room. Hanne would give anything to get down on her knees and help her gather them up. She closes her eyes, listening to Sasha move around the room, murmuring, "Here's one. Here's one." This search takes a long while, but finally she returns to the chair beside Hanne's bed, and in a small, fragile voice, says, "Can you read me a story?"

Hanne shakes her head. I'm sorry, my love. More than anything, I wish I could.

Sasha nods gravely, then with a sharp twinkle in her eye, without any prompting, says "Ich liebe dich," I love you.

Hanne's eyes water. She taught Sasha that German sentence a year ago. Hanne realizes that for days she's thought of herself only in disassembled pieces—a brain, frontal lobe, nose broken, arms paralyzed, gashed forehead—but now something below the fragments congeals.

When Tomas walks in and pulls up a chair, Sasha quickly climbs from her chair and into his lap, hugging and kissing him. "Daddy." She leans up to his ear, cups it in her hands and tries to whisper. "Is Grandma going to die?"

"No," he says quickly, studying Hanne's face. "No, sweetie. She had an accident, but she'll be fine."

Through watery light, she looks at her son and his daughter, watches them snuggle into each other's warmth. A throb of joy fills her, and she feels, for a moment, full of grace.

Several days later, the first sign of improvement arrives. A nurse with big front teeth has removed Hanne's sweaty hospital gown of dull blue and is now administering a sponge bath.

"Still having hot flashes?" says the nurse. "No fun, are they? My mother had them until she was fifty-nine. Can you believe it? Hated them, absolutely hated them. Think what I have to look forward to."

The nurse wipes down her arms, her neck. "Until you're up and about, this is the way a bath is given. My mother used to call this a spit bath. Ha! A spit bath, can you imagine the germs? How's your head feeling? More painkillers? You can have a certain amount each day, you know, and you could have more if you liked. In fact," the nurse studies the bag of clear liquid hanging from an IV pole, "you've barely used any." She laughs. "Usually patients gobble it up. Oh, your nose looks better. They've set it perfectly. Less black and blue around the eyes."

A torrent of words, this nurse. Hanne knows she should feel indebted to her, the care, the concern for clean feet, it goes far beyond what she's ever done for anyone, except her children.

"Your big big toe."

Hanne wouldn't be surprised if as she cleaned it, she wiggled it, the big piggy toe. And she does! Hanne tries to think about something else. To drift from this, the talking to her toe. She conjures up Jiro, but he has nothing to say. Hanne can't seem to escape this moment. Tomas is not here, Anne and the girls have gone home. She is stuck in this room with a nattering nurse and her head is pounding. She pushes the button and gives herself a dose of morphine.

On and on about her toes, how this nurse likes to paint her toenails, doesn't mind the smell, any color, changes it once a week, and the time she tried black, a horrid color on her—

"Please be quiet," says Hanne, with some effort.

The nurse stops talking and her face opens. "I don't know what you just said, but it's a good sign." She says she'll be right back.

Hanne feels a crackle of excitement. She stretches her lips over her front teeth, opens her mouth wide, runs her tongue along the soft inside of her cheeks. Be quiet. Please be quiet. Her mouth muscles feel like a new toy.

By the time the doctor arrives, she's carefully formed her speech, but can only manage a short sentence: Time for me to go home. The concentration required for that one, coherent sentence has worn her out. If granted more energy, she'd say "Thank you for such thoughtful care. I can't remember when I've been so well attended to, but it's time to resume my life. After nine days here, this place is beginning to sap my soul." "Sap my soul" is her sole utterance.

He nods, staring at her more intently than he ever has, his eyes alight, alert, and says he'll be right back. He returns with the copper-haired doctor and a timid-looking Japanese woman with bony arms. The doctor introduces her as Keiko Matsuko. She is doing her residency in neurosurgery.

"Please tell her what you just told me," says the doctor.

Hanne repeats her statement slowly. The Japanese woman translates.

"Fascinating," he says, smiling, looking at Hanne as if she's a glorious star. "You're speaking Japanese."

She is doing well. Walking now, urinating, bathing on her own. Everything seems to have returned, except her ability to speak her first languages. Though she can hear them in her head, sense the texture of the words in English, Dutch, German, she can almost feel the English word in the front part of her brain travel over a bridge to Japanese, a language she learned in her teens.

It seems that a second language learned in adulthood, says the doctor, is spatially separated in the brain from the native language, or in Hanne's case, the languages of English and German and Dutch. Both are located in the brain's language area, the Broca, but they are not in the same spot.

Tomas stands beside Hanne's bed, and the doctor's eyes flit from Hanne to Tomas, as if not certain to whom he should speak. The doctor had done some research and found a similar case in Israel involving a 41-year-old bilingual man. His mother tongue was Arabic, and he learned Hebrew later in life. A brain injury knocked out both languages, but rehabilitation eventually brought back his Arabic. His Hebrew, however, remained severely damaged. He could understand it, but not speak it proficiently.

"He represents the typical case—the mother tongue is recovered first. But you, you've retained the language learned later in life. That's unusual. There've been some cases where the later language returned first if it was used the most around the time of the accident. Is that true of your Japanese?"

Hanne shakes her head no. Despite the year-long effort to translate Kobayashi's novel, Hanne's primary language was always English. And even when her husband had been alive, English was their preferred language. For Hanne, Japanese has always been too quiet, too passive. With its verb at the end of the sentence and changing its form, depending on who one was speaking to, it made her too aware of what she was saying and to whom. When she spoke it, she could feel it shaping her private mental life into something more demure, indecisive, even wishy-washy. It would do no good to think this way, especially in dog-eat-dog America, where the winner takes all.

"Or the later language is the most practical—"

Again, Hanne shakes her head no.

"Another study suggests that the language first recovered might be motivated by unconscious factors. I'm speculating, of course, but maybe Japanese holds more significance for you. For some reason, in your subconscious, it's more important or meaningful for you to speak it right now."

What's most important right now is that she go home. "When can I go home?" she says in Japanese.

"What did she say?" asks the doctor.

"She just wants to know when she'll be released."

"Yes. Released. I should have used that word," she says.

"A couple more days of observation, and she'll be on her way," says the doctor.

"Observed like a monkey. And spoken of in the third person."

Tomas reminds her she's at a university hospital, a teaching hospital. She's become an intriguing case for students and for the doctors. "It's a way of contributing, Mother."

She frowns.

Before they can speak further, in comes a procession of medical students. She counts eight. Young, too young—five boys, three girls gather around her bedside, peering at her, the suture at the top of her head, where the tube was inserted. The copper-haired doctor tells them about her case. Describes the location of the impact, then asks the students for the patient's symptoms. The patient. Not Hanne or Ms. Schubert. The patient in room 272 is an odd case, Hanne imagines the doctor saying as a prelude. The students dutifully go through a list of symptoms associated with brain trauma.

"All right, Hanne, can you tell us how you're feeling? Please note, her first languages are German and English and Dutch."

The circle of students moves in tighter, closer, an arm's stretch away. They seem to be collectively holding their breath, though she smells coffee, something medicinal, and watermelon. Lip gloss? The girl with shiny pink lips? What if she sat there mute? Just stared at them. Or stuck out her tongue. Or barked like a dog. For a moment she lets the possibilities exist—all of them in their surprising glory.

She glances at Tomas, who's standing by the window looking out. But if she chose to bark or bay, they'd probably keep her here longer. Extend the observation period. Make her perform over and over for these blurry-eyed students. She's at their mercy. This is what she's been reduced to, a performance, an act, a patient in room 272 whose brain got rearranged in a most entertaining way.

She speaks. "Hello, my name is Hanne. I am a monkey." In Japanese.

A Japanese boy with a thin wisp of a dark moustache laughs, showing off crooked teeth. "Wow."

"Wow is right," says Hanne, now speaking directly to the boy. "The monkey does her little tricks and makes the audience laugh."

The young Japanese man laughs again.

"What did she say?" one of the interns asks the boy.

The doctor smiles. Clearly pleased with the performance.

With his arms crossed, Tomas comes over to her bed. She asks him please to get these people out of here. Tell them she's tired. Tell them anything. One good thing: at least she didn't yield to the Japanese language's love of politeness and decorum.

"You're in a bad mood," he says to her in Japanese, then turns to the students. "My mother would like privacy now." He frowns again at her. "But I do hope everyone learned something."

Chapter Five

THERE'S NOTHING CEREMONIOUS ABOUT HER departure from the hospital. She's outside, finally, and it feels remarkable, this quick pulse in the chilly air. Noises lie everywhere. Across the street, a group of kids are playing basketball, and the ball hitting the court aligns with the beat in the air. The squeaky shuffle of sneakers, the grunts, outbursts of "Hey!" are like instruments in an orchestra, all of it sends pleasure spiraling down her spine. She almost feels like her old self again.

In her apartment, she quickly unpacks, tossing everything into the laundry basket, and checks her voicemail. How odd, only David calling to find out if she went away on an unexpected vacation. She thought for sure she'd hear from the publisher. Kobayashi should have finished reading and signed off. And she expected a call from Claire Buttons, an editor at one of the big publishing houses, who'd mentioned several months ago she had a translation project for Hanne. She checks her e-mail. Nothing. Hanne announces she's going for a walk.

"Why don't you relax," says Tomas, who disappears down the hallway, carrying his luggage into his old bedroom. "We just got here."

"I've been cooped up for too long."

"I need to call the office first!" he calls from the room.

"I'll go alone, then," she says, grabbing her coat, closing the door, shutting out his likely protest. Fresh air, outdoor sounds, pavement underfoot, these are the things that will re-anchor her to the world of the living.

Across the street, the lone bottlebrush tree, stuck in its small patch of dirt, an island in a sea of concrete sidewalk, shows off its red-tipped branches. The blare of a car alarm, high-pitched, intermittent, pierces the morning. A robbery, she thinks, or a tap on a front bumper. Who cares; it exists and it's close enough for her to hear at least three different notes in the seemingly monotone blare. Just like Brigitte, Hanne has always had keen hearing. A girl with two dark braids bounces a red ball on the sidewalk, like the rhythm of a heartbeat. Next to the girl by the stairway, a tall birch tree flutters hundreds of heart-shaped leaves. Hanne heads down the sidewalk, where a man with a big belly lifts the hood of his beat-up car, plunges his head, a tangle of red hair, inside and starts to sing a sad love song.

She stops beside him. A big, stunning voice, made for the opera. Jiro would love this—there's a scene in the book where he's walking down the street and hears a woman singing in the shower. He stops and listens to the entire song. After a while, the man pokes his head out from under the hood and looks at her, curious, puzzled, before he dismisses Hanne, who has just been standing there, staring at him mutely. "Bunch of wackos in this town."

Still, she smiles at him. Pasted onto the sidewalk, leaves, the color of dirt; sheets of newspaper scuttling down the street; a man in a suit, his shirt robin's-egg blue. *Kireina*, beautiful, she murmurs, beautiful. She walks slowly, deliberately, aware of the sidewalk, the cracks and bumps, the dips and drops. Aware now of how easy it is to fall.

In the brightly lit lobby of her apartment building, she even lets her neighbor's collie press his wet black nose on her dress, leaving a long smear. "I'm so sorry," says the neighbor, whose blue-tinted hair seems remarkable today.

Smiling, Hanne strokes the dog's head. "What a lovely dog," she says. "She must keep you company."

The neighbor leans toward Hanne and tilts her ear. "Are you feeling all right, Ms. Schubert?" Her voice wavers and warbles with age. "I didn't understand a word you just said."

She forgot. She can't speak to her neighbors. Language, she remembers her mother telling her when she was a girl, is the umbilical cord to other humans.

By the time she returns to her apartment, she has a slight headache. Her brain, that convoluted gray mass, feels tender, like a small nocturnal animal that has been thrust into the sun. She sits at the kitchen table, watching Tomas attack an empty cardboard box with scissors. He thought he'd be useful, he says. He's replaced the light bulbs in the hallway, swept away cobwebs in the corners of her rooms, put oil on the bolt of a squeaky cupboard. Is there anything else he can do?

"There was a man singing, a beautiful voice, that man," she says in Japanese. "Baritone that swung into tenor."

"Just a state of ecstasy," he says, as he scissors through the side of the box. "The etymology of the Greek word," he reminds her, as if her fall had stripped her of more than her English, "being outside oneself. What you're experiencing is a complete forgetting of the past and future; you're conscious of only the present instant. I read about it somewhere."

One side of the box is cut in half. "Probably something to do with endorphins." He steps on it and crushes it. "Or maybe serotonin. I forget all the chemistry of the brain these days." He goes on interpreting and speculating about the possible reasons for her ecstasy—maybe something she ate, or the lighting outside, or some medicine they gave her—and as the list grows longer, she feels her ecstasy, if that's the right name for it, dissolve.

She's grateful when his cell phone rings. She fixes herself a coffee and rubs her temples. As he paces the living room, his voice rises and falls, circling around the word "contract." When he finishes the call, he says he should probably leave soon. Maybe tomorrow morning. "Do you think you'll be all right?"

For a moment, she feels cold panic. How will she negotiate this city speaking only Japanese? David doesn't speak it. Who will keep her company? But she can't ask her son to put his life on hold. He's done more than enough. "Absolutely."

She asks Tomas to call David—a friend, she says—to tell him what happened to her. "Tell him there's no need for concern. I'm on the mend." Tomas dials the number and leaves a message. And then could he please call the university and let them know at least for the foreseeable future, she will not be able to teach Japanese. She knows her students; they require a professor who can explain things over and over in English.

"I don't want you here alone," he says, frowning. "I'll arrange for a nurse."

"There's no need. Really, Tomas."

He reminds her to check in with her doctor.

She agrees to do just that. He nods absentmindedly.

In the morning, he slips into his coat, snaps shut his briefcase, no, no breakfast, tells her he's called a taxi and should head to the lobby.

He reaches for the door.

"Tomas."

He pauses.

"Any word from Brigitte?"

"No. Call if you need anything," then he closes the front door.

She looks around her empty apartment. There on the side table, Tomas forgot his yellow legal notepad. Not words, but a doodle, a man on his back, his legs lifted up in the air. At first she feels a flush of embarrassment, thinking she's intruded on his fantasy life. But the image reminds her of something else: Picasso's painting of a man on his back eating watermelon. Was her son contemplating delight? *Her* ecstatic delight?

With her son no longer here making calls, his voice scaling peaks of excitement, then sliding down into a hushed reassurance, his hard heels smacking the hardwood floors, his head bowed reverently over a notepad, his long fingers running through his inky black hair, there is only deathly quiet.

She hurries down the hall to the elevator. "Hurry up," she murmurs as it descends. She runs across the marble floor of the lobby, but by the time she pushes through the heavy glass doors, he is gone. Whisked away in a yellow taxi. What greets her is the rush of traffic, music blaring from god knows where, people hurrying by on their way to work, as if pushed along by a strong wind. She stands in the lobby doorway, trying to catch her breath, hoping to spot him, wave him back, one foot in, the other out. She glances down. How unlike her; she is standing in the foyer barefoot.

The next day, she cuts her morning walk short, deciding against a trek across the bridge in the fog, with the wet gray clinging to her. And she doesn't stop by Cecilia's Bakery because she doesn't want to dumbly point to her selection and nod like an idiot—yes, yes, that's the one. Cecilia, with the lines on her face filled with flour, will ask what happened in her heavy accent, and Hanne will be reduced to more hand signals or jotting everything down.

By the time she gets home, she's chilled to the bone. She picks up the phone to call David. Then remembers she can't. Fortunately, he comes by at noon. She can see he's startled by her appearance. Does she look that bad? He studies her, then looks away, then sneaks another glance before he walks into the foyer and announces in a voice deliberately loud and upbeat that he has brought a homemade meal of rosemary chicken, mashed potatoes, and salad. "I never claimed the English were good cooks," he says. "But, ta-da."

She smiles, nods, grabs a notepad and writes: *It smells delicious. Thank you.*

"How are you?"

Doing better. It's so nice to have your company.

He puts together a plate of food for her, then serves himself. For a while, they try to converse with David asking questions, and she responding via her notepad. But the conversation moves slowly, like drips from a faucet. He launches into a monologue, telling her about school, a tedious faculty meeting, his wonderful students, a concert he attended, his visit to the Monet exhibit at the Museum of Modern Art. She nods, smiles, gestures with her hands. About mid-way through the chicken, he runs out of stories and steam. A long interval of awkwardness settles over them. The lunch, she knows, is exhausting. For him. For her.

When they make love, it's not the same. A cotton layer has wrapped tightly around her, dulling her senses. She is just going through the motions. He must sense it because afterwards, he doesn't lounge around in bed. "Call me—" then he catches himself. He says he has to go to Sacramento for one of his kids' soccer tournaments. When he returns in a couple of days, he'll stop by, take her out to dinner.

I'd like that, she writes on a paper. She refrains from writing *Please don't forget.*

She can't sleep. Around midnight, half dazed, she steps into the living room, stretching her back to untangle the knots. The lighting seems different, brighter, a strange yellow glow. It takes her a moment to realize she's failed to perform her nightly ritual of shutting her curtains. Through her big wall of windows, her life is on display to whoever wants to peer in. She hurries over to shut them, but just as she's about to do so, she glances straight into an apartment across the street, where a woman in a blue dress is chasing a man around a couch. Or maybe he is chasing her. Around they go. The woman is barefoot and tosses her head back, laughing, exposing the long line of her pale throat. The man is running and now unbuttoning his white shirt, flinging it into the air, and it sails beyond the couch, as if caught in an invisible wind, and it floats onto a chair. She should look away, shut her curtains, but will he catch her?—she's decided he is chasing her— and he does, and now they tumble onto the couch, their arms and legs entangled, their bodies glued together. No one is watching her—it's she who is watching them. She yanks closed the curtains.

Four days go by and she slips into a great hole of silence. She can't while away the hours reading, because she's unable to focus on words without ushering in a headache. The doctor explained

71

it, but she didn't quite understand. She only clung to his final phrase—that, too, should return. Some day. She'd give anything to have the demands and absorption of her work, the reassurance of a new manuscript to translate.

When there's a firm knock on the door, she nearly runs to answer it. She's expecting David. Thank God. Finally back from his trip. A woman with straight black hair, as thin as a wire, is standing there in a skimpy black skirt, holding a fistful of balloons, one hip provocatively thrust forward. She's tottering on four-inch heels, shoes that are surprisingly large to accommodate the woman's surprisingly large feet. A tight red top accentuates her big breasts, but black fishnet stockings sag loosely on her rail-thin legs.

A trollop, thinks Hanne, frowning her disapproval. Who in the condo association would order such a woman? Probably that man on the ninth floor with the huge paunch and greasy hair, who has a permanent ring of sweat gleaming underneath his eyes. Hanne grabs a paper and pencil. *You have the wrong apartment.*

Pink foundation covers the woman's face, and her black eyeliner is so thick the effect is raccoonish. Garish red lips compete with the eyeliner, and Hanne's eyes dart back and forth, from eyes to mouth, as if both exaggerated features are clamoring for her attention. It's hard to see, let alone fathom the real face underneath all that gunk, though Hanne imagines this woman, surely a prostitute, is not much older than twenty. A drug addict too, thinks Hanne, too thin, unkempt, malnourished.

Snapping her gum, the woman runs her hand up and down the doorframe, as if stroking velvet, her charm bracelet jingling on her skeletal wrist. She glances at the door number, then the card in her hand, and, shaking her head, grins her slash-mouth. "Nope."

Are you sure? she scribbles.

"Hanne Schubert?" She lurches toward Hanne, who takes a quick step back.

You're not coming in.

The woman shrugs her bony shoulders to her ears. "Suit yourself." Her voice is low, grating, with a hint of an accent—Bulgarian?—and her tone amused. "Most people don't want it in the hallway."

From the streets, thinks Hanne, getting a whiff of the woman, who smells unwashed, oily. Now Hanne sees that the woman's foundation reaches only to her jaw line; her neck is ghostly white, as white as death. There is something familiar about the woman. *Who sent you?*

Looking straight at Hanne with hard angry eyes, as if daring her to do something, say something more, the woman spits her gum into a wrapper, clears her throat and begins to sing a song in perfect beautiful German. It's the lullaby her mother sang to her as a child. Hanne can still hear her mother's heels clicking across the wood floor as she came to Hanne's bedroom to tuck her in, smooth down the white quilt, and sing to her. It was the moment Hanne waited for all day. It didn't happen often, her mother too busy. But when it did, her mother's face came so close, wisps of her blond hair tickling Hanne's face, her red-wine breath, her voice, magically beautiful, singing, *Schlaf, Kindlein, schlaf. Der Vater Hut't die Schaf. Die Mutter schuttelt's Baumelein, Da fallt herab ein Traumelein. Schlaf, Kindlein, schlaf!* Sleep, baby, sleep. Your father tends the sheep. Your mother shakes the branches small, Lovely dreams in showers fall. Sleep, baby, sleep.

Hanne only remembers that verse, and perhaps that was all there was. The song and the presence of her mother swiftly delivered her into the arms of Morpheus, where she was held in the loveliest dreams. For a moment, Hanne closes her eyes, letting the song spill over her. When she opens them, she hardly knows where she is. But this girl—this young woman, with her black hair, her brown eyes faintly slanted, her big feet, reminds Hanne of her daughter. Brigitte, as a teenager.

Hanne tries to make the woman stop, but she keeps singing, her voice flatter, angrier. German, one of Brigitte's first languages. She spoke it with a perfect accent.

When the girl finishes singing, she says, "Here you go, lady." And as she gives Hanne the balloons, their hands briefly touch. "See ya," she says, baring her teeth, a streak of red lipstick marring her front tooth. The sarcasm lingers in the air, like a bad smell.

Hanne watches the girl saunter toward the elevator, hips swaying like a pendulum, not bothering to turn around. The farther she walks, the jerkier her gait becomes, as if she's having trouble negotiating high heels on the nubby carpet. Before Hanne can decide what else to do, she is gone. Hanne stands there, nothing in focus, the hallway rug a smear of slate blue. In her mind, she repeats the girl's phrase like an incantation, with the same accent, the same guttural growl, "See ya."

She looks over at the balloons in her hand and sees a small card attached to the one of the ribbons. Slowly she closes the door, locks it, and opens the card.

Welcome home! Glad you're out of the hospital. Love, Tomas, Anne, Sasha and Irene.

Hanne stands in the front hallway of her apartment and watches her hand release the balloons. They drift up, hit the ceiling, bounce off, then up again, where they stay glued. She slowly makes her way into the living room, as if tangled in a dream.

The wall that is all windows casts the day's light across a large open space, with maple wood floors, a white sofa, two white chairs, and a glass coffee table. Nowhere is there clutter, nothing extra, everything open, bare, pared down. A spaciousness that allows room to think, that was the intention behind the design. She can see it that way, but also another way. It looks uninhabited, an empty room staged with just enough furniture to persuade a prospective buyer to make the purchase. Who lives here?

She stands so close to the big window that her breath fogs a small circle. A handful of miniature people on the sidewalk, someone walking a small skittish dog. Cars and a yellow taxi zoom by. Six hundred souls live on this block, eating, shitting, sleeping, making love, and somewhere in this city a new soul is arriving, another departing. She leans her forehead on the cold glass, humming the German lullaby underneath her breath, wordlessly, until she catches herself doing so and makes herself stop.

Two more days go by and her loneliness has taken on sharp edges. Every sound—the floor creaking, a door closing, laughter drifting up from the street—seems loud and mocking. She waits a day, then breaks down and calls Tomas. She asks if he'd do her a big favor and phone David for her.

"Of course, Mom. How are you?"

"Better."

"Good. You sound good. Got the balloons?"

"Yes, thank you. And her German was perfect."

"Glad to hear it worked out."

Tomas puts her on hold and dials David. She looks down at her nightgown. Lunch time and she still hasn't dressed. Tomas comes back on the line. "He wasn't there. I left him a message to call you."

A chill runs through her along with a vision of her future— more of the same bleak silence. But she won't perish from that.

"Is there anyone else I can call?"

She asks him to call the publisher and find out what's happening with the translation. He calls her back ten minutes later. Kobayashi hasn't gotten back to the publisher. They aren't sure what's going on.

"Do you want me to fly out again?" he says.

She can hear a hint of reluctance in his voice. "I'm fine. I've got plenty to do." An entire closet of old clothes to sort through. She'll start her spring cleaning early.

The next day, when the unbearable silence bears down on her, when the highlight of her day is riding the elevator to the lobby to check her mailbox, which is empty, when David sends an e-mail apologizing, he's been stuck at home with two sick kids and now he's come down with something, she calls the Japanese Ministry of Culture. She knows it's short notice, but if it's at all possible, if they still have room, she'd like to be on their panel of speakers for the conference she'd turned down earlier. Her schedule now allows it. "It sounds so interesting," she says, hoping her tone isn't too eager.

"One moment please," says the woman on the phone.

Hanne refrains from pleading.

The woman says, in fact, they just had a cancellation. One of the speakers has a family emergency in London. Hanne has to stop herself from shouting with delight. The Ministry will secure her airfare, accommodations, and meals, as well as an honorarium.

"The Ministry is quite honored to have you attend," she says. "We are so happy."

"I'm so happy," says Hanne, reveling in the sound of her own voice. She asks about the weather and nearby restaurants within walking distance of the hotel. And shopping. What boutiques and specialty shops would she recommend? "I'm so looking forward to this."

"You are located in a very exciting area of Tokyo."

"Oh? Tell me." She just wants the woman to keep talking.

The woman rattles off some names, then says she'll send a packet of information in the mail.

"Wonderful," says Hanne, gobbling up everything the woman says. She keeps the woman on the phone a bit longer, asking how many attendees will be at the conference, from what countries, and a sample of the topics that will be discussed. Finally the woman apologies, but says she must go. A million things to attend to before the conference.

"Of course. Can you tell me if Mr. Yukio Kobayashi will be there?"

"He will, indeed."

"Good. Wonderful."

She looks forward to meeting him. Though he grumbled about the early chapters, after he reads the entire manuscript, he'll see she worked hard and gave him a beautiful translation, virtually guaranteeing him an English audience for his novel and all his future work. She imagines him asking her how she did it. What's her secret? Maybe he'll take her out for a celebratory drink or dinner. He'll set his glass down and wait. She'll tell him she's never understood a character as well as she did Jiro. It was uncanny. The longer she read, the more Jiro seemed to stand in her presence and speak to her directly. When she finished, she felt she had an intimate recognition of him. She knew what he was going to say before he said it. Like an old married couple. She's certain he'll request her to translate his next book. When a writer finds a translator who understands his work, it's like finding gold. And after all she's been through, she'd welcome the praise.

"I strongly advise against it," says her doctor. The Japanese medical student is on another line, interpreting. "If something happens to you, you're at the mercy of the Japanese medical system. It's not bad, but I won't be there to help you."

As she circles through the rooms of her apartment, her legs restless, she says she appreciates his candor, but she's sure she'll be fine.

"I can't say how it will or won't affect your condition. I just don't know. You could be taking a huge risk, but then again, it might be fine."

That's how she sees it too. How different is that from staying put? She loops twice around the living room.

"Let me be clear: I'm not giving my consent. But I can't stop you."

Her son is not so wishy-washy. "Don't go."

She pulls her suitcase from under the bed. "I'm an adult—"

"That's not what I mean. You don't have your languages back, which means something is still not right."

She doesn't want to bother him with her money concerns. "I'm looking forward to this trip. I haven't been there in years."

"I'll visit again. We'll take a trip together. Napa. We'll go drink wine."

He doesn't have time, she knows. "No, you're busy."

When she stares at her clothes hanging in the closet, her gaze lands on the boxes pushed to the far back corner, boxes of Brigitte's things. In one is a teddy bear with a loose felt eye. And a sweater she knitted for Brigitte, soft pink with milky white buttons. Brigitte picked out the yarn, and it took Hanne months to finish, unraveling row after row, knitting it again to make it perfect. She can still see Brigitte heading to kindergarten in that sweater buttoned to her neck. Her kindergarten teacher. What was her name? Mrs. Lapensko? Lapensker? A horrible woman. Hanne had fretted that Brigitte would be too bored. What would she do when the others were stumbling over the alphabet? Slowly spitting out the simplest of words? Brigitte already knew how to read—and not just in English. Hanne wanted Brigitte to skip a grade, but the school advised her to wait and see.

Not long into the school year, Brigitte's kindergarten teacher called Hanne and asked her to come in for a parent conference.

Hiro couldn't make it, she can't remember why, so Hanne showed up the next morning. Bright gold stars made out of construction paper decorated one entire wall. The letters of the alphabet were stapled around the perimeter, along with the numbers, 1 to 10, and self-portraits done with tempera paint hung above the blackboard. As Hanne took a seat across from the teacher's desk, she tried to spot Brigitte's.

The teacher said Brigitte was clearly bright, but too easily distracted; and during individual study times, she had trouble focusing. And she was always interrupting her classmates.

That was it? Hanne was relieved. "She's bored."

The teacher was probably in her mid-fifties and couldn't curb her sing-song voice intended to motivate, discipline, and guide five- and six-year-olds. She'd dyed her shoulder-length hair dark earthy brown, but near the temples the gray refused to be stamped out. "May I ask, are there problems at home?"

In an even tone, Hanne said that Brigitte had a stable, happy household with a loving father and mother. Who was this woman to pry? What gave her the right?

The teacher opened her mouth, as if she were about to ask another question. When she finally spoke, she said Brigitte never raised her hand. "It's strange. I know she knows the right answer. Maybe she's shy or she's afraid she'll say the wrong answer. Or maybe no one at home listens to her, so she thinks why bother."

What a thing to say!

"But that's not the biggest problem."

At least once a day, Brigitte wept—a girl who refused to sit beside her or play with her at recess; a toy she wanted, but was too late to retrieve from the box; a reprimand not to talk while the teacher was talking. Any failure went terribly deep, too deep. She falls apart. "I was hoping I could enlist your help."

"Once a day? Really?" Hanne couldn't keep the surprise and alarm from her voice. In the early weeks of school, Brigitte had cried in the car on the way home. Something about a girl who didn't want to play with her at recess. Hanne had a long talk with Brigitte, how, of course, these things hurt, but tomorrow was a different day, and she could make it better. Brigitte should find someone else to play with. "Don't bother with this girl who refuses your company," Hanne told Brigitte. "She doesn't sound like a very nice girl." How could she put this delicately? "Some girls are not worth the trouble." Brigitte nodded and dried her tears, and after that, Hanne never heard another word about it. Or any of the other things the teacher had mentioned.

Hanne finally spotted Brigitte's self-portrait. She'd painted herself wearing her pink sweater and a big red bow in her hair. A huge face but with a tiny body, as if the latter were an afterthought, squeezed in at the request of a teacher. Her eyes were slanted lines, her mouth wavy, not a smile, but not quite a frown either. To Hanne she looked hesitant to join the fracas of accompanying faces, her so-called peers.

At home, the teacher advised, Hanne shouldn't reward this infantile behavior. When Brigitte cried, Hanne should minimize the event. "Or don't even acknowledge her. Ignore her, the crying jags. The tantrums. Just go about your business as if nothing is happening. She will learn that this kind of behavior is not rewarded."

"I don't reward that kind of behavior," said Hanne, not restraining the fury in her voice. "Did you know my daughter speaks four languages? She comes from a very intelligent, hard-working household. At home, she basks in so much attention, and she never cries. She's happy. You've never seen a happier child."

Surely the woman was exaggerating about crying bouts once a day. And if Brigitte occasionally broke down and cried, it had to be out of boredom.

The teacher sighed. "I've been teaching kindergarten for sixteen years. I've seen a lot of children."

"And I know my daughter."

Hanne grabbed her coat and purse and marched out, vowing to find another school. What did this woman know about her Brigitte? Brigitte, who, as a baby, clamped her hands to her ears and cried whenever she heard a loud sound—a siren, the vacuum cleaner, the stove alarm, a person with a booming voice. The pediatrician had recommended that Brigitte's keen hearing be normalized—what was his word?—desensitized—or she'd have trouble negotiating the world. Every outing would be an ordeal for Hanne. Expose her to new sounds gradually, slowly raising the volume, and soon she would be fine. But that acute ability meant her daughter could hear and almost instantly speak different languages. Hanne would not crush her daughter to fit some terrible average, some awful norm.

Now still on the phone with Tomas, Hanne pulls out the rob-in's-egg-blue dress. Is it too early for a dress intended for spring?

"Come stay with us," says Tomas. "You won't be in the way."

Of course she'll be in the way. Anne and her granddaughters don't speak Japanese. She will be reduced to a ghostly presence, a museum relic, glued in a chair.

He sighs. "What did your doctor say?"

She chooses a cream-colored dress and puts it, along with the blue one, in her suitcase. "He gave the okay."

"What did he say, exactly?"

"It could be a wonderful time. He said to enjoy life. He's never been to Japan and wishes he could go." She gives him the name of the hotel and the phone number. "It's a marvelous hotel," she says. She hears him tell someone to wait. "I understand all the risks." She opens her top drawer and counts out pairs of socks, underwear, pantyhose. "It's a paid engagement to speak."

He groans. "You're so stubborn. So damn stubborn."

If he thinks he's reprimanding her, he's wrong. Stubbornness is one of her greatest strengths, she thinks. She can always be counted on, no matter how difficult the task, no matter the number of naysayers.

For the first time in a long while, she feels giddy. She showers, puts on makeup, and dresses in a white silk blouse with ivory buttons and a black skirt. A string of pearls. She's never let herself go. Not during pregnancy, not after Hiro's death. She always kept her figure; she still wears a size eight.

She takes a taxi to Japantown and heads to her favorite restaurant, Mifune. The place is crowded with Japanese, slurping noodles. She's seated in the corner. A young Japanese couple sits beside her, and she quickly learns that they don't suspect she speaks their language. She has watery eyes, they decide, a sharp nose that makes her look like a hawk. "At least she's not fat like most Americans," says the young man with a greasy sheen to his hair. And she doesn't have many wrinkles. It's hard to guess her age. Hanne listens with a mixture of horror and voyeuristic thrill, peering into her own life as if she, too, were viewing it, assessing it, finding it, on the whole, lacking.

"She sits alone," says the girl with a shine to her forehead. "No husband. No friends. It's so sad."

"That's how most Americans look to me. Lonely and sad."

"But this woman seems like she sits alone—lonely, sad, and also angry. Maybe she sits there, angry with her life."

She can't be quiet any longer. "Sits?" says Hanne, turning to them. "A present participle would be a better choice. 'She is sitting alone.'"

The woman covers her mouth with her hand. A few seconds pass, and Hanne hears a mumbled "*Sumimasen,*" sorry.

She knows she should have let it go. The waiter brings Hanne her bowl of wakame. While she eats, the couple sits stiffly, not saying a word. When the waiter walks by them again, the young man shoves the bill and money at him, and they quickly leave.

Chapter Six

"*HAJIMEMASHITE. DOZO YOROSHIKU,*" SAYS THE young Japanese woman who greets Hanne at the gate. How do you do? I'm very glad to meet you. A limo will take Hanne from Narita Airport to Tokyo. Stocked in the limo refrigerator are Hanne's favorites— inari, salted sea bream, and cold sake. Along with pears, mandarin oranges, mamakari fish, and sweet liquor. The young woman has a high, soft voice, made softer by a slight lisp and the dip of her head at the end of her sentences, as if apologizing for what she just said. Hanne will have the limo to herself. She must be very tired from the long plane ride, says the woman, whose name is Amaya. Amaya will follow in her own car and check Hanne into the hotel. The young woman bows low, lower than Hanne's bow. "We are honored to have you here."

"I'm very honored to be here," says Hanne.

As the limo speeds along the freeway, Hanne gazes out the window at the bleach-white sky, the billboards for every possible consumer product, the blur of cement tenement buildings. It's late winter, but soon the windows will be open, laundry on the line, fluttering like birds. She has mostly fond memories of living here as a teenager. After five years living with her Oma, who, by the end, wouldn't leave the house, who refused to let Hanne out, except for school and errands and while she cleaned, Hanne had finally been fetched by her mother. Her mother had secured a lucrative translation position with the German government, which was trying to make inroads into the Japanese car industry. They were moving to Japan.

Coming here felt like stepping out of prison. Now Hanne is filled with memories of feeling alive, vibrant, in the mix of things. In her mind, Japan is associated with the hot thicket of her teenage years when she discovered sex, and, more significantly, her power to allure by the simplest of gestures, a wetting of her lips, a tilt of her head. With her round eyes and brown hair, she was a desirable anomaly, sought after, at first tentatively and then more aggressively, by the Japanese boys. They thought she was American, but when they discovered she was from Europe, she became even more exotic, a real catch, but she was the one doing the catching. Hanne's mother saw only a bookish, studious girl, so she let Hanne at the tender ripe and ripening age of fifteen do what she wanted, go wherever she wished. It was a very safe country, her mother told Hanne. Her mother was so busy working, she had no time to watch over Hanne or realize what Hanne was doing. Hanne welcomed the neglect. She roamed and explored and the world was alive and vigorous and so was she. Her mother never suspected

Hanne's afternoons were spent with Japanese boys from her school, one in particular, his shiny-shampooed hair falling into his dark eyes, like a veil. She sees them wrapped around each other on the corduroy couch in the cramped living room, like lush vines, as she plunges her hand into the deep territory of his trousers, touching his rubbery penis, coaxing it into a hard shape. Not just once. His hand fumbling under her blouse, lifting her bra, stroking, fondling. When he pinched her nipple, she told him to cut it out.

She cracks open the limo window—cold air, mingled with car exhaust, the stink of rotten eggs, and tar, fills the car. Not much has changed since she was last here—more buildings, more cars, the same polluted air. She closes the window again and kicks off her shoes, stretching out her legs, soaking them in the cool blue light from the darkly tinted windows.

That Japanese boy wanted to keep going, but she had no desire to lose her virginity to fumbling hands and an awkward, boyish body. She wanted her first time to be better, more extraordinary; she had someone else in mind. He worked behind the counter of the café where she stopped after school and drank black coffee and smoked Sakura cigarettes. Five years her senior, he was tall for a Japanese man, smooth-skinned. He rarely smiled, so when he did, it felt genuine.

She began wearing short skirts to show off her long legs, and scarlet lipstick, and her hair curled so it outlined her ear, like a picture frame. Smiling at him a little too long, as if seeing deep into the dark core of him. After a month or so, she knew his shift ended at 3:30, and that he slouched outside on the porch to smoke and scribble in a small blank notebook. He liked D. H. Lawrence; a tattered copy of *Lady Chatterley's Lover* was always on the counter beside him. During a lull, he'd pick it up and head out back. She began joining him on the back porch to smoke, talking about Lawrence, his boldness, his sex scenes. One day she invited him to her apartment. Not in love, Hanne was curious about sex and mildly smitten with his cool exterior. When they entered the apartment, he wrapped his hand around her wrist and took her, as if he'd been there before, straight to her bedroom. He knew how to make love; it was why she'd picked him.

But then he started showing up at her apartment door, saying he had to see her, he missed her. She was irritated that he'd arrive, uninvited. What if he showed up when her mother was there? She told him she'd see him at the coffee shop. The third time he showed up uninvited, she lied and said she had another boyfriend, then closed the door. But at the end of the week when she stopped by the coffee shop and he barely looked at her, she softened. She went outside on the back porch with him, took his hand in hers. In her bedroom, she made love to him one more time. It was good, as good as the other time, but then the swelling, the nausea; not a good pick in the end, for he was no help. She took care of it immediately; took such good care, her mother never knew.

After that, her interest in boys waned. It rattled her, the possibility of her life derailing just because of a boy, because of what could happen from sex. What took its place was mastering the Japanese language.

The limo delivers her directly to the front steps of the imposing Imperial Hotel. A quick dash from the car to the high-ceilinged lobby, she escapes the crush of humanity that is Tokyo, though she can hear it all around her, a mesh of cars, taxis, buses, scooters, the metro. The density of this city is the main reason why she so rarely visits. Hiro, too, preferred more space, more breathing room. Because of that, he had no interest in living in Japan, especially Tokyo. Before she enters the fray, she needs to rest.

Amaya is already at the front desk and the bellhop carries her bags to her room. The other speakers are also staying in the hotel, Amaya says, handing Hanne a glossy conference program, opened to the page that shows Hanne will lecture tomorrow, the first day of the conference. "Please ring if you need anything," she says.

In her room, she opens the curtains and drags a bulky chair over by the window to sit in a patch of winter sun. Across the street is Hibiya Park. A cherry tree sapling looks like it was recently planted, a skirt of fresh dirt surrounding its small trunk. She watches it sway with the breeze. How peaceful. Already San Francisco is quickly becoming remote, receding into the past. Unable to speak to anyone, she was slowly disappearing in San Francisco. Here she feels she's someone again. Not just anyone, someone held in high regard. They are honored she's here.

A Japanese man in a dark gray suit stops and stands right beside the cherry tree. He lights a cigarette. Hanne is watching the smoke spiral and dissipate when the man's arms curve in front of him and he begins to waltz, the familiar 1-2-3 pattern, around the tree, as if dancing with an invisible partner. Hanne stands to get a better view. She can't see his expression; only now and then does he suck on his cigarette, exhaling a plume of gray smoke, as if his body is overheating and letting off steam. She watches, entranced by the public display of a private world.

After she found Brigitte dancing with that first boy, Hanne stood in her doorjamb, hands on her hips, and Brigitte cried that he was the only one who truly loved her, who truly understood her, now that Dad was gone. Brigitte's face was wet with tears. "He loves me," said Brigitte, "and I love him." Hanne's mind spun a hundred retorts: fleeting first love, it held you in its grubby grip, fumbling, a moment of pleasure that quickly vanished when someone new and shinier came along and that was the end of that. And just as that comeback faded, along rushed in—how could everything I've done for you—out of love!—be so casually and carelessly tossed out? Am I nothing to you? And are you having sex? You're still a child, for God's sake, so you'd better not, but the way Brigitte was looking at her with teary eyes, as if Hanne had just ripped out her heart, she knew Brigitte had and she would again. "I hope you're using protection," said Hanne icily. "Being a mother is hard work."

She was aware that she was being hypocritical. She, too, had been sexually active around Brigitte's age, but the word "love" wasn't part of it. Hanne was never in love with these boys. Love and girls were a dangerous mix. Love entered and a girl thought, why not a baby? It became even more dangerous when a girl believed it was true love and he was the only one in the entire world who loved her. He, who said he loved her, who would leave when it wasn't so fun anymore, when there was a crying baby at 3:00 A.M. and again at 4:00.

Now she regrets that. Her quick, angry retort. She could have explained herself better, could have told Brigitte her fears. The man waltzing outside abruptly stops. Looks up at the hotel windows, as if suddenly aware that someone might be watching. Does he see her? Is that why he departs in short rapid steps?

She's back in the doorjamb. Brigitte answered back just as sharply: "You just make mothering hard. It doesn't have to be that way."

Hanne looks down and sees she's crumpling the conference program, the cover of which is scattered with words in all different languages. Flipping through it, she reads the names of her fellow conferees, most of whom she does not know. She hesitates before turning to her listing: a professor at Colbert University, a long-time translator, whose work has received "rave reviews" from critics, who call her translations "music to the ear, you forget the original was written in Japanese."

Something settles inside. She made the right decision to come here, she thinks. She finds Yukio Kobayashi's name. "An acclaimed Japanese novelist who is about to make his debut in America with the English version of *Trojan Horse Trips*, which in Japan sold over 1 million copies. Called a tour de force by *The Japan Times*, a stunning debut by *Asahi Shimbun*." "Kobayashi peers into the soul of Japan. His language is charged and playful and poetic." He is scheduled to speak tomorrow.

She calls Tomas and tells him she's arrived safely. Everything's fine. It's lovely.

He pauses. "I wish you hadn't gone. Anything might happen."

"Such as?"

"What if you fall again?" She's startled to hear his voice, now astonishingly bare, stripped of its authority, the voice of a small boy who used to play for hours with his Matchbox cars, lining them in neat little rows. "Your languages aren't all back. Something isn't right."

"Please, Tomas, I'm sure you have many other things to worry about."

"I just don't think you should have gone." The overlay of irritation has returned to his voice. She imagines him rubbing his eyelids, pinching the bridge of his nose.

"I'm fine. By the way, I'll get to meet Kobayashi."

"I hope it goes well."

"Of course it will."

"Well, he certainly has taken his time getting back to you."

She sighs. When did he become such a worrier?

Tomas says he'll be traveling for the next week or so. An unexpected trip. They leave it that she will call if she needs him.

Jet-lagged, she falls into a deep sleep. A man's face appears, but the face is missing eyes, mouth, and nose. She hunts everywhere for his features, in the tall grasses, cupboards, a swimming pool, hunting in a methodical way, not frantic or even particularly fearful. She hears herself calling for the man. The man waits calmly, pushing back his cuticles. Toward early morning, she settles into what feels like another long dream. She's leaning over to blow out hundreds of candles on a cake, a birthday cake, hers—how did she get to be so old?—leaning so close that she feels the heat of the flames on her face, smells the burning wax, hissing as it melts, and she's planning to blow the candles out in one big whoosh—"Make a Wish!" when her hair catches on fire. Crackling and sizzling, and she's shouting for help, running madly, trying to find water—water!—faster and faster, the stench of burning hair thick in the air, her ears filled with the whir of the flames and wind.

She wakes to the air conditioner running full blast and morning's white light. It must have turned on automatically. It's cold in the room. What could the dream have meant? She looks around, locating herself in time and place. The dream was in Japanese. It has been years since she's dreamed in Japanese. But she has no time to ponder this. It's morning, and if she's going to take a walk before her presentation, she needs to leave now.

Weaving her way through throngs of people, mostly busi-nessman in gray suits and heavy coats, she catches snippets of conversation, "—tomatoes . . . ripe—"; "—trip to—" "—work on Saturday—" and as she strides at a brisk pace to stay warm, she feels part of the great big beat again, part of progress up Uchi-saiwaicho Street, past the shops with jade bracelets and skimpy skirts. As she reads more signs, she becomes aware of a change in her brain. Prior to the fall down the marble stairs, a second or two had lapsed between reading a Japanese word and recalling its meaning. It felt like following a bridge that attached the word to its meaning. The more obscure the word, the longer the bridge. Now there is no searching, no bridge. She knows the Japanese word and simultaneously knows the meaning. No need to search for meaning in English. For the first time, she's living inside this language. As if this were her native tongue, as if she had been born and raised here.

At a construction site, a crane smashes a wrecking ball into a building. Walls of brick collapse, windows shatter, support beams tumble, and up rise great plumes of gray dust. She can see straight into the building now—office cubicles with gray carpet, filing cabinets, an employee lunch room with a bright, white refrigerator, a photocopy machine, a water cooler. Another woman comes up beside her.

"Soon it will all be gone," Hanne says to the woman wearing a black cardigan sweater.

"*So desu ne.*"

They stand there together watching.

"Then something new," says the woman, who points to a picture of the new building posted on a board near the sidewalk. From the rubble a fifty-story building with bluish-tinted glass. "*Kireina,*" beautiful.

They chat about it a bit longer—why this design, who thought of it, marvelous, isn't it?—with Hanne taking pleasure in the ease of conversing and watching her mood shift to something lighter, even buoyant, from the simplicity of interaction with another human being. She finds out this woman is a secretary and is worried about losing her job. "The world can be a difficult place," says Hanne.

"*So desu ne.*"

On her way back to the hotel, she stops into a department store to buy gifts for her granddaughters, two kokeshi wooden dolls, with big round heads and cylindrical bodies. Not particularly cuddly, nor can they do much—they lack arms or legs—but they are traditional Japanese dolls, staring at you with bright black eyes that will never blink, as if they don't want to miss even an instant of life. "For my granddaughters," she says to the shop clerk. The clerk smiles and points to candy shaped like sushi. Made out of gummy, says the clerk. Hanne adds it to her basket. On impulse, she also buys a bottle of black hair dye.

Three phone messages from Amaya are waiting—"Does Ms. Schubert need anything?" "Please contact if you need anything." "If there's anything Ms. Schubert needs." Wrapped in red cellophane on the coffee table, there's a gift basket overflowing with rice and seaweed crackers, Satsuma oranges, chewing gum, Pocky Shock, chocolate pretzels, and red apples. A small note is tucked between the apples, "Welcome to Japan!" from the Ministry of Culture.

She slices into quarters what is probably a $5 apple in this expensive island of a country, where most everything is imported; she tries to eat each section as a Japanese person would, savoring it, like a treasure, a luxury, but to her it's just an apple and she's hungry.

She steps into the bathroom. Her hair has always been non-descript, the color of mud, she called it, though at the beginning of their marriage Hiro referred to it as beautiful dark cinnamon and made her promise not to change it. When she began to go gray, she dyed it and tried to match her natural color. But that was long ago—is that why she's pulling on the thin latex gloves and rubbing in dye? Or is it that she's in a different country with a language she speaks exclusively and doesn't quite feel herself?

Against the emerging darkness of her hair, her pale skin glows; her green eyes are darker, a forest green. For a long time she stares at herself in the mirror. Not mesmerized by beauty—that would be too generous—but the sense that she's both herself and someone else, both the subject and the object.

She puts on what she calls her performance suit—a dark gray skirt and jacket, a white blouse—and clip-on gold earrings. With her new black hair, she would have to call herself striking.

She has ten minutes before she's due downstairs. As she dries her hair, she reads over her lecture notes. Written during the eleven-hour flight, she must have been under a spell of sustained optimism. She's about to give her audience a glowing picture of the wonderful powers of translation, an elixir to the human tragedy. There's no mention of the difficulties, the inability to do a literal translation, the issue of fidelity—to what? To whom? She can't do anything about it now, and she's not sure she wants to.

In the cavernous conference room, only a smattering of chairs are filled. Well, she'll give her talk, collect her fee, and that will be that. She hopes Kobayashi isn't in a rush, so maybe they can go to dinner tonight. Amaya is wearing a red suit coat and a red skirt. A good-luck suit. Amaya motions to her that it's time. Hanne is introduced with fanfare, a renowned translator, an impeccable speaker of Japanese as well as many other languages.

When Hanne steps onto the stage and to the podium, she is unexpectedly overcome with stage fright. The blinding bright light makes it impossible to see out to the audience; and in that gap, her panicked mind imagines that everyone is intently watching her, waiting for her to fail.

"Welcome. Thank you for coming. Let me begin with a personal anecdote," she says, her voice cracking from nerves. "Early on, I was drawn to making sense of the incomprehensible. When

I was seven years old living in Holland with my parents, I invented a language, which I called Lombot. It contained 72 characters and was syllabic. I wrote plays and stories in this strange language that looked a bit like Arabic and sounded—I found out later—Japanese. At the dinner table, my parents asked me to translate, which I did with great joy, turning Lombot into Dutch or German, depending on their preference that evening. It was my first experience with the joy of translation, my first encounter with the translator's array of alternatives. This activity brought great pleasure to my parents, who, between them, spoke thirteen languages. We were like a familial United Nations, though our negotiations usually concerned my failure to clean my room."

There's a titter in the audience, which relaxes her a little. But she feels exposed, so vulnerable. She normally doesn't talk about herself. She tries to calm herself down by remembering why she's doing this—she was terribly lonely. And the money is a help. At least here she can speak, and right now she's speaking too fast, but at least her hand is no longer shaking. There's no elegant way to segue from her private disclosure to her prepared speech except to proceed.

"For centuries, people have posited that we once spoke only one language, an Ur-Sprache. With this language, we understood each other with perfect ease. This language supposedly contained the original Logos, the words giving us direct knowledge of the nature of things, providing an intimacy with the world that we can't even begin to fathom today. This first language gave us not a representation of reality, but reality itself. Words spoke not of things, but the truth; and it was with this language that man once had total understanding of the world and of each other."

Her throat is dry. She pauses to sip water. Is anyone listening? Is anyone there?

"But when we were tossed out of Eden, our true home, and later when the mythical Tower of Babel fell, we lost this language and our understanding of the world. Besides creating the question—what's the meaning of our existence—as Humboldt said, 'all understanding became at the same time a misunderstanding, all agreement in thought and feeling is also a parting of the ways.'"

She hears movement in the room, hushed voices, but she can't tell what's going on. A door opens and slams shut.

"How to access this common language again? Is it possible? For centuries this question has plagued us. In the sixteenth century, Paracelsus believed divine intervention would restore the unity of human tongues. Not wanting to wait, the Royal Society of London commissioned a man to create a universal language, which was so complicated that its only suitable purpose was to be satirized by Jonathan Swift in *Gulliver's Travels*.

"Some posit the language after Babel can never lead us to our primal tongue—only silence will do that. Remember Kafka's narrator in 'Josephine the Singer, or the Mouse Folk,' who asks 'Is it her singing that enchants us, or is it not rather the solemn stillness enclosing her frail little voice?'"

Metal scrapes against metal, followed by a long hiss. Is someone opening a can of soda? Too rude to be Japanese; probably an American who wandered into the conference hall and is eating his lunch. Will the crunch of potato chips follow? The ring of a cell phone? The grunts of monosyllabic speech?

"To date, no one has located this first language, the language of home, if you will. Translation, then, is a necessary evil; but for our exile, we'd have no need for it. Then again," she says, feeling an old excitement dust itself off, "perhaps translation is also our blessing."

This is what she used to believe, what she used to argue as a student to others about the importance of her subject matter. Why bother mastering so many languages? they'd ask. No one cares about translation anymore. You could do so many other things. The State Department. The United Nations. Years have gone by since she offered up her reason for choosing her profession. "Maybe it holds the key to our understanding each other, to the meaning of our world."

Sweat trickles from her underarms down her sides. There's a flurry of footsteps on the hardwood floor. Are they reprimanding the soda drinking? Escorting the rude *gaijin* to the door?

"Might it be that a translation from language A into language B creates a third presence—almost like the birth of a baby, pure, uncontaminated, truer? Might that third presence hold the essence of what lies underneath both languages? As evidence, consider what it takes to move language A over to language B—it is a search for the true meaning of the words. A hunt for what lies buried under colloquialism, culture, gender, age, all the layers of skin on a language. If our first common language was scattered around the world, might we come closer to it if we combined the two languages and formed another entity based on meaning? A purer speech. Translation then is about the birth not of A or B but C. And C, it could be argued, is the closest we get to truth."

She goes on for a while longer, talking about language C, but her voice is fading. Somehow she's lost her original enthusiasm. She senses that something in the room has stirred, flexed. She finishes quickly and looks up, removing her glasses. A smattering of applause.

Well, that's done. When she steps down from the stage, a Japanese man is waiting for her at the bottom of the wood steps.

He's frail, bony, almost delicate in his tan trousers and dark brown sweater vest.

"You are Hanne Schubert?" he says.

She smiles, nods, slips her glasses back on. "Yes. And you are?"

The man smells of cigarette smoke.

"What you speak of. It's idiotic. This idea that translation is purer than what the author creates."

Her mind goes blank. She had imagined him as a younger man, full of vitality.

Kobayashi takes a deep breath. "You may be a very well-educated woman, speaking Japanese and English and other languages and all that, but what you have done is wrong."

A couple of people nearby stop talking. Hanne feels them listening.

"You were supposed to translate my words, my story, not rewrite it and make your own story in the hopes of uniting mankind. I don't know where you get your ideas about translation, but no author in his right mind would want you to translate his work. I put my trust in you to bring my story to the English-speaking world. My story. Not yours."

Now a small crowd has gathered. Hanne feels her face burning.

"There's only the author," he says, his voice rising. "You don't exist without me. That's something you seem to have forgotten."

The event organizers appear.

"My character had a beating heart—"

One of the organizers tries to interrupt him.

"Go home," Hanne says finally.

Go home? What does she mean by that? It sounds like a command to a feral creature, a creature following the scent of something, its ferocious instinct driving it onward. She needs a stick to beat it back. Go home.

"Over a year I spent," says Hanne. She feels herself finding her bearings. "I worked hard—"

"Let me tell you something. You ruined my main character. Turned him into an asshole. A class-act jerk!"

"Jiro?" she says. "You're talking about Jiro?"

Hanne smells his breath weighted with whiskey.

"I am ashamed of what you did to my Jiro," he says, the line between his brows deepening. "You should be ashamed."

Amaya is speaking into a walkie talkie.

"If Moto read what you did, he'd hate it. That makes me ashamed. Deeply ashamed!"

Moto? For a moment, she can't think. Then she recalls Jiro was modeled after this man, Moto Okuro, the Noh actor.

"If this Moto saw what I had to work with, he'd give me a medal," says Hanne, filling with anger and his horrific accusation. She loved Jiro! She understood this character better than Kobayashi did himself. How can he be saying such things?

The man's face pinches. "You know nothing. If you knew Moto, you'd see."

A security guard approaches and tells Kobayashi he must leave. She watches the guard escort him to the door. Kobayashi's shoulders are hunched, his head bowed. The room is quiet. With trembling hands, Hanne gathers her notes together. When she slips out a side door, into a dark hallway, she has no idea where she is.

Chapter Seven

SHE NEEDS FRESH AIR. IF she could find her way across the busy street into the green. Green of a park with bare winter trees. The name escapes her, and for a moment she worries that her head injury has asserted itself again. Brought on by the public humiliation, no doubt. But then the name rushes at her. The Shinjuku Imperial Gardens, where, for the first time since she's arrived, she hears birds—blue jays and brown sparrows fluttering tree to tree. It's a relief. She and Brigitte used to escape the city on the weekends and drive across the Golden Gate Bridge to Bolinas Lagoon, where they'd wander the shoreline looking for birds. Tomas didn't like bird watching, and so Hiro would stay home with him.

That one Saturday, Hanne packed a picnic and as they ate, they saw four great blue herons, a flock of willets, and then Brigitte spotted a rare black-crowned night heron. They'd never seen one before, and she saw it along the shoreline in the tall reeds. Brigitte talked about it for weeks afterward and couldn't wait to go again. She must have been ten, maybe eleven years old. Hanne offered to teach her bird calls, but Brigitte said she didn't want to learn. "They seem so content," she said, "I don't want to disturb them." She just wanted to sit and listen.

Whenever Brigitte suggested they go, Hanne put everything aside. Let it wait. Everything could wait. By then, Brigitte had her own language teachers and didn't need Hanne. Brigitte's teachers were more blunt: it was best if Hanne didn't interfere. "It's hard to listen to more than one teacher," they said. Brigitte was studying advanced German, French, and Japanese—and, Hanne found out later, Sanskrit. Bird watching was the one thing they still shared. And Hanne loved it as much as Brigitte, but more than that the long drive there and back, with its windy road that ushered in a meandering conversation. They talked about everything: her new favorite shoes, or what she was learning in school or why it is that every living thing must die. It was on one of these drives that Brigitte asked if Hanne could take her to church. The one near their house, a small white thing. She just felt the need to go.

The next day, Hanne sat beside her daughter and watched her pray. The priest told the story of David and Goliath. A good enough story, thought Hanne. A clear moral, Hanne could see its mass appeal. David's belief in something bigger than himself gave him a different view of Goliath. Not a giant after all; a measly mortal. Brigitte sat there transfixed. Which baffled Hanne; what was Brigitte hearing that Hanne wasn't? As the sermon went on, Hanne's mind wandered to the different translations of the Bible. The Septuagint, the Greek translation, which sometimes omitted entire verses. The King James, with its seventeenth-century English, the New International Version, with its modern-day English.

101

The next Sunday, Brigitte wanted to go to church again. Hanne said she had too much work to do. What she didn't tell Brigitte was that she found religion with its moral codes, rules, and promises of an afterlife far too easy. But more than that, too patronizing, too infantilizing. Life and its meaning were for you to decide, and she wasn't going to turn that decision over to anyone or anything else. So Hiro went with Brigitte. Then they went to a different church. Brigitte kept going and another life ensued, one that took up the weekend with church activities, one that Hanne knew little about. She wishes now that she had accompanied Brigitte, if only to find out what she was learning. Tomas says it's not technically correct to call the group she's now with a cult, because Brigitte could leave at any time; she just chooses not to. Just as she chose to go to that little white church all those years ago.

Now Hanne calls to a blue jay. It calls back. Back and forth. A handful of jays gather in the branches of a pine tree. She can see them, their dark blue feathers and black beaks. She remembers when she used to make Hiro laugh with her calls. "You are a very powerful woman," he'd tell her. "You're probably changing the migration of these birds."

She sits on a park bench, her mind still reeling. She doesn't understand what has just happened. Jiro, an asshole? A class-act jerk? She doesn't know what to make of it. Because the Jiro she put on the page is honorable and courageous, full of generosity and patience. Her Jiro is anything but a jerk. She smelled alcohol. Maybe Kobayashi was drunk. Maybe he said those things to get attention, though he doesn't seem that type of man. Maybe his English is so bad, he didn't understand her translation. What just happened seems almost dream-like, a bad dream. She knows she isn't wrong. She knows Jiro.

In her hotel room, the glass table is covered with bouquets of flowers and gift certificates—free sushi at the Imperial Hotel's restaurant, free massage, a manicure, a trim. The conference organizers send their apologies.

Amaya calls. "If there's anything else we can do—"

Maybe she'll go meet this Moto Okuro. See for herself what kind of man he is. That's exactly what she must do. "Do you know where I might meet the Noh actor Moto Okuro?"

Amaya says she will find out immediately. She knows of him, remembers her parents going to see one of his performances and raving about him for days afterwards. "We apologize for the disturbance this morning. It was most unfortunate."

Mid-afternoon, Amaya calls. Moto lives in a small town called Kurashiki, about two hours from Tokyo by bullet train. "It's quite beautiful," says Amaya. "It wasn't bombed during the war, so it retains its natural beauty."

She should have known. Kurashiki is where Kobayashi set his novel.

Mr. Okuro, however, is not working right now, says Amaya.

"You mean he's not in a show?"

"No. Not working. He is not with a theater company right now. Technically he'd be considered unemployed."

"What happened?"

Amaya doesn't know. She falls back into apologies. "We are so sorry for what happened this morning. We would like to make it up to you. Perhaps you'd like to visit Kurashiki?"

Indeed she would. Amaya says she will secure a train ticket and find a hotel. Five minutes later, Amaya says she's booked a seat on a train that leaves at 8:00 in the morning.

"Thank you," says Hanne. "That's very kind."

She doesn't doubt that she'll find Moto Okuro; Kurashiki is a small town, and he's probably its biggest export. Hanne has one more night here. She finds it impossible to sleep. She decides a drink might help. The hotel bar is dimly lit with flickering candles on round tables, a counter where one can sit and talk to the bartender. She chooses a corner table and orders a brandy. What seems moments later a tall man, impeccably dressed in a good tweed coat, approaches her.

"May I join you?" he says in Japanese.

He has a foreign tinge to his Japanese—Danish, she guesses. Not appearing any age in particular, with his thick sandy-brown hair, and his eyes a beautiful ice-blue. His tan, slightly ravaged face suggests he plays golf or tennis or perhaps spends time sunning by a pool. Definitely Northern European, so many months spent in darkness, they develop an unquenchable craving for the sun.

"Oh, I'm not here for very long," she says, glancing across the room, willing the waitress not to come so she can get up and leave. But there she is, with Hanne's drink on a tray, ice cubes tinkling against glass, and a complimentary plate of sushi. The waitress sets the drink in front of her, and he slides into the seat across from her and tells the waitress he'll have whatever she's having.

In fact he is from Denmark. Copenhagen. He introduces himself as Jens Radmussen. Passing through, unable to sleep. Someone in the room next to his with a loud TV. "And you're not from here either," he says.

She supposes they've reached that point in the conversation when she's supposed to divulge her personal information. An awkward silence follows, and he's looking at her, his eyes alert, glittery. "In fact I've spent years in Japan," she says. Why is she inventing? She spent three years in this country, then her mother moved them to Germany, then to the United States. "My parents were missionaries. That's how most Anglos and Europeans learn the language."

"And what do you do?" he says.

Before she answers, before she gives herself over to a definition, a noun, she floats in the excitement of becoming something other than what she's been. With the elevator music twinkling in the background and this man enjoying her, she feels another landscape, a different life running parallel to her existing one. "A surgeon," she says, surprising herself.

From the expression on his face, he is duly impressed. More than he'd be if she told him the truth of her profession.

"A surgeon," he repeats, his voice full of awe.

"Cardiac pulmonary," she says, then adding when she sees his puzzlement, "heart and lung." What is she doing? If given the chance, if handed another hundred years, this is hardly what she'd choose. She can barely watch a nurse stick a needle in her arm to draw blood. Jens is watching her, his eyes bright, interested, his elbows on the table, leaning toward her. She asks, out of politeness, of his profession.

"Sales. Software, networking," he chortles. "Stuff I don't really understand."

The waitress brings out his drink and Hanne scoots the plate of sushi over to him. "Please. Help yourself. I'm not that hungry."

He pops one in his mouth. "Have you ever saved anyone?"

It's becoming ridiculous. She should leave. "Maybe. Maybe not. But that's not what interests me. It's when in the face of tragedy there arises the divine in a human being. An almost pure selflessness. You don't always see it, but when you do, it's breathtaking."

They are both humbled by her statement. And she's startled— where did that come from?

The sushi is gone. The drink is too, gone straight to her head. She probably should not be drinking in her current neurological state, she realizes, too late.

"I should do something else with my life," he says, looking out across the tables, as if the answer lay on the other side of this room. "I travel too much. None of this is worth anything and I'm really out of shape." He pats his stomach. For a moment, the mood feels gloomy. Then he smiles. "But if I didn't travel, I wouldn't meet interesting girls like you."

Girls. Does he not know the Japanese word for woman? She feels the small spark of desire flicker, fade. "I've got an early morning. It's been a pleasure," she says, standing, hearing the sound of silk as she uncrosses her legs. She extends her hand. His large hand envelops hers, sending a rush of unexpected heat through her, and she can't suppress the accompanying thrill.

"A pleasure to meet you," he says with respect in his voice. He stands, smiling down upon her. "A real pleasure, doctor."

She can feel in his gaze a promised intimacy. For a moment, she flashes on their intertwined nakedness. How would his hands grip her? But then someone walks into the bar and the landscape of her fabricated life collapses, like a wilted flower, leaving her with herself again.

Chapter Eight

ON THE TRAIN SHE QUICKLY falls asleep. Two hours later when they pull into the station, she stirs awake, blinks in confusion, and stretches her aching neck. On the window, water has created a lace-like pattern of loops and circles. She touches the cold frosty glass. Through the clarity of the small streams, she sees a platform, a newly shingled shack, where twenty or so Japanese in dark coats are huddled inside, as if waiting for a performance to begin. In the distance, the neon signs of McDonald's, Burger King, The Gap, on and on—an eerie glow. She is in Kurashiki.

Outside, standing on the platform, she sees more of the town. In addition to American fast food franchises and clothing chains, there are the shops with tables out front displaying the usual Japanese junk—fake fans and made-in-China teapots; postcards on a circular rack, kites with long tails. She was hoping otherwise, but it's as she read in Kobayashi's novel—flat, lifeless descriptions of a place he called *true Japan, an amalgamation of Western and Eastern crap, leading to supreme crap.* She remembers fiddling with that word—crap? Garbage? Shit? Kitsch? She eventually kept his word—crap.

Hanne already knows what waits in the direction she is heading, down the narrow, squiggly alley dotted with small rice and tea and camera shops. And there they are, the rows of bone-white warehouses, hundreds of years old, adorned with shiny black tiles, which she translated as "looking like fancy party skirts, all dressed up with nowhere to go." The warehouses, once used to store rice, with their steady determination stand erect along either side of a slow-moving canal. Kobayashi called it "murky," and she was faithful to his word, but seeing it now, she prefers the more vivid "dark green" to contrast with the orange koi swishing by, breaking the smooth surface. With cars banished from the Bikan Historical Quarter, she can, as Kobayashi wrote, hear her hard-soled shoes click against cobblestone. She's already spent hours and hours here in her mind. And he was right again, no overhead electrical wires net the sky, so it does resembles the look of the Meiji period.

She heads across a stone bridge, and when she reaches the center she leans over the railing, watching the water flow underneath. Maybe "green," she thinks, looking at her reflection, the water stretching her face twice as long as normal, turning it into something grave and austere and ghostly. She opens her mouth and it becomes a looming black hole.

The other side of the canal is a mirror image of the side from which she came—the same warehouses, same cobblestone, same weeping willows dipping their branches into the dark green water, as if tentatively deciding whether to dive in.

Not exactly how Kobayashi put it—*the old part of town, a tourist trap. Shops selling high-priced trinkets to wide-eyed tourists, who wander the museums, quickly passing by the old men floating in nostalgia. A dead place. Listen closely, you can hear tormented ghosts.* Of course, that's going too far. Like any place pinned to a particular era, this part of town has its charm, a quaintness from another world, lulling you into believing time's flow has stopped and tomorrow's mistakes and misfortune can be averted if you just stay put.

She yawns. Staring at buildings was her husband's passion, never hers. Hiro could wander inside a building for hours, looking at the squared beams supporting the roof, admiring how they were mortised one into another and put in place with wood dowels. After a while, she'd find a bench and pull out her book, telling him to come back and get her when he was done. Besides, all of this, every bit of it is known to her. She must concede, begrudgingly, Kobayashi got the setting right.

She wanders into a gift shop and looks at the ceramics. She circles back to the front counter and asks the pock-faced shop clerk if Moto Okuro is from this town.

"Oh, yes," she says, smiling. "The great Noh actor. He's really handsome."

Hanne asks if she knows where she might see him. "Does he live in town?"

The woman doesn't know.

Hanne asks in a couple more shops. He comes to town now and then, usually for dinner or drinks, Hanne is told; no, he doesn't live in the center of Kurashiki. Somewhere in the countryside at the family's house. Hungry, Hanne steps into a small sushi shop, barely a slit in between two buildings. The building is old, including the window pane, which lets in a pinkish light, accentuating streams of floating dust. Only three tables, empty. She tries to imagine what it's like to live here. The willows along the canal, the cobblestone roads, probably wonderfully quiet at night. If she lived here. . . . Ah, the power of the conditional, how easily language lets you walk away from a past, she thinks.

A waitress wearing a dark blue kimono brings Hanne a pot of tea and a menu.

"Excuse me," says Hanne. She asks the waitress if she knows Moto Okuro.

"He grew up here," says the woman proudly. "He recently moved back."

"I'd love to meet him. I admire his work so much. It would be a great honor." It's not exactly a lie, she thinks. She would love to meet him. And she's sure it will be an honor.

A thin man with crooked teeth comes over to the table. He introduces himself as the proprietor. Hanne explains she is a translator of Japanese literature. She just finished speaking at a conference and thought she'd spend more time in the countryside, especially the hometown of Moto Okuro. She's fascinated with the Japanese culture and in particular Noh theater.

"You will have to see a Noh play while you're here."

"I want to." She's raving about something she's never seen—of course she knows about Noh, the oldest surviving form of Japanese theater from the fourteenth century. It continues in much the same form, with many of the same plays performed today, plays filled with uncanny things, gods, ghosts, demons—but it's painfully slow and hours long. She's never wanted to make the time.

"I am honored to say that Moto comes to my restaurant for dinner," says the proprietor, smiling broadly, turning his face into a fan of wrinkles. His older brother eats here, too. "Moto comes here because we serve the freshest fish."

Hanne smiles and orders sashimi. The owner is right; the fish is wonderful. She tells him she'll be back for dinner.

It's not Moto who shows up, but his older brother, who must be in his mid-sixties.

The proprietor makes the introductions, telling this man, whose name is Renzo, that Hanne is a well-known translator who is a big fan of Noh, and particularly his brother.

"You've traveled so far to meet my brother," says Renzo, whose voice is reedy thin, like his body. He smiles, showing off his tea-stained teeth. He's a dapper dresser, decked out in a warm gray suit and crisp white shirt. "He will be quite honored. He loves Americans."

"I'm sorry to disappoint you," she says. "I'm not American. I come from Europe first, Germany, to be precise. Only lately has it been America."

"Oh, he loves all foreigners."

The proprietor shows them to a table by the window.

"You speak Japanese so well," he says. "You must be a very great translator."

She spares him the story of her fall down the stairs, and the lecture that knowing a language is only a fraction of what makes a good translator. "Thank you."

Over dinner, Renzo turns out to be a chatty fellow, telling her Moto is considered a master of Noh. He began training when he was just a boy, around age three. That's not unusual, mind you, but he showed talent even then. It's clear from Renzo's bright eyes that he loves his brother.

"So young," she says, thinking of Jiro, who began playing the violin when he was five years old. Jiro demanded an adult-size violin, and once he began to play, it became his passion. Except, of course, during that difficult year with his wife. What's happened to Moto that caused him to no longer act? Did his wife fall ill too? She supposes she'll find out soon enough.

The Okuro family has produced six generations of superb Noh actors, Renzo tells her. Hanne probably knows about Bon, the annual ceremony, which is one of Japan's most important rituals to honor one's ancestors. Loyalty to one's family has deep roots in Japan, going way back to the samurai. "That's all changing now. But my generation was raised to honor our ancestors, to honor our family name and legacy."

Hence the legacy of the family tradition of Noh, thinks Hanne. The similarities between Jiro and Moto are striking. Jiro also inherited a family tradition. At least seven generations of males played some instrument in a symphony or for the imperial court.

"I had a dose of that, too," says Hanne. She remembers sitting with her mother at the kitchen table, conjugating German verbs. To speak, speaking, spoken, have spoken. A rigorous schedule instituted by her mother and never questioned by Hanne because she wanted to earn the praise of her mother. She lapped it up, her mother's "Good, good," which came rarely, but just enough to feel earned and urge her on. That Hanne would in some way specialize in languages was never questioned. Looking back, Hanne is glad her mother prodded and pushed; she approves of knowledge handed down through the generations. Though she has no idea what Brigitte would say about that. Does she even use her languages now? Renzo is still talking about his family legacy.

"I was supposed to become a Noh actor, but I was no good at any of it," says Renzo. When Moto came along and could dance and sing and act, he was promoted to the role of eldest. Renzo's name was changed from Ichiro, first son, to Renzo, or third son.

He laughs. "I know what you're wondering—but there's only two of you, why third son?"

There's Moto, then the character Moto plays in the Noh play. "I come after that," says Renzo, smiling. "He had talent and it's what our family has done. What the Okuro family has contributed to Japan."

Hanne wants to ask what the Okuro family is contributing now that Moto is unemployed. Renzo tells her he used to own an antique shop, and he still dabbles in buying and selling antiques.

Hanne pays for the dinner. "My treat."

"I can't accept."

"You must," says Hanne handing the proprietor her credit card.

Renzo insists on picking her up tomorrow around 6:00 P.M. for dinner at their house. "We would be honored."

"I'm looking forward to it."

She's never been to this part of Japan. The buildings dwindle, vanish, and then acres of open fields of greenery, with grazing brown cows, barns, stables, tractors, a few houses with dirt driveways dotting the horizon. She thought by now the whole island had been mastered, cultivated, roped in and scraped away for houses, buildings and shopping malls, hotels, golf courses, and driving ranges. But here large swatches of arable, fertile land, growing what—wheat? Corn? Alfalfa? Pastoral, she thinks. Or maybe bucolic. In the hills, a ring around the valley, there are real trees, an actual forest. They drive through a small village—only a grocery store, a pharmacy—and Renzo points to a lone house on a small hill in the distance. "You can see it from here."

The glossy black roof tiles gleam like dark water. A traditional Japanese house, it looks huge. He parks the car by the iron gate. In the front yard, a large stone Buddha with a big belly greets them with a big smile. Someone has planted a bonsai garden of dwarf pine trees, but she's drawn to the rock garden next to it, with five big gray boulders. The huge rocks are surrounded by a sea of gray, white, and black pebbles, neatly raked, the tongs making flawless lines that never cross, never touch. Such order, she thinks, and precision.

Inside they remove their shoes, setting them beside a jumble of men's black dress shoes, brown, sneakers, boots, slippers, moccasins; it looks like five men live here, not two. A wooden bodhisattva stands by the shoes, as if guarding them. This one's smile almost seems smug, as if it knows something you don't. The house is still, only the occasional sound of a twig or pine cone pinging the roof. It's freezing and it's so quiet. Too quiet. Is the great Moto even here? She buttons her coat to her chin and pulls on her gloves again.

Renzo takes the stairs two at a time. She hears him above her, opening doors, closing them. A big drafty house. He calls out, "Make yourself at home!"

Wearing her socks, she pads into the first room, a long stretch of golden tatami mats, and two Buddhas, side by side. In front of both Buddhas are incense holders, a line of stubby white candles, and two mandarin oranges. Shrines to Renzo's deceased parents, most likely. Another Buddha, this one larger than the others, sits like a sentry in the corner. It, too, has candles, incense, oranges, and also apples in front of it. Probably offerings to the beloved ancestors.

She slides open a shoji paper wall; nothing but a fish tank with goldfish and a dark wood table hovering over a square recessed area in the floor. The room could be called empty, but she doesn't feel a lonely vacancy, only an essential elegant beauty, everything subtracted except that which appeals to the eye. She's always felt

114

comfortable in Japanese-style homes. When she lived with her mother in Tokyo, they decorated their apartment like this, with tatami mats made of stiff rice-straw, paper walls from the inner bark of mulberry trees.

She slips her legs underneath the table and, leaning under, finds the knob to the kerosene space heater. The coils glow orange with a hint of rose.

Renzo finally joins her. "He said he'd be here." His face is creased with worry.

"Maybe he stepped out," she offers.

He sighs deeply.

"Or something came up," she said, hoping her tone doesn't sound too disappointed. Did she come all this way for nothing?

"I'm sorry to tell you this." He hesitates. "Moto has not been himself lately." He looks down at the table, as if embarrassed, then excuses himself and steps into the kitchen.

An actor. She can conjure up the handful of actors whom she's met. Performers, entertainers, solitude makes them lonely, and private love is a pale version of what they really want—the unwavering love of an audience. With their expanded presence, they make you feel part of something larger, somehow exalted, more vast, playing a bigger role than you ever imagined—but not necessarily the role you would have chosen. He's probably very charming. And now he's out of work. Maybe Renzo invited her so he'd have a new member of his impromptu audience. But, out of practice, he didn't feel ready, so he skips out on dinner.

By the time Renzo reappears, he's fully recovered his cheerful self. "Here we are," he says, bringing out bowls of miso and rice and a plate of homemade sushi and sukiyaki.

"This looks lovely."

After a bottle of sake, Renzo begins to tell her more. She remembers this about Hiro's Japanese friends. So shy and reserved at first, but with a little alcohol they became red-cheeked and loquacious. Moto had a dishonorable thing happen. He lost his job.

"What happened?"

Renzo swallows. "He says he can't act anymore."

"Why?"

"I don't know." Renzo tells her Moto's wife left him. "But they were unhappy for a long while. Or so it seemed to me."

Kobayashi must have met Moto when the marriage was on its last legs, she thinks. And he changed it, so in the novel the wife was dying, which put immense strain on the marriage, versus the slow dying of a marriage from more mundane trivialities. If that was truly what happened to Moto and his wife, Hanne knows that terrain very well.

"What was your brother's wife like?" Hanne is thinking of Aiko and her gloomy moods, the days spent sprawled on the couch in the dark living room.

Renzo hoots. A powerful advertising exec, he says, she had the Viagra account. Did Hanne ever see the Japanese ads on television? The old man sitting at the bar counter, fawned over by beautiful young women. The old man turns to the camera and says "I'm sixty, but I feel like I'm sixteen." Seven million impotent men in Japan, and she hands them a way to shrug off old age and throw themselves into sexual ecstasy.

Renzo opens a second bottle of sake and tips back a glass. "And now Moto wastes his time doing silly voice-overs for commercials." That admission seems to take something out of Renzo, because he abruptly falls silent. The room fills with the gurgling from the fish tank.

She stares at him in this strange, suspended moment. With his thin, dry lips and forced cheerfulness, he's as interesting to her as a head of cabbage. When he begins talking again, it is a long rant about how Moto is ruining the family name, ruining his life. Though Renzo was demoted to younger brother in their youth, he is Moto's only remaining relation, and it was to him Moto turned for help, and Renzo has been paying his bills. He let Moto move in with him, but it isn't ideal, not at all.

It does not seem Renzo enjoys the reversal of roles, thinks Hanne.

Renzo runs out of steam. The food is cold, the second bottle of sake almost empty. And Hanne is tired. Renzo pushes himself up from the table. "I apologize again for Moto." His face quickly brightens. "You must come tomorrow night. I will make sure he is here."

How he plans to do that, she doesn't ask. "All right. I'd love to." She offers to call a taxi.

He laughs. "You think I had too much? No, I'm fine."

As he drives her back to her hotel in Kurashiki, he talks about what he'll make for supper, and she half listens, looking out the window at the pitch black night, the occasional glow of a house light. She's aware of a weight lifting; she wouldn't call it euphoria or even happiness. It is something more subtle, quieter. She feels a forward trajectory again.

Chapter Nine

THE NEXT EVENING, SHE TAKES a taxi back to their house. This time Renzo is missing. There's a note taped on the door: *Hanne-san, Please come in! I've run to the grocery store. Say hello to Moto!*

As she walks down the hallway, she's surprised by the adrenaline rushing through her. What does she think will happen? It's just a first meeting. Yet she also knows that first impression, her sense of him, matters. But it's more than that. She's about to meet the man who gave rise to Jiro. Jiro, for whom she had such deep affection, and who was, frustratingly, the root of the confrontation with Kobayashi.

In the eating room, a muscular man sits hunched in front of the fish tank, watching the goldfish swim aimlessly in circles. He has a formidable head of hair, wavy black with coarse strands of silver, shoulder-length and disheveled. There's a stillness to his being, as if he has been in that position for hours and might stay that way for days. Most striking, on his right cheek, a fiery red birthmark blazes in what looks like the shape of Montana.

"You must be Moto. *Komban wa. Hanne desu.*" Good evening. I'm Hanne.

He doesn't acknowledge her, not even a turn of his head. She's about to speak again, louder, when he sits up and shudders, like a mangy dog freeing itself of water.

What to make of it? Dressed in faded blue jeans with a rip in the knee and a white T-shirt, he's barely made an effort to spruce himself up. Did he forget she was coming? Or maybe he plans on skipping out on dinner again. There's also the rebellion of his hair. From his appearance, he looks like an adolescent revolting against conventions, except he's no teenager. In his fifties, at least. She has never approved of men who circle back on themselves, attempting to relive a perceived glorious youth. Don't they grow bored traveling known, predictable territory—as bored as people are with them?

After a long silence, he grunts something, maybe a word, his voice a laconic rumble, as if used up long ago. Whatever he said, it wasn't a long enough utterance to be an apology for not appearing last night. He has yet to look over; the fish seem to be the most fascinating thing in the room.

He may be an actor, but he's not the least bit charming. He seems to have no need for an audience. Jiro had these moods: withdrawn, even prickly around people, preferring solitude above all else and feeling resentful when disturbed. He could spend hours in his study alone, playing his violin or composing music. He wasn't beyond barking at someone to leave him alone.

She'll let Moto have his privacy. She steps into the kitchen and suddenly the room is tilting, sloping downward. Her hip smacks into the counter. A delayed aftershock from her fall down the stairs? A clot in her brain? She hears a high-pitched ringing in her ears. Not exhaustion, she can't remember when she slept as deeply as she did last night.

She looks out the window to steady herself. Water from last night's rain has pooled in the leaves. In the back yard, a large, twisted apple tree reaches its spindly, leafless branches in every direction. Large lumps line its trunk, as if something lives inside it and is trying to punch its way out. It probably hasn't ever been sprayed for bugs or pruned. Each year the old tree must meet spring with a flourish of flowers, only to have the birds and a frenzy of bugs devour its fruit. What a waste.

A chill jerks her shoulders. The house is cold, and the sole source of warmth is where Moto is sitting, the heater beneath the table. When she turns, she's startled to find Moto standing in the kitchen. She didn't even hear him cross the cold floorboards. He's a handsome man, compact, not an ounce of extra fat. When he walks to the sink, he moves without bobbing his head, as if he's wafting on a breeze.

She tries again. "Your brother Renzo invited me—"

He fills a glass of water from the faucet. She watches his Adam's apple dance as he drinks until the glass is empty. A water droplet glimmers on his cheek. She can see his birthmark more clearly now. It's changed to a softer red, or is it the lighting, she can't tell. Stretching from the outside corner of his right eye down to the tip of his nose, it distracts from his deepset eyes, unusual for a Japanese face, a face that is unreadable, an expressionless mask, like the Noh masks he wears on stage—or used to wear.

"Hello," he says.

His first clearly articulated word, and it's almost civil. But it's not just the word her attention veers to, it's the sound, a deep timbre emanating not from his chest, but lower, his belly. And from that one sound a whole series of sounds runs through her, as if he's not just one man but many—shouts of anger and joy, cries of ecstasy, moans and laughter. How did he do that?

"It's a lovely house," she stammers. "Post and beam, with paper walls that move. A constantly changing house," why doesn't she stop rambling, "you can have a wall or not."

He wipes his lips.

"You're a Noh actor?"

"Was."

"Yes, I heard. I'm sorry. It must be difficult."

He looks at her. "*Shikata ga nai*," he says. It can't be helped.

It's a fairly common Japanese expression. When she was shopping in Tokyo for her granddaughters, Hanne heard a woman in the check-out line utter this phrase as she relented and bought her crying child a bag of candy. The woman said it whimsically, a meaningless bit of verbiage. Moto's tone, on the other hand, held more gravity. It reminds her how Jiro must have sounded after he called the doctor and turned over the care for his wife. An acceptance of a bad situation and the need to move on.

It's this attitude that she found so appealing and admirable about Jiro: faced with the demise of his marriage, he exuded from his constitution a steady fortitude and resilience to march onward. In her opinion, his response was not heartless at all. In fact, she'd argue that it's one of the more admirable traits a human can have. Not selfishly mired in a haze of self-absorption or pity, a person with this quality is responsible, full of integrity, available to others. To carry on. It's a courageous act to move on from an unexpected, unfortunate event. And look at Moto: except for his hair, Moto hasn't let himself go. He is a physically fit man, and he holds down a job, though it may not be the kind of work that Renzo approves of. At least he's carrying on. Bravo. Bravo for him.

"You seem to have the right attitude about all this," she says, not bothering to conceal her praise.

Then he is right beside her, his long fingers approaching her face, his breathing near her ear, steady, loud, low. And now he's so close she sees the filigree of intricate red veins that make up his birthmark. She freezes. What is he doing? From her shoulder, he plucks a single strand of her newly blackened hair and holds it in front of him as if it's the most enchanting thing he's ever seen. He twists it this way and that before he lets it go. They watch it slowly fall. And it keeps falling, it's taking forever to fall, as if he has thrown it into a world where time operates differently, if at all. Her strand of hair is still falling through space when the front door opens. The loud creak of the door hinges breaks the spell, then Renzo's chipper voice. Her first thought: Why did he have to come back? The black hair lies on the wood floor, a scribbled pencil mark on an otherwise pristine canvas.

Renzo comes into the kitchen and stops. "Well, finally. You meet Moto."

Now that they are standing side by side, she can see the resemblance. The same coarse hair, though Renzo keeps his cut short; the same broad forehead; they are almost the same height, though Moto is slightly taller; but Renzo, with his hunched shoulders, concave chest and baggy trousers, looks almost malnourished and dried out, while Moto has the build and stance of a young athlete, ready to tackle someone.

Renzo wants to know where Moto was last night. Renzo turns to Hanne. "He didn't come home until 2:00 A.M."

"Something came up," says Moto. "But we're all here now."

"You haven't served our guest a drink," says Renzo. Hanne is a distinguished translator of Japanese literature, says Renzo, giving the Western world the best of Japanese writing. "And here you are, treating her so poorly."

Hanne senses she's caught in a longstanding feud. "Oh, I'm fine."

"You mustn't be mean to our guest," says Renzo. Though he's trying to be playful now, there's still an edge to Renzo's voice. "That's what my mother always said to Moto. Remember how you'd whine about the other schoolboys and their dull minds, their dull lives? Only if someone had a limitless capacity for tragedy or comedy or passion would you befriend him."

Moto leans his back against the counter, his arms crossed, his expression not giving anything away.

"You might have judged me wrong, Moto," says Hanne, smiling, trying to lighten the mood. "Maybe I have limitless capacities."

Magically, Moto's whole face fans out, as if something has finally unclenched and is bursting open. In his new leonine splendor, he lets out a loud, deep belly laugh. There is his warmth, his charm. That smile, that laugh, he keeps it hidden, she thinks, until it is earned.

The dinner isn't spectacular; what is spectacular is the amount of sake consumed by Moto. No longer taciturn, Moto has opinions about everything—cars, photography, suicide, rice growing, boredom—one opinion is as good as another, and he won't be pinned to any of them because, moments later, he contradicts himself. It's as if he isn't listening to anything he says or simply doesn't care. An illogical force of verbal nonsense. Hanne can barely believe this is the same monosyllabic man she first encountered at the fish tank.

"Japan has never truly opened up its doors to foreigners," he says, opening another bottle of sake. "Its true heart can't be known by a foreigner."

Is he taunting her? "What is its true heart?" she says.

Before she can stop him, he refills her glass, then his. Wagging his finger at her, he gives her a great big smile. "You might speak perfect Japanese, my dear, but you won't ever understand Japan."

"Try me."

"It takes more than perfect Japanese to understand."

"Aren't you judging me a bit early?"

"Surprise! It has no heart," he says, laughing loudly. "Nothing in the center."

"Oh, come now," says Renzo, who's sitting at the head of the table.

"A beautiful heart right here." Moto pounds his chest with his fist. "We Japanese got a bad reputation. The truth is we are passionate, as passionate as the Italians." His face is flushed, his birthmark is blazing deep scarlet, as if the alcohol has lit a fire inside. "No. Wait a minute. A heart split into thousands of pieces. An ugly shattered mess." He tips back another drink. "Watch out! This fractured heart can change in an instant because nothing holds it together. It can turn into a clod of dirt. A wild river. A manga figure."

"And that's a heart?" she says.

"No," he says, sticking out his lower lip, pretending to pout. "Too bad. There is no heart. Empty. Vacant. Nothing. It fills with water after each rain."

"This is a very good meal," says Renzo, the little muscles flinching along the line of his jaw.

A futile attempt at changing the subject, thinks Hanne. Was Jiro ever this drunk? There was that month when Jiro went to a karaoke bar every night after work. That one night, he drank so much whiskey, he ended up singing the Eagles' *Heartache Tonight* at least twenty times, hogging the microphone. The owner of the bar came out and barked at him to sit down and give someone else a goddamn turn.

Moto leans toward her until he is about seven centimeters from her face. His pupils are huge and he seems to be studying her face, as if he sees something that doesn't belong there. Or something he's never seen before. The moment stretches out until it becomes embarrassing. What? Is there food on her face?

She takes a napkin and wipes her chin.

"Moto marinated the salmon," says Renzo. "Everything Moto makes is a marvel to me."

"Noh is the purest expression of the Japanese soul," says Moto, his eyes a little out of focus.

"Finally," says Renzo. "Let's hear the sensei talk about something he knows."

"You've probably never heard of the founder of Noh," says Moto to Hanne. Then he turns to his brother. "Don't call me sensei. Zeami is the sensei. He figured out a way to produce the essence of Japan, Japan's heart, the deep reality of all things."

"The deep reality of all things," she says. "That's pretty vague."

Renzo tells her Noh means the perfect art or accomplishment. "Usually the plays involve the main character returning in ghost form to revisit a significant event in his or her life—"

"I don't care about any of that," says Moto, waving his hands in the air, as if clearing it of a stink.

Maybe she's had a lot to drink too, because she asks directly: "Is that why you can't perform anymore? You're no longer in touch with this so-called reality?"

"The stage is a place of shared mortality," says Moto, ignoring her. "The superb Noh actor creates this space because theater is about the moment, an intense moment that's gone in an instant."

"So you and your audience must live and die together?" says Hanne.

"Yes! A million times. You probably don't believe in life after death. Neither do I. But guess what? On stage, it happens."

"Well, I guess I'll have to forgo a Noh play because I like being alive," she says.

He puts down his glass and stares at her. "Do you? Do you?"

What does he mean by that?

"Noh demands a great deal from both the actor and the audience, more than any other art form," he says, balancing a chopstick on the end of a finger. "To experience it fully, the audience must undergo a blossoming, an upheaval, a complete collapse of reality. That's what the good actor experiences on stage. But for a foreigner," he says, shaking his head, letting the chopstick fall, "impossible. Someone like you will sit there baffled, muttering, what the hell is going on? Or fall asleep." He pretends to snore, then looks directly at her. "Especially a woman."

"Really?" she snaps back. "I didn't know you were a misogynist and an elitist."

He laughs again. "This is going to be fun."

"Oh?"

"You. You're so easy to get riled up. You've got a temper."

Hanne stiffens. "Funny, none of my friends would say that about me." The truth is, she rarely sees her friends. And when they do gather, the conversation is usually about the university or problems with their translation projects. Safe topics.

"Maybe I'm seeing a new side of you. Or maybe I'm more honest."

Coming from him, almost a complete stranger, the comment seems inappropriate.

"Okay," Renzo claps his hands, a forced cheerfulness to his voice. "Let's turn on the music and dance."

Miles Davis's "Fat Time Shout" cascades into the room, vibrating the table, the floor underneath her. Renzo slides open the paper walls, and now the eating room flows into the other room, giving them a perfect dance floor, empty of furniture. Renzo shuffles his feet, slowly making his way to Hanne, and extends his hand. "May I?"

"I don't know about this," she says, laughing nervously. When was the last time she danced? Hiro didn't like to, so it must have been when she was nineteen and lived a year in Paris. A man named Jacques comes back to her. Dark hair, a smooth way of talking, smooth hands and lips, far too beautiful to be trusted with anything, let alone her heart. She didn't give him anything but her hand and body to move around the dance floor, to make love to in his one-room apartment with the red-beaded lamp.

Renzo's eyes sparkle. He's a boy again, moving and twirling her, enveloped in the music, but there's nothing carnal about it. It's like dancing with your brother.

"Now you're getting it," he says.

But she isn't. It's been too many years, and her body in space is a strange, foreign object. She stumbles along, following Renzo's lead, until the next song, when he swings her over to Moto.

She has no chance to decline because his hand is in hers and he has slipped an arm around her waist, pressing her against his chest, until there is no space between them, his arm firmly clasped behind her. His birthmark is no longer the shape of Montana, but seems to take up his entire cheek. Most remarkable is how they are moving: How are they circling around the room? Not a foxtrot or waltz or anything she can name; they are, it seems, floating an inch off the floor. It's the same silent, fluid motion she witnessed earlier in the kitchen, but now she's experiencing it, as if she's under his skin and now skimming the surface of the world, unleashed from gravity.

"You move," she says, slightly out of breath, "seamlessly, no heel toe, heel toe, no beginning, no end—"

Despite her failure to find the right words, she keeps trying, tossing word after word after word, until he says in his deep, resonating voice, "*Hanasanai de kudasai,*" Let's not speak.

A shiver of excitement runs through her. They are in the middle of a scene from the book. She remembers it perfectly. Three monosyllabic words, a softened imperative, the intonation, hushed, intimate, spoken close to her ear—they already live inside of her. Jiro said them to his young lover not long after his wife was checked into the hospital. Chikako was cooking stir-fry on the stove and Jiro flicked on the radio. A song came on—something American—and he grabbed her around the waist. They'd never danced before, but he was flush with his new life. As the chicken sizzled in the wok, he danced with her across the kitchen floor, while she agonized out loud about the dinner party in a couple of hours; what if no one showed up? Didn't he see the way the wives of his male friends glared at her, as if to say, aren't you ashamed of yourself? "But don't you see my male friends looking at me with immense envy?" He kissed her earlobe. "I have someone young and beautiful and they do not." And that soothed her, and she laughed and talked on and on about the things they'd do together, their future, a trip to Florence, until he touched his finger to her lips and said, "*Hanasanai de kudasai.*"

When Hanne initially encountered them, she fretted; should it be, "Don't talk," or "Please don't speak." "Let's not talk," or a curt, cold, "Don't say another word," or simply, "Don't." She ultimately decided: Let's not speak.

The music is still playing. The way Moto is smiling, humming in her ear, running his hand along her back, says to her he's not too upset about his divorce. What's it been? Over a year since his wife left? He's just like her Jiro. But her thoughts are interrupted by a vision of Brigitte. Brigitte dancing with that man, that first young man, and earlier in the morning before Brigitte left for school, her face had been drained of color, her eyes dull, but dancing with that young man, her face was lit up, dazzling like a bright star. That moment right before Hanne told the young man to get out, right before that, Hanne stood there captivated and bewitched by her lovely daughter. She couldn't remember the last time Brigitte had looked so beautiful, so happy. Now she wishes she could crack open that moment again, tell that to Brigitte, "My, you look stunning," instead of scolding her.

Hanne realizes Moto has stopped dancing. His eyes seem to be full of tears. What's happening? "Are you all right?" she says. "Do you need to sit?"

She glances over at Renzo, who is lost in his own fog.

Moto's arms hang limply. He opens his mouth, as if to say something. He is, in fact, crying. Her breath catches. Before she can ask him anything else, he rushes out of the room.

It's too late to call a taxi, Moto is holed up somewhere, and Renzo confesses that this time he is too drunk to drive.

She follows Renzo outside to the guest cottage. It's fully stocked with everything she might need—toothpaste, toothbrush, shampoo, lotions, even a terrycloth bathrobe. "It's not much," he says, "but you'll have privacy."

A small white Scotty dog prances around his heels. Renzo introduces her to Morsel, who was in the other room during dinner so as not to disturb them. He lights the wood-burning fireplace, shows her the bathroom, the fresh towels, then excuses himself. "Good night. I've got to put this head on a pillow."

The guest cottage contains solid, clunky pieces of furniture: a Western-style bed, a nightstand, a lamp, an empty chest of drawers, a hard chair. She sits at the sizeable polished oak desk and opens the drawers; full of blue pens, and a pencil, sharpened to a fine point. Oddly, a woman's shiny green pantsuit with silver buttons hangs in the closet. She checks the label—Ann Taylor. Perhaps this is what these two brothers do: bring home foreign women.

She gazes out the window. Outside, only darkness, tar black, no streetlights, no gas stations or bars or cafés, not even a car passing through, as if this is the center of the earth. What happened to Moto? She felt like she stepped into a scene from the book during that dance, but was then abruptly tossed out. She tries to remember how Kobayashi wrote the scene between Jiro and Chikako, but the exact words are lost to her. Her overall impression was that Jiro was swept up in the moment, swept up in love with Chikako.

She sits on the edge of the bed. Maybe Moto was overwhelmed with joy instead of love, because how could he possibly be in love with her after one meeting?, and that joy moved him to tears. But she sees in her mind his quivering lower lip, his sad, dark eyes. Maybe while he was dancing, he remembered acting and the stage and suddenly missed it. Maybe she's making something out of nothing. He did seem like someone who was prone to emotional swings, and after all, in that scene Jiro was with Chikako and Hanne is nothing like that young woman, so why on earth would Moto be swept up by her?

The dog is scratching at the door. She finds Morsel on the stoop. The dog bounds inside and sits in the middle of the room, watching her, thumping his tail on the floor, waiting—for what? Cold air rushes into the room, crowding out the heat. She shuts the door and stares at Morsel. Shivering, her teeth chattering, she gets into bed, and Morsel jumps up with her and turns around and around, as if trying to grab its tail, then settles at the foot of her bed, a perfect circle. She has never liked the idea of dogs on beds or, really, dogs in a house, shedding their fur, polluting the air with their gamey smell. Her first impulse is to push it off. "Itte," she says, go. She points to the door. But after a few more tries, she gives up. Through the heavy blanket, the dog's body heat warms her feet and she quickly falls asleep.

Chapter Ten

SHE WAKES, UNSURE WHERE SHE is. Sunlight blasts into the room, and the walls blare bright white, telling her she has a hangover. Not since her fall down the marble stairs has her head throbbed this badly. And now Morsel is flitting around the room, leaping onto the bed, jumping to the floor. She untangles herself from sweaty sheets and pulls one leg and then the other over to the edge of the bed. When she finally stumbles to the door, Morsel darts out, as if on fire.

She takes two aspirin, showers, dresses, and heads to the main house. What she needs is coffee. A few chickadees are hopping along the stone path, and the trees are stubbornly bare. As the house comes into view, she sees it is still dark. She enters through the back door and steps into a house of silence. Both Renzo and Moto must be asleep. She quietly shuts the door and returns to the cottage.

What day is it? It feels like she's been in Japan for weeks. She has a suspicion that her fall down the stairs not only affected her languages, but her sense of time. Though she'd never tell her doctor that, for fear he'd imprison her at the hospital for a litany of more tests. And they'd find out she suffers from headaches a lot more often than she let on. Well, she won't go back to the hospital. She doesn't care if she's putting her health in danger; her health was in far more danger being cooped up in that hospital and her apartment.

In the back yard, Morsel is running in circles for no apparent reason. She lies back down and naps. When she wakes, she's disoriented again. Only a few minutes have passed, but it feels like hours. She throws cold water on her face, calls her message machine at her apartment. Nothing. She rings Tomas to let him know her whereabouts.

"How are you feeling?" he says.

On the yellow blouse that she wore last night, she sees a big stain near the collar. What is it? Soy sauce? Red wine? "Fine."

"Where are you staying?"

"With friends." She pauses. "I met Kobayashi at the conference. There was a bit of a confrontation." She tells him what happened.

"What's going to happen to your translation? Have you heard from the publisher?"

She's surprised that she hadn't even thought about it. "I'm sure it's all a big misunderstanding. Kobayashi was drunk. He misread a passage and since we were both at the conference, it was convenient to complain to me." She stops herself from saying, and convenient to publicly humiliate me.

She steps into the bathroom, takes off her blouse, and tries to scrub out the stain.

"Some Japanese newspaper is probably going to write about it," he says. "If Kobayashi hasn't already spoken to your publisher, they'll soon find out they have an unhappy author on their hands. This doesn't sound good to me. Where are you again? Are you sure you're feeling all right?"

"I'm fine. Perfectly fine." She tells him where she is. "I thought I'd meet this man, Moto. Judge for myself."

"Why? What does it matter?"

"Moto is here and I want to see, to explore for myself what kind of man he is. Though I know what I'll find, what I'm already finding. That he's Jiro. The Jiro that I translated."

"Who's Jiro? What are you talking about? Are you sure you're all right?"

"And I know what you're thinking, but it's not just a matter of pride, Tomas, it's my work. It's everything. It's what I do. Who I am."

She hears Morsel scratching at the door.

"Is it safe? I mean, is this man, Moto, safe?"

The stain appears permanent. Since she has no other clothes, she will have to wear a stained blouse that is now wet. "Of course." He's also exasperating, she thinks, and intriguing and handsome, just as she knew he'd be.

"I think you should head back to San Francisco and check in with your doctor."

"Oh, I don't think so. Not just yet."

"This could jeopardize your health."

"It won't. Besides, this won't take long," she says.

Tomas sighs again. The wind picks up and the branches from a nearby boxwood whack the window. Outside, the sky is doing a changing-of-the-guard, with the last bit of murk leaving and now there is steel gray. He tells her he's heard nothing from Brigitte. "I wish I'd never gotten that call about her being in the hospital. It's agonizing to hear that and then nothing. But," he says, "you know all about this."

Even before the long silence of six years, Hanne endured days of silence. On the weekends, she was off doing some sort of church-related thing. On the weekdays after school, Brigitte would return to the apartment and immediately head to her bedroom and shut the door. Hanne would set aside her work and stand outside Brigitte's door, debating whether to knock. The couple of times she did, Brigitte was sitting on her bed, knees drawn up to her chest, arms folded. She said she was studying. But often there were no books in sight. The way she looked at Hanne, those sad eyes. Hanne could see Brigitte was trying to hold back the tears. She learned that if she asked Brigitte too many questions, her daughter said nothing; if she was quiet, her daughter might speak. A sort of game, Hanne thought. When Brigitte was little, they played actual games, crossword puzzles, Scrabble, dominoes, cards; and now it was playing a game that involved guessing all the rules. Hanne missed the days when Brigitte was little, always asking "Why?" Eyes shining with curiosity.

She once overheard her teenage daughter tell someone on the phone, "This is where my mother lives. I don't really live anywhere. I don't have a real home anymore."

At dinner, Hanne said she expected more from Brigitte. That she'd given up far too easily. "If it doesn't feel like a home, change it so it is."

"I haven't given up. It's just the way it is," said Brigitte. "It's the way it feels to me." And she stretched out the word "feels" as if it were a foreign word that Hanne didn't understand.

Hanne let the implicit jab go. She suggested Brigitte try harder. "If you quit, you have only yourself to blame."

"That's always your answer. What if I told you it's not a home because Dad isn't living here? How can I change that?"

Now Hanne says to Tomas, "When she's ready to call you, she will. That's the way it works."

When she heads to the main house again, she sees the warm glow of a light on in the kitchen. Renzo is in the eating room, reading the newspaper. "Good morning," he says, setting down the paper.

"Good morning."

"I guess we all got carried away last night," he says. "I apologize for Moto's behavior."

"Oh, don't. I enjoyed him. I really did. I'm usually the one who instigates the verbal sparring. It was nice to have someone else do it for a change."

He pours her coffee. "Well, you're a rare one, then. Say, if you're not in a rush to get back home, why don't you stay a while? We'd love to have you."

"I don't want to be a burden."

"You're not a burden." Since he's retired, he loves having company and entertaining. What better way to spend one's time? Over the years, because of Moto's position, whenever Moto came to town, Renzo would host a dinner party. That's why they had built the cottage—to house visitors.

"It's so kind of you," she says. "Maybe a couple more days." But she won't stay on without paying him something.

"You can stay as long as you like. And there's no need for payment."

"It's so beautiful here. I didn't know Japan still retained some of its natural beauty." She means it. She thought she could never live in the country, too slow, too boring, but this place reminds her of her childhood years in Switzerland, so much space saturated emerald green and burnt umber. The hills lined with pines and dense conifers. If she had had good years of childhood, it was in Switzerland, where she and her mother spent hours together. Her mother would wake up and ask "What should we do today?" Together they'd hike the hills and mountains, traveling through clouds of flower scents. Now Hanne says she might go for a walk. "Is Moto still sleeping?"

Renzo smiles. "He's a man who loves to dream. Nothing can wake him when he's dreaming. He dreams even when he's awake. When we were boys, after school we'd play for hours in this very back yard. He'd make up entirely different worlds." A jungle, the moon, they scavenged for berries or fought off demons and ghosts. For hours, they were dogs, cheetahs, birds, warriors, never small boys with mud on their scraped knees, never something as ordinary as that. "I couldn't come up with half of what he did."

"You mean he has an active imagination."

"No, I mean dream. You know how a dream can feel real, as real as reality. He has this way of making his dream real for you. It's like entering another world."

She's sure Renzo is exaggerating. He is enamored of his brother despite the strained interaction she saw last night. Regardless, Hanne never had that deep capacity for dreaming or imagining. The closest she came was setting out alone in the forests, listening to birds and trying to identify them from their songs and calls. Tomas wasn't inclined that way either, but Brigitte spent hours inventing with her best friend, Maria. Maria, who moved from Russia and was placed in Brigitte's third grade class. Maria and Brigitte. They looked alike with their black hair in braids and pale skin and bright red lips. Hanne heard them more than once whisper in their knot of intimacy that they could be twins. Separated at birth and thank goodness they found each other.

Nearly every night, they called each other to decide what to wear to school. Brigitte insisted that Hanne buy her a pair of shiny black Mary Jane shoes just like Maria's. Bright pink headbands pulled their hair from their faces. They read the same books, watched the same movies, they refined the art of common interests. It reminded Hanne of the girl world that had remained closed to her growing up. She was happy for Brigitte, pleased she had gained entry. And she approved of Maria, who was articulate and looked you right in the eye when she spoke.

After school, Maria came over and they did their homework together at the kitchen table. Then they'd spend hours in Brigitte's room, in their tent, a card table covered with an old plaid blanket, and pretended to be characters from a book. Hanne bought Brigitte costumes—a green elf outfit, a pink tutu, a red boa, a big felt hat. Hanne overheard them talking about magic and spells and how to defeat an evil wizard who lived at the top of the mountain. "You have a wonderful mind," she'd tell Brigitte later. And Brigitte would look at Hanne, puzzled. It just came naturally to her; there was no need to marvel.

Hanne once heard Brigitte tell Maria that her father used to be in the circus. An expert trapeze artist who traveled to Russia and met Maria's mother. "That's how we are twins," said Brigitte, "my father is also yours."

"You shouldn't lie to your friends," Hanne said later.

"I was just pretending."

"It didn't sound that way to me."

"Maybe you weren't listening right," said Brigitte, her voice soft.

"If people can't take you for your word, you're not worth much."

After that, Brigitte closed her bedroom door and Hanne couldn't hear a thing. She regrets that now. She wishes she had picked a different time, a different way to teach Brigitte about the power of words. How flimsy they can be, how indelible.

Renzo is still talking about Moto. How those long afternoons spent in the back yard conjuring up different worlds were perfect preparation for his life as an actor. "To become anyone—a man, a woman, a young girl, a dying old man, a ghost."

"You think that helped him?"

"I do. Absolutely." Then he says "Except he can't seem to do that now."

Late morning, when Moto still hasn't woken, Hanne heads outside for a walk. Fog has rolled in, and it looks as if the sky has inverted and she's among the clouds, unable to see anything but shadowy shapes. Even the sounds of cars, birds, the occasional barking dog are slightly distorted.

She hopes by the time she returns to the house, Moto will have risen and be eating. Jiro rarely deviated from his ritual of white rice and a bowl of miso soup, with bits of tofu floating in it. Black coffee, the newspaper—sports page first, then the front page—and when his wife was still living with him, he'd kiss her on the cheek, a quick "See you soon," before heading off to the symphony. What will Moto's routine be?

Indeed, Moto has risen, and he's not alone. As Jiro found himself many mornings after his wife was gone, Hanne returns to find Moto sitting at the table with a sylph. Smooth-skinned, her long black hair coiled at her neck, she is demure in a way that seems purposely designed to seduce. Petite, she is caught between adolescence and womanhood, but to Hanne all the Japanese women look this way, even the so-called chubby ones.

Moto introduces her to Midori, a fellow voice actor.

Here, she thinks, is Moto's Chikako. "A pleasure," says Hanne, bowing slightly.

Hanne feels Midori size her up as women do, a quick inventory of features, redeeming and otherwise, and then dismiss her.

"Didn't you do a commercial recently?" says Renzo.

"Bubble bath," she says, smiling proudly.

Midori and Moto sit side by side, the young woman nearly nestled into his arm. Like a child seeking warmth or comfort from her daddy. She supposes every country has the phenomenon of a sugar daddy.

Though Midori's sugar daddy looks pretty worse for the wear. His face is puffy from last night's drinking, and strands of his hair are floating out to the side, charged with static electricity, a salt-and-pepper dandelion puff.

"Moto taught me everything I know about my voice," she says, her tone flirtatious, her smile beamed on Moto. She wears a tight white top. She must be the owner of the white high heels in the front foyer. And maybe the green pantsuit in the guest cottage closet. The room smells of her jasmine perfume. Her only flaw is a slight droop of her lower lip, as if she's contemplating a pout but can't quite make up her mind.

"How long have you known Moto?" says Hanne, taking a seat.

"About five years," she says.

Well, that fits. Jiro had known Chikako for years. She imagines Kobayashi sitting right here, perhaps in her spot, watching, his blood pressure rising as he felt the making of a scene. Or was this the spark for the novel itself? These two, nuzzling and groping. And in his mind, he's busy scribbling notes for his novel. Midori, meaning green, thinks Hanne, young to the world, fresh, a fresh start. Is Midori the reason for the marriage's demise? The seductress, whose beauty and poise—the droop of the lip can easily be overlooked. Of course last night Moto wasn't swept up in the moment dancing with Hanne; in his drunken stupor, he was pining for his lovely Midori, distraught that this lovely wasn't the one in his arms.

"I'm sure you were talented before you met Moto," says Renzo, sitting at the head of the table.

What is she? Twenty? Or slightly younger than Jiro's paramour? Why isn't she thrilled at finding another similarity between her Jiro and Moto? Certainly this reveals something about Moto's character: that after his marriage, he is soon in the embrace of another. Because Moto, once the inventive boy inventing worlds in the back yard, has chosen such a fatigued narrative. Both Jiro and Moto using youth to plunge themselves back into life. At least Chikako was a talented musician with a promising career. This Midori seems a bit of a bimbo. Hanne stifles a sigh.

Midori whispers something in his ear and she laughs, or rather giggles, covering her mouth.

Moto puts his head in his hands. "Not so loud. My lousy head."

"Moto is the great Noh actor," says Midori. "He's had such great training with his voice, and I've had none." And now she yields to her drooping lip and pouts. It's a tremendous pout, the lower lip extended in such a way that she manages to convey sex appeal. Out of curiosity, Midori had recently gone to a Noh production by Moto's old theater group. "Moto's replacement is no good. Another ten or twenty years, then maybe. What can I do to get you back to the theater?"

Hanne imagines a whole host of things. All of which involve her creamy, smooth skin.

"When I'm ready," says Moto, "I'll be ready."

"Which says nothing," says Renzo.

"That's right," says Moto.

Midori laughs.

"I say a lot of things that amount to nothing," says Moto.

"You're stubborn," says Hanne.

"No," says Moto.

"Though you can be," says Midori.

"I can be a lot of things," says Moto.

Hanne sits up. She's heard that sentence before. Right after Chikako complained that her kitchen sink was leaking, and she'd have to call a plumber but didn't have the money, and why did she have to deal with this now? Jiro said he'd fix it. In response to Chikako's surprised "You can?" Jiro smiled, "I can be a lot of things." After that, he grabbed her and kissed her cheek, her neck, and whispered that he loved her, as he slowly unbuttoned her dress.

And, as she anticipated, Moto leans over and kisses Midori on the cheek. He places both hands on the table and, groaning and grimacing, heaves himself up, as if he were made of solid brick. "I've got to eat something," he says. "Then I'm heading back to bed. See you all later." He winks at Midori. A signal for her to join him?

A moment later, Hanne hears the hiss and spit of eggs cooking in a frying pan.

Midori laughs. "He's in bad shape."

"You must be very pleased about this toothpaste opportunity," says Renzo.

Midori goes on, how this is likely to lead to many other things, great things, ideally a movie, but she'd settle right now for an acting job on a TV drama. She's auditioning for a couple. She'd love to be on the program "Long Vacation," or "I Want to Be In Love." She'd accept any role, anything—the wife whose husband is cheating on her, the woman who is sick with some terrible disease and will, by the end of the season, die.

Hanne excuses herself, blaming it on jet lag, and says she needs to lie down.

"Hey," Moto calls out as she passes through the kitchen. "Aren't you coming in here to help me cook breakfast?"

"Looks like you've got it all under control."

"Here." He hands her a glass. "Bloody Mary. It's supposed to help."

"Thank you." When's the last time she had a drink in the morning? She takes a sip and hands it back to him.

He smiles, crossing his arms in front of him. "Sorry. You'll need to drink more than that."

"You're a bad influence. Last night, and now this." She hears herself. Is she flirting with him?

He grins. "Good. I mean, I'm glad I'm a bad influence. I'm determined to make your visit memorable."

And is he flirting with her? But there is Midori calling for him. Hanne takes her drink, gives him a little wave, and heads out to the cottage. She sits at the bare desk and stares at the dog sleeping outside in the grass. So long ago, it seems, she was fretting over words, *dry, dried up, drying*. What she's feeling is relatively new: that most of her life is behind her, no longer ahead of her. Unlike Midori, she doesn't have a thousand options, a huge expanse of possibilities. It's called getting older, she says to herself, and she doesn't particularly like it.

She has a vague sense that this feeling also has to do with her encounter with Kobayashi. It's one thing to see his name on a piece of paper; it's quite another to see him in the flesh. She can picture him now. His hunched, bony shoulders, his dark eyes, his frown, smell his whiskey breath, feel his fury. A human being who thinks she sabotaged his art. *I am ashamed.*

Over the years, she's narrowed down her options, finally confining herself to a small island, the art of translation. Her work, what she's deeply cared about, devoted herself to like a faithful servant, and sacrificed so much for—Kobayashi feels she failed miserably at it. How can that be? If, indeed, he read it, how could he have such a skewed reading? It matters, Tomas, she composes to herself. It matters because if I find that I've successfully translated Moto onto the page, then the itch of doubt will be gone. In her mind, she can see Tomas raise an eyebrow, as if to say: doubt? Yes, doubt, Tomas. That Kobayashi would make such a scene, spewing his accusations in public for everyone to hear, his charges are not so easily dismissed.

She lies down on the hard bed but can't sleep. Something is nagging at her. She showers and heads over to the house. Inside, she hears the slurred words of the singer Tom Waits, who to her ear sounds like a drunken derelict, his voice trampled by cigarettes and alcohol and who knows what else. She knows him because Brigitte used to listen to him too.

In the big empty room, where last night they floated along to music, Moto is stretched out on his back on the tatami mats. He's reading a book and listening to the dreadful music, his head propped on a pillow. She glances at the book's title: *Dead Souls*, Gogol's unfinished novel. An English translation. Of course Kobayashi took artistic license, changing superficial details, but Jiro never read anything but the newspaper.

"You can read English?" she says. "And you like Gogol?"

He leans over, turns the music down. "Yep. And I speak fairly good English. I'm full of neat tricks."

"I'm envious."

He raises an eyebrow.

She tells him what had happened, the fall, the loss of her first languages. She doesn't mention the hospital or the surgery or much of anything else, so by the time she finishes, it hardly sounds like anything at all.

Still, he murmurs, "All the things one can lose. Would it help you if I spoke English? Maybe it would jar something loose."

How kind of him to offer. "But that's asking too much of you."

"If it makes you feel better, I get to practice my English." He tells her that long ago he had an American girlfriend, so his English isn't too shabby.

"If it's not too much trouble."

He studies her. "I offered."

She takes a seat at the table and asks who translated his book. He shows her the name on the title page. "Nabokov approved of the Bernard Gilbert Guerney translation," she says. "Nabokov said the plot didn't really matter, it was the writing, which in Russian reads much more like a poem than a novel."

"I forgot," he says. "You're a translator."

He speaks American English, not British, and his cadence and rhythms are quite good.

"What are you working on now?" he says in English.

You, my friend. "I'm in between projects," she replies in Japanese.

She tells him about her play, and he mentions the Noh play about Komachi.

"Yes, I've read it. I plan on doing something very different." She points to his book. "When you're done with it, I'd like to hear your opinion of this translation."

He glances at the book. "I don't know if I'll finish it."

"No? Why not?"

He shrugs. "I might lose interest."

"But you're more than halfway through."

"So?" he says, smiling faintly. Watching her, he closes the book and sets it down on the floor.

"It seems you've already devoted so much time to it. It'll be a waste just to quit."

He doesn't answer, just smiles as if he knows something she does not.

Without warning, a memory of Brigitte comes to her. An argument with Brigitte, who wanted to quit her French lessons. She had decided she didn't like French anymore and wanted to learn Mandarin. Hanne had just picked her up from school, and Brigitte rushed to the car with an armload of library books about China. Her fourth-grade class had begun studying China and Chinese history. "They invented the compass and paper and printing and when I get older, I want to travel there and maybe live there," she said, her eyes the hue of thrill. With the extra hours freed up if she quit French, she'd study Mandarin. She smiled shyly at Hanne. "And that's a language you don't know, is it?"

But to walk away from five years of French lessons. It seemed so rash, so impulsive. Her French teacher called her his best student. All those hours spent learning verb tenses and nouns and sentence structure and exceptions to the rules.

As she drove home, Hanne lectured Brigitte about the often-grueling nature of life, how it's far more difficult than she might ever imagine, and she needed to learn to persevere. "When your father, brother, and I set our minds to something, we don't give up," she said. "No matter the odds or risks or difficulties. It's gotten us where we are today, and that's no small feat. Other people meet with hardship and tread no further. We forge ahead. You have to decide what kind of person you want to be."

"I'll probably be both," said Brigitte.

Hanne didn't know if Brigitte meant it, or she was just trying to be infuriating.

Moto is still smiling at her, as if he's thinking "So you've found me lacking. What are you going to do about it?" And he's still looking at her, studying her, as if he wants her to know he sees right into her, her views, her judgment, and is amused.

"I can't do something if my heart isn't in it," he says.

"So you give up when things become difficult," she says.

"I didn't say that." He still has that smile, though bigger, as if he's even more amused than before. "I've enjoyed many things that are difficult."

The tea kettle whistles. Moto tucks his knees to his chest and rocks himself onto his feet. Instantly, he is on his feet. In a million years, she couldn't do a move like that.

Hanne and Brigitte had argued about her quitting French lessons all the way home and into dinner. No, she's not remembering right. Hanne lectured and Brigitte sat there stone-faced, not saying a word. Finally Hanne forbade her to quit French. If she wanted to take up Mandarin, she'd have to find a way to fit it in. And now she sees her daughter slumped in her chair, her face pale, shoulders rounded, a posture of exquisite dejection. How cruel, how unrelenting Hanne was. And the worst thing about it is that she can still hear the excitement in Brigitte's voice as she bounded into the car and said she wanted to study Mandarin, the excitement that Hanne ultimately crushed.

In the kitchen, Moto takes the kettle off the burner and opens cupboards, finding the canister of green tea and two cups. A stack of dirty dishes in the sink diverts him. A rarity: a Japanese man his age who serves tea and does the dishes. He rolls up his sleeves and scrubs hard at the stuck food, and, when he finally removes it, puts the wet dish in the dish rack.

"Do you miss acting?" she says.

"Do I miss it? Not particularly."

"Years and years of acting and you don't yearn for the audience? The lights? The thrill of performance?"

He starts in on another dirty white plate. "I guess I've fallen out of it."

Fallen? Like falling out of a habit? A dream? Perhaps he doesn't know the English word for what he's trying to say. "What does that mean?"

He's running the sponge around and around, as if considering her question. "Or maybe it released me. I don't remember it," he says slowly. "I can remember how to move and dance and sing. But I can't feel it anymore."

Moto sets the plate in the rack, then puts his hands under the faucet, letting the hot water run on them. Steam rises up, fogging the window above the sink.

"Has that ever happened to you?" he says. "Something you once loved with every cell of your body is sucked of all of its juice?"

If anything, her work holds her even more firmly in its grip. If someone called her up right now and offered her a translation project, she'd jump at it. "I can't say it has."

He turns the water off and says, in a soft voice, "Are you happy, Hanne?"

How quickly they've moved from being mere acquaintances to something familiar, intimate, and most likely contentious. "I'd love to have my language faculties back. But I won't let myself complain."

"Why not?"

"I don't find it very becoming."

"You should give it a try. You might enjoy it," he says.

"And you, are you happy? All is well?"

He shrugs. "It is how it is."

This time she hears in his voice profound resignation. "So you're a fatalist? You're dealt a hand and you just resign yourself to it?"

He laughs at her. "Is that what translators do? Put a name to everything?"

Not just one name, she thinks.

That night, she cooks supper for the three of them. No one feels like driving to Kurashiki, so she uses what's on hand—nothing fancy, vegetable soup, red beet salad, garlic potatoes.

"Just with this soup, you've earned your keep," says Renzo. He explains to Moto that Hanne wants to pay them to stay in the cottage.

Moto studies her a long time before announcing, "All right. That meal just earned you three days."

"No," says Renzo. "Four. And why are you speaking English?"

Hanne explains what had happened to her.

"I thought it might help Hanne to hear English," says Moto, turning to Hanne. "And before you object, Hanne, I get to practice."

Renzo says he's so sorry to hear about the accident. Unfortunately, his English isn't very good, so he won't be able to assist. Then he smiles. "But I'll grant you five nights for this meal."

"You two are making fun of me," she says.

Renzo laughs.

"Four it is," says Moto. He pounds the table with his fist.

"I was raised by very proper and dignified Europeans who believed in decorum and etiquette," she says, "and above all honor and decency." She could go on—good shoes and an ironed skirt, clean socks and underwear before exiting the house, a thank-you note for every gift or kind gesture, and a written invitation required to attend any party, any function.

"Okay. Only three nights," says Moto.

After supper, Moto gets his coat and heads out. To where, he doesn't say, but Hanne guesses to Midori's. Hanne retires early. When the dog scratches on her door, she lets it in and pats the end of the bed, hoping it will settle there and warm her freezing feet.

Chapter Eleven

THE NEXT DAY, MOTO IS up early. He's driving toward town to go swimming. She informs him Renzo has invited her to continue to stay in the cottage.

"Renzo loves company," says Moto.

"And you?"

"Depends on the company." He smiles. "Stay. As long as you like."

"Thank you. Just a couple of days."

And now she must impose again. Can she accompany him to town so she can retrieve her luggage from the hotel? She's wearing the same clothes from a day ago and they've begun to feel like a second, oily skin.

"My god! What an imposition," he says, mocking her. "Told you it would be fun having you around."

"I'm glad I'm entertainment for you."

"I'm just playing around."

Which you always seem to be doing, she thinks.

They head out to the garage. She's expecting a dirty clunker filled with old newspapers, crumpled receipts, empty soda cans, torn upholstery with dirty foam exposed. Instead, he drives a shiny black Mercedes, as pristine as if it had been bought yesterday.

"I wouldn't have guessed," she says, touching the shiny hood.

"I like to keep you guessing," he says, opening the car door for her.

She climbs into the passenger seat. The car still has its smell of newness. He doesn't get in right away. It seems something across the street has beckoned to him. He walks across the street, then comes back over to her side of the car. "You have to see the clouds. They look like huge ships sailing across the sky." He makes her get out and look.

She sees clumps of white billowy clouds. No ships, not even a sail.

"Quixotic, that's what you are, Moto," she says, getting back in.

"Oh, yeah. The woman who must name everything," he says, backing out on the gravel driveway and heading down the narrow two-lane road.

"We've kept ourselves busy over the centuries, naming and organizing and categorizing. Why not use them?" she replies.

"Do you ever wonder when you're busy naming, what you might be leaving out?"

"That's the beauty of knowing more than one language. The act of naming conjures more than one word for me, and each word hauls with it its own nuances, as well as cultural, associational, and etymological overlays. Suddenly, that one word has expanded into a large world."

"Of words," he says.

"Of course. What else?"

"I would think the beauty of speaking many languages is that you could talk to people. You know, travel to a foreign place and not feel foreign." He points to a squirrel on a bare birch tree branch and smiles brightly. "He's moving so fast, he's making that thick branch bounce. See it?"

She watches the squirrel leap to a telephone wire. "I don't travel much anymore. Occasionally I visit my son and his family, but that's about it. Besides, I've been reduced to only one language."

"Lucky for you it's Japanese. If it was Armenian, we wouldn't be talking right now."

The morning air is cold. She didn't come prepared for this weather. She needs to buy a heavier coat and a scarf.

"You mentioned a son."

She tells him a son and a daughter. Tomas and Brigitte. "And you? Do you have children?"

He takes a deep breath and for a long time doesn't speak, as if he's lost all memory of English words. "Unfortunately, we were never blessed that way."

"I'm sorry."

They drive by fields of soybean and barley, and then a lake. He points out the geese, says they look incandescent, as if they'd swallowed light bulbs. "Such beauty for no obvious purpose."

Hanne always wished she had that impulse: to be drawn to the world in front of her, not always reaching for something beyond herself. Jiro had it. Brigitte, too. "You're fortunate, Brigitte," she told her daughter many times. "This world is enough for you, isn't it?"

Now Moto says: "Your daughter. You don't travel to see her?"

"That's for another time, I think."

"Fair enough." Minutes seem to go by. "And what about translation?" he says. "Where does the beauty lie there?"

"I've always explained it as an effort to deepen the connections of the world. One culture converses with another, and the recipient culture receives a new vision of the world."

Even before she finishes, she's assaulted by the memory of Kobayashi humiliating her—*your hopes of uniting mankind.*

She concedes it's a romanticized version of translation. She's making it appear grand, and making herself appear far more magnanimous and generous than she really is. By the way Moto is smiling, as if there's an old joke between them, he must be aware of that too. Why does it always feel as if he's seeing right through her?

"And it enchants me," she says. "It gives me pleasure purely for what it is."

"You mean you like it."

"Yes. I like it. Love it."

"You know, I'm a pretty informal guy. You don't have to talk to me as if you're giving me a lecture."

"I'm just speaking. It's the way I speak. I was raised in a very proper household."

"I'm just saying you can lighten up with me."

"I thought the Japanese language with its proper, polite—"

"Yeah, well, not me." There's a long pause. "You know, it's like you think it over before you speak. It puts a lot of distance between you and everyone else." He glances at her. "You're guarded. That's why you do it, right? To protect yourself. But listen, I promise I won't bite."

Guarded? Why is he scrutinizing her? "I pay attention to what I say and how I speak, that's all."

They drive on in silence. Out the window, she looks at farmhouses, pastures filled with brown cows. She has no idea where they are. They pass by a temple and an orchard of bare fruit trees. Hanne considers all the ways to broach the subject and finally settles on something simple, direct. "So I understand you're no longer married."

"That's right."

"You've moved on, then."

He smiles faintly.

"Is Midori your girlfriend?"

"Back to the labels," he says, smiling. "Why? Are you going to make a move on me?"

She feels herself blush. When is the last time she's done that?

He laughs. "Let's see. She's an aspiring actress. A fairly good voice-over actress. A woman who has a closet full of pantsuits and shoes. A pretty lousy cook. Should I go on?"

"I meant in relationship to you."

"A woman who wants to learn everything about my voice. Who likes to hang out with me when I'm in a good mood. When I'm not, she'd rather not. And I don't blame her one bit. I can be a real stick-in-the-mud."

Did she really think this elusive man would give her the answer? It's almost as if he is intentionally vague, hiding from her, playing around, ducking away each time she probes. Why is that? He's tapping his thumbs against the steering wheel. Hanne looks out the window at the rice fields. Maybe it's early in his relationship with Midori. In the beginning, before Jiro and Chikako became a couple, Jiro dated other women. When Jiro was asked about his relationship with Chikako, he, too, was noncommittal.

Moto pulls into the parking lot of the hotel and she runs in, checks out, and gets her luggage. She's not sure she's doing the right thing, camping out in their cottage, but Japan is exorbitantly expensive, and, as she'd hoped, she's getting to spend time with Moto.

It's a short drive to what apparently is the swimming pool—a long building that seems to be constructed out of polished metal, glimmering in spite of the overcast day.

"We're here," he says, lighting up a cigarette.

"You smoke?" she says, getting out of the car. Jiro did too, but that's like saying he had black hair. Nearly everyone here smokes, she knows that, yet somehow it surprises her with Moto.

He closes his door. "Only before I'm about to swim," he says, his voice playful, as if he might be teasing her.

"It's not good for you."

"Yeah, well, breathing this crummy air probably isn't good for me either."

"I smoke only when I speak French," she says, opening her luggage and digging out her suit and clean clothes.

Moto begins to laugh, as if this was the most hilarious thing he's heard in a long time.

"And I only eat dark rye bread when I'm speaking German," she says, laughing with him, which prompts her to go on, "and pickled herring when I speak Danish. I think I look my best when I'm speaking French. My clothes, my hair, my complexion, French brings out a shimmer."

"Oh, you don't look so bad speaking Japanese."

"That's kind of you."

"And Japanese?"

She tells him it's too humble, too yielding, too ready to get down on its knees and apologize for the smallest thing.

"Everyone's so polite here, always saying you're sorry. Except you, of course."

He laughs loudly.

"I meant that as a compliment, you know. But maybe it's because you're speaking English, a rather blunt language."

"No. Doesn't matter what language. I'm always impolite. And rude and loud and disrespectful, if you ask my brother. He says I offend everyone." He picks up his swim bag. "My American friends who speak Japanese say it makes them aware of the other person. Your relationship to someone. You know, should you use honorific or standard or informal verb when you talk to someone? That kind of thing."

"Yes, that too. The other person."

Getting into the pool involves a procedure more suitable for entrance into the United Nations. Moto pulls out his membership card, which shows his picture—expressionless, staring straight at the camera. He produces his driver's license with a similar photo, and she's asked to do the same, in addition to paying the rather extravagant entrance fee. They must sign in, state their purpose (to swim), and walk through a security gate, which presumably will buzz if it detects too much metal on their persons.

Once they get inside, she sees what all the fuss is about. It's not a pool. It's a beach with fine white sand, blue waves rolling onto a shore, and the aroma of coconut suntan lotion drifting by. People are stretched out on bright, colorful beach towels, sitting under sun umbrellas. Straight ahead, a turquoise sea. All enclosed in a huge building.

The indoor sea went over so well in Miyazaki, says Moto, they built a smaller version here. Over by the lifeguard's chair, there's a statue of a monkey holding a cold drink. Down the way, a group of teens plays volleyball.

"Nature's so unreliable," she says. "Better to create your own sea."

"After a while, you'll forget it's fake."

He points to the women's locker room. "You can swim," he says, "or not."

She watches him walk toward the men's locker room, that flowing graceful gait again, his head not bobbing up and down like a normal human's. She watches until he disappears.

She steps into the locker room. White floors, white walls, white benches, white lockers. Not just an off-white, a bright white, as if designed to make someone go a little blind. She quickly changes into her black one-piece suit, a piece of clothing she threw in her suitcase at the last minute, thinking she'd never use it, and studies herself in the mirror. Still trim, she can wear a bathing suit without embarrassment. For a moment, she tries to see herself from Moto's point of view. No Midori, that's for sure. But not too shabby. For a woman her age. She steps outside, or rather inside, onto the fake sand.

The shore is crowded with people, the water filled with swimmers. She sits alone on the white sand. She has no idea where Moto is. Her skin is ghostly pale, though most everyone is the same anemic coloring; the Japanese, like her, avoid the sun. She is self-conscious, like a bystander. Oddly, she starts to sweat. Maybe a heater is used to mimic the sun's warmth.

Wading into the warm water (unnaturally warm), she can't remember the last time she went swimming. She does the breaststroke, but her legs are not kicking hard enough. And she's out of breath. She floats on her back, until someone swims by, kicking hard, splashing drops of water on her face. She resumes the breaststroke, her chin in the water, and tries to spot Moto. Is he the fanatical freestyle swimmer, charging just outside the waves in a beeline, then doing a flip turn? Or the steady one slowly raising his arm over his head, his hand a perfect cup, entering the water delicately, without a splash?

Jiro would be the charger, throwing himself into his strokes. Before she became ill, before he sent her away, Jiro had told his wife that if he ever became sick with no hope of recovery, he'd commit suicide. He wouldn't put up with a withered body, a demented mind. She argued with him, a big fight. His life was valuable, even if he was ill, even if he was a vegetable. She'd love him regardless. She'd never let him kill himself, never! How ironic, then, when she became ill, she tried to end her own life. One never knows what one is capable of, thinks Hanne. You can only speak from the circumstances you currently find yourself in; change the circumstances and you might have an entirely different view of things.

Truthfully, she can't say for sure that Moto would be the charger. She could just as easily see him floating on his back, staring at the ceiling just because he wanted to. She feels herself slowing down, her bottom half sinking. When a young woman swims right into her, hitting her shoulder, she has her excuse to swim to shore and get out. She stretches out on her towel.

A boy appears and sits about five yards from her. He's looking at her. He looks away. Then back again. "This is a pen," he says in English.

This is a pen? There is no pen. Not in his hand. Not in hers.

He repeats it, smiling bigger, clearly pleased with his statement. He must be seven or eight years old.

In Japanese, she tells him her name and unfortunately she doesn't have a pen. "*Sumimasen.*" She raises both hands up in the air to show they are empty.

"*Eigo ga dekimasu ka?*" Do you speak English, he asks politely.

"*Iie*," she says. No.

He looks at her, puzzled, then laughs and laughs.

She steps into the locker room. Quickly she strips off her wet suit and changes into her clothes. When she comes out, Moto is sitting in her spot, waiting. His wet hair is combed. Has he known her whereabouts the entire time? And decided to stay away? She tells him about the exchange with the boy.

"That phrase," says Moto, "is one of the first English phrases that a young schoolboy learns. He wanted to practice and thought you were American or European."

As they head to the car, she wonders: if not American or European, then what am I?

On their way home, Moto stops at a coffee shop. Even with his wet hair, T-shirt, and ragged jeans, he has celebrity status, as if dipped in gold. Though to Hanne he looks tired, those weary eyes, as if he's played too hard. The young waitress flirts with him, giggling her way through their order. Another woman with perfectly coiffed hair waves hello. A third, who is passing by the shop, rushes in and says she'd love him to come to her dinner party. She stands so her bony hip brushes against the edge of the table, near his hand.

He could have his pick of women, thinks Hanne. Yes, he's moved on and is probably sampling a wide range of women, like fine desserts. Not just Midori. Look at him smiling. He's happy, playful, engaged; all is right in his world. Fifteen years of marriage and the world has opened up for him again. Back in the social whirl.

The proprietor brings him a plate of mochi. "So nice to see you," he says to Moto. Moto thanks him and scoots the plate toward Hanne.

Moto asks, "You asked about me. What about you, Hanne? You're not married?"

"A widow."

He looks at her for a long minute. "I'm sorry. Truly sorry."

"It was a long time ago."

Moto sips his coffee, watching her.

She shifts uncomfortably. "Like you, I've moved on."

Back at the house, she heads to the cottage to hang up her wet bathing suit. When she returns to the main house, Renzo says Moto has left.

"To where?" Hanne says, trying to hide her disappointment.

Renzo shrugs.

She spends the rest of the afternoon working in the garden with Renzo. He's determined to weed it out and plant vegetables—daikon, potatoes, burdock root, lotus root, and radishes. The dirt is dark, rich, suitable for planting. Hanne and her mother used to plant a garden every spring, no matter where they lived. Even if the garden was confined to a two-meter-by-two-meter swatch of poor soil. Her mother was a very determined woman.

That night she helps Renzo cook dinner. He teaches her how to make Japanese sweet potato cakes using cooked sweet potato, butter, sugar, eggs, flour, and a bit of cream. When she inquires again where Moto might be, Renzo shakes his head. "He's a funny guy. He could be with Midori. Or a surprise visit to a friend. Or he might be at the library reading about van Gogh. He says if he could see as well as van Gogh did, he'd be a better actor. There's times he watches me so closely, it's almost like I feel his gaze rub against my skin. Have you noticed it?"

In fact, she has.

"That's a good sign, don't you think?" he says. "He's preparing to return to the stage."

"I hope so," she says, thinking of Jiro's return to the symphony. She's aware that she's listening for Moto. And there, she thinks she hears the front door open. She waits, expecting him to wander into the kitchen. But there is no one. A new wave of disappointment.

She mixes the ingredients together and puts cake-size blobs onto a greased cookie sheet. "Can I ask, has Moto always been so unanchored?"

Renzo is at the stove, stirring miso soup. "Unanchored? What does this mean?"

Unsettled, she wants to say, unbalanced, unhinged. "Drifting about. Following a whim."

He thinks about it. "Yes, I think so. But when he was acting, he was anchored and unanchored. Acting out different characters, so he was drifting, as you say. But anchored to the role of actor no matter what. You see?"

Like Jiro. The wide landscape of human emotion washed over him when he played the violin, one series of notes leading into sadness, another into delight, but always anchored to the violin. He told his wife that when he played he felt fluid, the boundaries of himself evaporating, and he became everything. He was no longer himself, or maybe not only himself. "What a relief for you," said his wife. "That you have a way to escape this world."

She goes to bed in a good mood. Overall, she's found no flaws in her translation. Moto is like her Jiro. Late that night, Hanne hears the dog barking. She gets out of bed and steps outside into the cold. A half moon casts light on the frosty ground. She smells the rich dirt from this afternoon's digging in the garden. A breeze stirs and her white nightgown billows around her. She doesn't see the dog anywhere. She's about to step back inside when a car draws up in the driveway. A door slams. He's walking toward her.

"Look at you in this moonlight," says Moto, smiling. "What a shame my English is so lousy. Everything I can think of saying is a cliché."

She smiles. "Best to remain quiet, then."

"Your hair, with the moon stroking it, looks like black glass. Your gown glows like a sun ray. Your skin—"

"Okay. Enough," she says, laughing. When she turns and he follows her into the cottage, she feels her old recklessness dust itself off. Lust, yes, he's a very attractive man. Before Hiro, before marriage, she had plenty of sex for the sheer pleasure of it. Another appetite of the body was how she saw it. She reaches for his hand, a warm, firm hand that grips hers. Lust, she thinks and also curiosity—does he make love like Jiro?

He's smooth, his chest hairless, as sleek as a stone. Like her Jiro. Moto smells of alcohol, but what does she care. A morning spent with him, and now the slow burn of desire has somewhere to go.

His hand finds the curve of her lower back, guiding her to the bed. "Not so guarded," he murmurs in her ear. She turns him around, kisses him, feels the fullness of his lips, of him, tastes the bitterness of beer. He kisses her neck, fingers, until, restless, she pulls him on top of her. He takes his time, until she's quivering under his fingers.

When they're done, they lie in each other's arms and listen to Morsel howl. Moto joins in.

"Stop, you'll wake Renzo," she says, laughing. She picks up Moto's hand and fiddles with his fingers. It's how she imagined sex with Jiro. Intense, passionate, playful.

"Spoilsport." Grinning, he slips back into his clothes, bows low. "I depart."

"Until we meet again."

He heads out the door. The bed is too small for the two of them. Besides, she'd rather sleep alone.

Chapter Twelve

OUTSIDE, THE WEATHER IS RUNNING itself through the tree branches, with the day gathering into a dense dull presence of rain clouds. Before she heads to the house, she makes the bed. How unexpected, she thinks, untangling the sheets, noting the wet spot. A nice unexpected, she admits, though she thinks it shouldn't happen again. She's here to observe, not become involved in something.

It's early morning and the house is astonishingly cold. She buttons her sweater and steps into the eating room. Moto is there, busy sewing a button on a white shirt. Thankfully, he's turned the heat on full blast. He offers her hot tea.

"You're up early," she says, cupping her hands around the mug.

He has a voice-over gig and has to go to Kurashiki to record it. "I'm trying to look halfway presentable," he says, holding up the shirt.

"Another talent of yours?"

Renzo is the one with sewing skills, he says, but he has gone to Kojima to look at a tansu and visit friends.

"I'd like to hear you," she says. "It sounds interesting."

He shrugs, finishing a button. He snips off the thread. "Not much to it."

It seems last night will be folded up, tucked away, forgotten. For the best, she thinks, sipping her tea. "Renzo really hates these voice-overs, doesn't he?"

"I suppose." He points to her sweater. Two buttons are missing. How hadn't she noticed it? "I think I have a match," he says, digging through his box of buttons. She hands it to him. He threads his needle, shaking his head and smiling, his birthmark bunching up like a pretty rose. "Renzo has this idea that our parents and all our ancestors, all the way back to the beginning of time are watching our every move and I'm disappointing each and every one of them."

She smiles, thinking of her mother's expression—a mixture of expectation and disappointment. "Isn't it a given that we disappoint our parents?"

He reaches over and touches her hand. "A pleasure, last night."

She nods. So it won't be forgotten. Might it happen again? She finds herself unexpectedly hoping it will.

"So does that mean your children have disappointed you?" he says.

More rain clouds must have blown in because the room fills with a brownish light. She tells him about Tomas. Responsible, intelligent, driven, a good father and husband. "I could go on and on."

"And Brigitte?"

She's startled that he remembered her name. To hear someone else say it out loud, it makes her feel as though Brigitte is present, sitting at the table with them. "She's on her own path. Isn't that what every parent wants? A child who is out in the world, doing what she wants to do?"

He leans forward with his elbows on the table, as if trying to get underneath her words. He's waiting for her to say more, and the silence elongates until she feels the need to say more.

"For years she wanted to be a translator. Then it was a veterinarian, then an emergency medic, then a poet, and then the Peace Corps, then I forget. There were so many iterations of possible careers, I lost track. And she could have done any one of those things. A million other things too."

"A girl with many interests," he murmurs.

"That's one way to put it."

"How do you put it?"

"Oh, I don't think about it anymore. We haven't spoken in a long time. Six years." That last part came out fast.

A pause. "That sounds hard."

"In the beginning, but one learns to carry on."

"How?"

"The way one does. Life isn't beyond mending, Moto. As you know."

Minutes go by, it seems. The wind picks up, rattling the windows. Her right leg feels incredibly hot. She must be too close to the heater. She shifts, but still her leg is burning. And now her stomach aches, as if it's shrunken into a tight fist. His gaze is fixed on the fish tank behind her. His birthmark is an intense red, almost in the shape of a crescent moon. "She sounds like an artist, your daughter," he says, as if speaking to himself.

"I suppose. There was that phase of poetry."

"That's not what I mean. She sounds like she's struggled to find her place in the world. Sensitive people are like that. When a way of life isn't working, you have to get rid of it. The alternative is to feel a part of you, a big part has been forgotten. Eventually it just dies off."

Hanne feels slightly disoriented. Is he trying to tell her something about himself? Or does he suddenly claim to have special insight into Brigitte? "You didn't struggle to find your place." She says it as a statement, not a question.

"No. But that was just damn luck. The path chosen for me by my parents was the right one."

"And now?"

He shrugs. The light drains completely from the room, as if the day has rolled by in an instant and now it is evening. She watches him sew a new button on her sweater. A feeling of apprehension sweeps over her.

"Were you and Brigitte ever close?" he says.

Why is he so interested in her? What's he fishing for? "When she was little," she says. "Back then, she loved languages and, as you know, that's my forte." In her mind, she sees Brigitte, with pudgy baby-fat limbs, hears the pitch of her voice as she wrapped her mouth around German. How hard she'd grip Hanne's fingers, as if she never wanted to let go. Hanne tells Moto about their birding expeditions. "But," she takes a deep breath, "she made things hard for herself by dwelling on her problems. Or perceived problems. Or other people's problems." She almost says she took every little thing to heart. But stops herself. She hears Moto's explanation from the other night as to why he might not finish Gogol's novel—how his heart might lose interest. Is that why he's intrigued by Brigitte? Might he hear an echo of himself? "I tried to help her, instill some hardiness. Some fortitude. Life is rarely easy, as you know."

When he says nothing, she finds herself telling him about the time Brigitte found a mangy gray kitten rummaging through their garbage can. She must have been eight years old, and she insisted that she keep it. Its mother had been hit by a car. The big black birds were in the street, picking at it. She had to take care of the kitten. From the moment she held it, Brigitte worried that it, too, might die. "I don't want it to die. Will it die? What can we do so it will never die?"

Her anxiety was endless, but Hanne refused to lie. She told Brigitte that just like all living creatures, the cat would eventually die, but they'd give it a good life and when it came time, give it a proper, dignified burial in the back yard. That solved nothing. Brigitte continued to fret and Hanne wouldn't budge. Hiro was no help. He was teaching more classes at Stanford, and during the week he was sleeping in the spare bedroom of one of the other faculty members, driving home only on the weekends. Tomas, who was sixteen at the time, finally cornered Hanne in the kitchen. "God, mom. Tell her someday that cat will go to sleep for a long time. Just tell her that."

"I won't disrespect her like that."

"Dad does it. Whenever Dad drives by a dead animal on the road, he tells Brigitte it's sleeping."

"Oh, hell." She scoffed. "How weak, how cowardly, how—"

"It works."

Hanne refused. Brigitte wasn't a baby.

The cat soon died of distemper. Hiro took a week off from his classes and spent his free time with Brigitte, who was inconsolable. They went out to lunch, to the museum, the movies. Hanne and Hiro fought about it.

"You're sending her the wrong message," said Hanne. "You're teaching her to wallow when something difficult happens."

"I'm not sending her any messages. I'm just being with her."

"You're not considering the consequences of your actions. You're encouraging her to be spineless. To fall apart when something hard happens. That won't serve her well in life."

Hanne suggested getting a new cat, but Brigitte wouldn't hear of it. You can't just replace one with another. How could you think like that? She loved that kitten. Eventually Brigitte stopped all her language lessons and spent every afternoon at the animal shelter. Hiro had suggested it. Her job was to feed the cats and clean their cages. But soon the tasks went beyond that, to walking the dogs and helping the veterinarian administer shots. Her dream changed from becoming a translator to a veterinarian. She planned on saving all the hurt and abandoned animals in the world.

When is the last time she has told that story to someone? Or even thought of it?

"She sounds very tender," says Moto. "To realize that everything will perish. To fear the death of something or someone you love so much." He shakes his head, as if amazed by her depths. "So wise."

"Not that wise. And not that tender."

"No?"

She takes a deep breath. "It's a commonplace story. A girl hits teen years and rebels. Drugs, most likely. Sex. Nothing I said or did mattered. She could be cruel."

Her teen years came, unfortunately, at the same time Hanne's husband died, she tells Moto. "We weren't living together at the time. The decision was mutual, but Brigitte, I think, blamed me. If only he had been living with us, if only we'd been there, we could have saved him. Called an ambulance. Rushed him to the hospital. Maybe that's true. Maybe it isn't. But after that, Brigitte was lost to me. I became the enemy. The hated one." She doesn't tell him about the many nights she heard Brigitte crying in her room. How at first Hanne tried to console her. When she couldn't, she tried to ignore it, hoping it would subside.

"I felt the best thing for us, all of us, was to carry on. Hiro would have wanted that, I think. Not pull her out of school, not grant her a leave of absence, a stretch of idleness. All those things she wanted. What would she have done? Just mope and sulk around the house some more? Get into more trouble? A girl of fourteen can easily meet with ruin. I was teaching Japanese and translating, the equivalent of full-time work. I couldn't monitor her. She was failing school. Refusing to study, cutting class, hanging out with the wrong crowd. I don't know where she met these boys. She wouldn't listen to me. In the end, I suppose, she found a way to take her leave of absence."

She stops. How out of character, going on and on. Why is she laying out her life story before him? As she picks up her tea, she sees a slight shake of her hand. To her surprise, she feels like she must say more—as if she's trying to convince Moto of something.

"She's a very bright girl and she was throwing her life away. I couldn't just stand idly by. I located a boarding school for her. A very good school. Perfect for her. It was the right thing to do. She didn't want to go, of course. Her friends were in San Francisco, not Connecticut, where the school was located. I didn't find that hard to understand," she says. "But I *did* find it hard to understand why she made such a mess of her life."

"The heart can be a mysterious thing," he says quietly. He hands her back her mended sweater.

She makes herself stop. Enough airing of dirty laundry. They sit in the quiet for some time, and it feels as if he's still listening, threading through his mind everything she has just said. No longer smiling, he looks in deep concentration. The fish tank gurgles and bubbles, as if they've fallen deep underwater. Hanne has the urge to grab her coat and head out, anywhere, but now it's not only her leg that's hot. She feels feverish, nauseous. "I'm suddenly not feeling very well."

"You don't look well."

"I think I need to lie down."

"Let me help you."

He takes her arm and helps her out to the cottage. She slips off her shoes and, shaking uncontrollably, climbs into bed. He leaves and comes back with hot tea, a tray of rice crackers, and aspirin.

He places his hand on her forehead. "You're burning up."

"I feel foolish."

He opens the bottle of aspirin and hands her two. She feels like a child as he holds a glass of water to her lips. "Now rest."

"I'm sure it's nothing serious. Please just go about your business."

She's in bed for four long days. Renzo and Moto take turns bringing her food and herbal drinks. She tries to put on a cheery face, but in the back of her mind she's worried her decline might have something to do with her fall. The doctor warned her there might be unforeseen complications. He couldn't guarantee anything. So here she is, drifting in and out of sleep. Babbling in a feverish state. Sweat pearling on her forehead. Staying here far too long and requiring so much from them. So weak, it's an effort to lift a glass of water. Sounds are amplified. Sometimes it seems like the dog is barking directly in her ear, even though when she opens her eyes, Morsel is nowhere in sight.

A doctor comes and determines she has the common flu. She should feel relieved. It has nothing to do with her brain. Still, she is concerned. She can't remember the last time she had the flu or even a cold. That part of being human, she always thought, didn't apply to her. The doctor says she is to rest and get plenty of fluids. Whenever Moto or Renzo appear, she apologizes. For herself. For this inconvenience. For imposing. As soon as she is better, she will leave. They will never have to see her again.

"If you apologize one more time," says Moto, "I'm going to make you stay for another five weeks."

"But you didn't intend for a visitor to stay for so long, let alone become so demanding."

"People get sick."

"But this isn't what you signed up for."

"So?"

He pours her a cup of tea. The smell is horrible, a mix between boiled grass and underarm odor. "Chinese herbs. I use them all the time. Can't hurt."

"Surely they can." In an effort to be a good patient, she drinks it. "It's horrible." She puts the cup on the nightstand and gulps down water to cool her burning throat.

"Now, you must be bored. So I'll read to you."

"I feel bad enough about this." She tries to shoo him away.

He pulls up a chair beside her bed. "You know," he says, "some people take great pleasure in caring for others."

It is the same way Jiro viewed tending to his wife. He felt needed, and many sweet hours were spent caring for her. Until he realized he'd done all he could. And it was still not enough.

Moto pulls out Gogol's *Dead Souls* and smiles. "And since you were so interested in my opinion of the translation, I thought I'd read it to you. Let you come to your own conclusions."

On the fifth day, her fever finally breaks. She is weak, her limbs reluctant to move, but she makes herself get out of bed and dress. Enough lying around, staring out the window. She wants to go to town to buy gifts for their generosity, their patience, their caretaking. By now, she feels like part of the family: a bad relative who has stayed far beyond her welcome. They have seen her without make-up, sweaty, her hair puffed out by a pillow, her breath stale from not brushing her teeth.

"The fallen rise again," says Moto. He's in the kitchen, stirring a raw egg into his orange juice. "Welcome to the land of the living."

"Thanks to you and Renzo, I am standing again. I want to repay you for your hospitality."

"I'll add it to your bill," he says smiling.

"Are you going to town anytime soon?"

In fact, he has another voice-over.

She gets her bag and they head to the car. Outside, the landscape erupts in feverish colors. It's been so long since she's looked at anything but a wall. She inspects herself in the visor mirror. "Back to normal," she says, but the truth is that her face is drawn, gaunt, as if she's aged ten years. It seems months ago that she and Moto were intimate. And now? She feels so old, she's sure any scrap of beauty is gone. Moto finds a radio station that plays American jazz. He hasn't bothered to brush his hair, but she supposes it isn't necessary—it's his voice the company wants, and, she guesses, his fame. His birthmark is smaller today, or so it seems, and in the shape of an egg.

He pulls out of the driveway and starts to drive. "Help yourself," he says, pointing to the two cups and a thermos of coffee.

She raises an eyebrow. "You'd risk sullying your fine leather seats?"

"Only for you," he says. "Before you say no, since you don't seem to want anyone to ever do anything nice for you—"

"Is that how you see me?"

"You're one of the worst patients I've ever had. Always apologizing. Always saying you don't need a thing. You're 'perfectly fine'—at a 103 temperature."

She pours him a cup and one for herself. "Growing up, I wasn't allowed to get sick. My mother didn't have time for it. Nor did my father. I learned not to get sick."

"You can will yourself not to get sick?"

"I just don't. I wasn't allowed."

"Except," he says, smiling, "you did."

As he drives, he runs his thumb along his right earlobe, stroking it absentmindedly, almost tenderly. When a car barrels down the road in the opposite direction, he drives with one hand on the steering wheel at twelve o'clock, while gnawing the inside of his cheek. He points out for her a woodpile stacked up to a house's rafters, a thick cluster of bamboo, a pond that, in the dead of winter last year, froze over and became an impromptu ice rink for the neighborhood.

"I've been thinking about your daughter," he says. "Maybe you just go to her. You know, show up. Where is she now?"

It feels like he's picking up where they left off, before she got sick. Has he been thinking about Brigitte the entire time? Hanne buttons up her coat. "I don't know."

He raises an eyebrow.

"She keeps in touch with her brother, but only because he doesn't tell me what she says."

She's glad he doesn't say for a second time it sounds difficult. Drops of rain splatter on the windshield. She watches a drip trickle down the glass. "In the beginning, no one knew where she was. It took a couple of months for her to inform Tomas where she was. That was kind of her." Hanne doesn't try to keep the sarcasm from her voice. She knew Brigitte had taken a leave from college and gone to Eastern Europe with an organization called Safe Houses for the World. They built prefab houses for low-income folks. "Admirable, yes, but I wasn't in support of this, not that she asked me. I no longer had any financial strings to pull, because she'd rejected my help and signed up for financial aid. She declared herself no longer my dependent. She was supposed to return and finish her final year of college, but she never did. And that had been my fear all along. That she wouldn't finish. That something else would come along, something that would yank at her heartstrings and throw her off course. The group's president had no idea where she'd gone to and everyone was frantic. Finally, she called. She was in Cologne. She'd joined some spiritual group and had gone on retreat."

Moto says nothing. Then, "Was she religious growing up?"

"She found a church. Church friends." What was it? Presbyterian? Unitarian? She's ashamed to say she doesn't know. "But as a family, we had no religion. No regular attendance at a church. I suppose you could call Hiro a Buddhist."

"And you?"

"Me?" She laughs. "Do I think there is some great power that will, when the grand curtain of life closes, judge my character and condemn me for my many failings? Do I believe there is some inherent meaning to existence? Unfortunately, no. Though we need meaning, I believe that. That's one thing I firmly believe. We are meaning-making machines. It keeps the storytellers and entertainers and psychologists and translators—yes, I benefit—in business."

He slows down for a stop sign. "Maybe your daughter found a different way of viewing things."

"Such as?"

"The world has its own inherent meaning. There's no need to do or make anything. It's just there. It's life in all its glory and, what's the word in English? Banality. That's the meaning."

"Is that your belief?"

He smiles. "If you're asking is it a habit of my mind to think this, then no. It just is. A truth. And I was lucky to discover it."

"Why lucky?"

"Sounds like a lot of work, trying to make meaning all the time. You can just sit back and enjoy life's meaning. No need to do a damn thing."

Does he really believe this? Why does she always get the sense he's toying with her? Poking her in the ribs? The rain falls harder. Moto turns on the wipers, and she listens to their steady, hypnotic beat. The car ahead of them is spraying a white tail of water. She watches the rain with something like tension.

"I went over there," she hears herself say. "To Europe. I went to her, hoping to bring her back, but I was denounced and rebuked by her so-called spiritual leaders. Hardly generous, these leaders. I was told I'd failed my daughter. She'd found her real family. Basically I was told to go away. I didn't know her defection would be permanent."

She was going to add "I was found guilty without a trial and as punishment banished from my daughter's life," but when she imagines it spoken out loud, it sounds too excessive, too self-pitying. And she doesn't feel self-pity. For years now, she's lived without knowing her daughter's whereabouts, without speaking to her. She's at peace with what she did, how she handled it. It was necessary, all of it necessary. She doesn't fault herself for trying to save her daughter.

Why is she dragging up the corpse of those hard times? It seems she forgets her purpose for being here. "May I ask, why did your marriage end?"

"It just did."

She waits for him to say more. The rain is coming down in great silver sheets of water.

"And Midori?" She almost says "and all the others."

"Yes?"

"Did she come before or after the demise of the marriage?"

"Right smack in the middle. Confusing for someone like you, isn't it?"

"What do you mean?"

"Someone who needs things to have labels, definitions. Someone who isn't allowed to get sick." He smiles. "Midori wasn't the cause, if that's what you're asking. She just appeared in the middle. And she isn't a girlfriend, she's a friend who happens to be a woman. Nothing is neat and tidy."

Moto hums a little overture, a resonating baritone rising from deep in his body. A wondrous sound; Hanne could listen to him all day.

Then, "My ex-wife, she's an amazing woman. Not just a businesswoman, but a painter, on the board of the public school and hospital, and a million other things."

She hears the awe in his voice. Jiro loved his wife, too, and devoted himself fully to her well-being.

"But we couldn't have children and I didn't think we could move beyond it. It's what she wanted more than anything. For years we tried."

It's her turn to say she is sorry.

"I had to let her go," he says. "She didn't want to part ways, but I insisted."

Like Jiro. Moto sent his wife away. He had to, if he wanted to do the right thing.

"Two years she's been gone. She met someone who could give her what she wants. She's forty years old and eight months pregnant."

He rubs his eyelids.

"How generous of you," she says, her voice quiet. "Not everyone could do that."

"Not that generous. It feels as if part of me is off doing something else," he says, "and I'm left waiting until she comes back."

"She'll fade, by the by. The dimensions of the pain will contract. You'll forget about her."

"I don't want to."

"It's our nature to forget."

"Not my nature. Besides, I couldn't bear it."

"But wouldn't that make it easier? Happiness is often about forgetting."

"Maybe. But I'm not able to do that."

"Of course you are."

"No. I'm not. I am who I am today because of her. She's threaded through every fiber of my being."

"Is this something that's particularly Japanese?"

He slows the car down and turns to look at her. "No. It's something human. You haven't forgotten your husband, have you? Even though it's been years?"

Hanne stiffens. "Well, I'm sure Midori or someone else has helped you move on."

"No."

"So Midori means nothing to you?"

"I didn't say that. She's kind, and kindness goes a long way these days." He talks some more about her, how she puts a little bright light into his otherwise gray day. He doesn't mention love of Midori, how she, or anyone else has swept him up and hurtled him back into life. No mention of how passion has made him new again. How in the years since his wife's absence, he's put one foot in front of the other and walked away from tragedy.

They drive by a dilapidated white barn, part of the side caved in, threatening to take the other side down. She tries to smooth the wrinkles from her skirt. A shiver runs from her scalp, down her arms, her legs, as if a cold wind just blew over her. Her skin feels like ice, and all her warmth has rushed out of her. She glances at Moto. He looks tired, a deep sadness in his eyes.

Jiro wanted to live, let the past drift away like a stick in the current so he could go on with the living. A year after his wife was placed in an institution, Jiro, her Jiro, was in the full embrace of another life, another woman. Or that's how she translated it. She remembers this line: *He was tired of feeling waterlogged with sadness.* She sensed in him an insatiable thirst for life. A refusal to be confined to the narrow space of loss. Didn't she translate the line: *He wanted to use himself up before he died?* Those dreary, melancholy sections of darkened windows and corridors, tear-stained pillows, she didn't give those to Jiro; she gave that messy malaise to Jiro's wife. But now she has a seed of doubt.

"Do you know an author named Yuri Kobayashi?" She can barely keep her voice steady.

"Sure. Years ago my ex-wife hired him to do a commercial. I can't remember what it was for. He became a good friend of mine."

"He said he based the main character of his latest novel on you."

"I wouldn't know about that."

"You haven't read it?"

"No."

She recites a passage to him: *Sunlight streams in through the bedroom window and he becomes aware of vast acreage in his mind that is wonderfully uninhabited. Where just yesterday it was populated by worry, anxiety, and vigilance, there is now a small country of nothingness. He wasn't even conscious of how much of his mind was devoted to, no, obsessed with her well-being. He feels a funny little smile on his face. He is a free man.*

She studies him closely, trying to gauge his response. His face remains blank. "Does that sound like you at all? Since your wife left? Have you ever felt this way?"

"Some days. But most days, I can't do anything but stare at a damn wall. I've spent enough days like that to describe the way my blood feels coursing through my veins. Every day I miss her. Every day I wonder if I did the right thing. If I should have let her go. That's the truth of it. Maybe we could have made it work."

She's sinking into a mood she can only describe as unfamiliar. "The other night when we danced, you said 'Let's not speak.' Do you remember? It's a scene straight from his novel. That scene ends quite happily, on an upbeat, but you, you wept."

"My wife. She loved to dance. I was remembering the times we'd open up our living room and dining room, just like we did the other night, and turn on the music and dance. After a long day at work, we'd set aside time and dance. It was such a wonderful way of finding each other again. When we were first a couple, we went dancing all the time. She looked radiant on those nights, so happy and full of laughter. What's this all about?"

"I translated Kobayashi's book into English. I was the translator. And he accused me of mistranslating it. Of turning Jiro, of turning you, into a heartless man."

A pause. "I don't get it. You've come here to prove to yourself you're right?"

To have it put that way, so crass, so boorish. "I wanted to meet you. If I've offended you—"

"Oh, come on. You must know by now that's pretty hard to do." He slaps his hand against the steering wheel. "Hanne the sleuth! Slinking around, gathering facts for your case! Who'd have thought."

Moto puts on the blinker and pulls into the parking lot of a modern five-story office building with dark, reflective windows.

"We would all like things to be simpler," he says, opening his car door. "But we humans are complicated. Even you, Hanne."

A man with a white silk handkerchief in his front suit coat pocket greets them, bowing low to Moto. "We are so honored you are doing our commercial," he says.

Hanne excuses herself, saying she needs to run some errands. Under the heavy clouds, she heads down the street. She feels as if a block of ice has been dropped down her throat, straight into her stomach. People pass by with folded black umbrellas, the tips poking and stabbing the sidewalk. The world is huddled in on itself. Sad people. Everywhere, gray or black coats, faces blank. She remembers this about living here—the pervasive decorum and politeness seemed to stifle and kill off more than rudeness; something far more vital. And everyone seems resigned to this state of affairs. The constant refrain, *Shikata ga nai*, there's no way out.

One time, riding the train home from school, Hanne had sat across from an old lady who was slumped across from her, asleep, her head bowed, as if it grew straight out of her chest. That day Hanne intentionally had put on a hot pink blouse and bright robin's-egg-blue pants, a leopard scarf around her neck, because she wanted someone to say something, anything about it, about her—too loud, too ugly, too much—so she could spit something back. "Go to hell!" But the woman slept on and the people around her stared straight ahead or buried their faces in newspapers. When Hanne's stop came, she stepped hard on the old woman's toe. And the woman finally woke up and shrieked, "Barbarian! Foreigner!" The entire trainload of people sat up startled. Hanne was delighted, and for days afterward, she heard that shout bounce around in her head—anything but the polite "Sumimasen," or the girlish giggles or the way the women spoke in high-pitched voices, pretending to be dolls.

But now look at her, her black hair, her black coat, her perfect Japanese, she blends right in. What has she become? But more importantly, what will become of her? If she made a mistake. A grave error of enormous magnitude. What then?

Hanne enters the department store and the two greeters by the door call out "Irasshaimasu!" Come in! We are ready to serve! The polite imperative, she thinks, said with just the right amount of cheer so you almost believe it.

She mindlessly picks up a miniature plastic hamster. It turns out not to be a toy, but an eraser. And the bag of cookies? They contain some herb that supposedly enlarges your breasts. Nothing is as it appears, she thinks. She makes a pencil mark on a piece of sample paper. As she erases it with the hamster, a possible scenario comes to her: Moto said he knows Kobayashi. A good friend. Couldn't Kobayashi have called Moto and told him about their blow-up in Tokyo? She's probably coming your way. Look out! She's an intense woman, convinced she did a superior job on that translation. Have a little fun with her—for my sake.

Moto gets a good laugh out of this—sure, he'll play along. Why not? Couldn't this be what happened? He's an actor, after all, and knowing what she's up to, he finds every opportunity to toy with her, trip her up, make her doubt herself over and over. "Keep her guessing," she imagines Kobayashi counseling Moto. No wonder Moto seemed wholly unsurprised to meet her that first day—he'd been expecting her. Probably rubbing his hands together in delight. Moto tells Renzo to extend a generous invitation—stay as long as you like. And Renzo, happy Moto is interested in some form of acting, willingly obliges. His role? Simple, refuse to be pinned down or turned into a type, especially the character she translated. Moto doesn't miss acting because he's acting right now! Perhaps that was it. She wasn't wrong. She was being toyed with.

She buys the hamsters for her granddaughters, skips the cookies, buys toothpaste, coffee, shampoo, and three bottles of sake as gifts to replenish the dwindling supply. When she returns, she finds Moto inside a small recording booth, eating an apple. The businessmen stand and bow as she enters the room. One of the men finds her a chair. Over the speaker system, she can hear Moto making every possible sound.

He stretches his mouth wide open, as if he's going to shout, then snaps it shut. Over and over, and with his flowing hair, he looks like a tiger about to devour its prey. Now he's a frog, his tongue out, holding his mouth open wide. Next, he's wiggling his lower jaw side to side, an old man having trouble with his false teeth. Finally, after warming up his voice with scales, he reads in a beautifully rich, commanding voice, "For relief of acid indigestion, heartburn, and sour stomach, try Stomach Guard."

The businessmen murmur and nod their approval.

Moto reads it again in a lower tone. The businessmen ask for more rhythm, then more seriousness, compassion, spunk, humor, and finally they murmur "*Soo desu ne. Totemo yokatta,*" very good.

Yes, he can be so many things. The man who can so easily disguise himself, become someone else, even an emotion. She feels the first stirrings of fury. An hour later, Moto emerges, looking the same as when he entered, as if the entire session has taken nothing from him.

Outside, it's torrential rain. She covers her head with her shopping bag and runs for the car. When she's inside, soaked to the bone, she turns to him. "No wonder Renzo is concerned. It requires so little of you."

"It's all I've got in me these days."

"How much do you know about me?" she says, her tone wintry.

He takes a towel and rubs his hair. "What?"

"What do you know about me?"

"Only what you've told me."

"That other night at dinner, all those arguments about Japan. A heart, no heart. One minute you're hung over, barely awake; the next, you're ready to swim. You say you don't want to forget your wife, but you're with Midori. But she's not your girlfriend, you say. And so you're with me. You seem to be everything."

"And?"

"Are you toying with me? Deceiving me?"

He turns and looks at her.

"Did your good friend Kobayashi call you and tell you to do this to me? To put on a grand performance and twist and turn in the wind, never allowing yourself to be pinned down to any defining trait? You are everything, so you defy description? Especially my description?"

She glares at him.

When he says nothing, she goes on. "You are performing beautifully, probably your best acting ever. Bravo."

"You're not a very trusting woman, Hanne Schubert," he says, switching to rapid-fire Japanese. "Not trusting at all."

"It seems highly coincidental that every time I think I understand you, you act in a way that undermines my understanding."

He throws the towel on the back seat. "Have you ever considered that you got your translation wrong? Completely wrong? To even accuse me of somehow putting on a ruse shows how little you understand me. What vanity! To think I'd go to such lengths to turn your world upside down. That's too much work for me. Lazy old me, wasting myself with commercials. I hear the judgment in your voice."

"I didn't judge—"

"I guess you've never met someone who doesn't fit neatly into one of your labels. Or maybe you've never really understood anyone because I don't think any human being fits neatly into one of your damn labels. It's a simple way of viewing the world. And you are the worse for it because what doesn't fit the label is blocked out."

She's about to say something, but he puts up his hand. "Please. Don't."

They drive the rest of the way in heavy silence.

By the time they get home, Renzo has returned and prepared supper for them, but Moto grabs a bottle of whiskey and pounds up the stairs to his room.

She hears a door slam.

"Must have gone poorly," says Renzo. "Good. Maybe he'll give it up."

She sits with Renzo, who has prepared udon, but she can barely eat. He chatters about his day. Something about an elderly woman with a bird cage. She fell and broke her ankle. A new couple planting trees.

She realizes she's waiting for Moto to come downstairs. Then what?

Renzo asks about the voice-over. "Was it horrible to listen to?"

"He's very good at it. Very good."

"I don't think I could stand to hear it. Even if it was good."

Hanne hears music coming from upstairs—Frank Sinatra's syrupy voice sliding over "Fly Me to the Moon." Renzo invites her to join him and walk the dog. She says she's too tired. It's been a long day. After he leaves, she washes the dishes, then heads out to the cottage.

She picks up her play, but can't seem to get beyond the first sentence. She remembers what Brigitte once said to her. It was not long after Hiro died. Tomas was away at college and it was just the two of them, living in the high-rise apartment. They were eating dinner and Hanne can't remember how it came up, but Brigitte asked her if she believed in an afterlife. This was their first serious conversation in a long time.

"I'm sorry to say I don't. Life doesn't care one iota about you," she told Brigitte. "It is neutral. Nothingness. It just is. You live, you die, it doesn't care."

When Brigitte said nothing, Hanne went on about Albert Camus's short story "The Guest." A schoolteacher who was given the assignment of delivering a prisoner to the police. But he could have easily led the prisoner to freedom, which was the teacher's preferred choice. Instead, the teacher did nothing and the prisoner walked himself right into prison.

Brigitte said she'd read it at school and hated the ending. "The schoolmaster should have done something," Brigitte said. "He could have chased after the man when he saw he'd made the wrong choice. He could have led the man to freedom. Why didn't he help? He just turned his back and walked away."

"But that's the point of the story. And though it doesn't seem like it, it's actually good news. You get to create the purpose and the meaning of your life. The schoolmaster starkly refuses to do so, and look where he ends up—miserable—but of his own choice and making."

Brigitte violently shook her head. "There was the moment the schoolmaster could have done something. He could have saved the man. It's not human, what he did."

Hanne took a deep breath and began again, explaining that Camus wanted the reader to feel the nothingness, the bleak, dismal, condemned nothingness of life.

"It's not nothing. Since Dad died, so many people have been so kind to me," said Brigitte, looking at Hanne with what Hanne remembers now as pitying eyes. "I feel like I've seen the very best part of people."

"Well, I've found few agents of sympathy," Hanne said. "People see me and turn the other way, like I have the plague. I've had to do this all alone. To fend for myself, and none of it has been easy."

Brigitte stared at her plate. "You don't trust anyone, that's why," she whispered, still seeking refuge with her plate. "How can anyone get close to you? You don't trust anyone. You think no one is capable, at least not as capable as you. Not even me."

Now Hanne stares at her play. Komachi has been thrown out of the palace, banished to a poor rural village, fifteen kilometers from the capital, Kyoto, but it might as well be thousands. Outside the city walls, the peasants work fifteen, twenty-hour days, subsisting on rice and vegetable broth, suffering from diseases unheard of within the court's walls. Death comes easily to children, to women, to men. No one has time for poetry. No one cares. In the end, Komachi is left with a talent no one wants, a talent that's the sole reason she wants to live another day.

Hanne rests her forehead on her hands. She wishes she hadn't barked back at Brigitte. "What's there to trust? Half the time you're truant, and when you do show up to class, your homework is not done, you're failing two classes. Oh, I know about that, young lady, and I catch you here alone with some young man. Tell me, what is there to trust?" She wishes when Brigitte began to cry, saying she missed Dad, she missed him so much, that she'd gone to her and held her, that she'd broken down with her and said how much she missed him too, how her heart, too, cried out for him. How, twelve years after he died, she still has not found someone whom she loved as much as Hiro. But instead, Hanne silently cleared the table, then put the leftovers in plastic containers in the refrigerator.

How easy it is to become this Komachi. The one tossed out. Forgotten. Komachi who tries to talk with the villagers, but the villagers back away, treating her like a foreigner. She hears the gossip: that strange woman uses strange words and phrases, and her proper, courtly way. Who does she think she is? Did you see how soft her hands are? Has she ever worked a day in her life?

In this village, living in this hut, there is no one to serve her, no one bringing her three meals a day. No parties, no banquets, no lovers beckoning to her under her window. How will she survive here if she's cut off? She is so ill-prepared. If the shop clerk at the grocery store refuses to serve her, as he did this morning because she did not have enough money? And she didn't have enough money because she has no idea how much things cost. If she's refused access to the water well, as she was yesterday because she lives on the upper part of the street, which doesn't receive water on Wednesdays?

Chapter Thirteen

SOMETHING JARS HER AWAKE. HANNE bolts upward in bed. She hears a bird chirping, sees the pale yellow light of morning, a moment of lightness before the weight of dread collapses on her chest, turning her breath, short, shallow. The translation, mistranslation, mistake, *mis*, meaning bad, wrong. The word "incompetent" burrows in, refuses to depart.

She lies down again, squeezes her eyes shut. The heaviness in her chest is quickly coating her brain, making her thoughts confused, slow. Those dreary, weepy scenes she gave to Jiro's wife, they actually belonged to Jiro. Some part of Jiro, of Moto, remains forever tangled up in the pain of loss. Doubting whether he should have let his wife go. Like a wounded animal licking old wounds, reopening them. Again and again. And that error has led to other errors. She stops breathing for a moment. She'd made Jiro far more heroic than Moto—Moto who lets himself be battered by every emotional wind; who chose to let his wife go and now refuses to forget and move on; who drinks to wallow some more.

The publisher will hire a new translator, who will discover all her errors. The International Translators Association might decertify her. She failed, failed miserably at the thing she values the most, so why shouldn't they strip her of her credentials? If anything means something to her, if anything is holy, it is the art of translation.

Yes, Brigitte, I do believe in something. Not an afterlife or a god, but my work. In her mind, what she has done to Kobayashi's novel is sacrilegious. Kobayashi was right. She put too much of herself into the work, what *she* wanted it to be, instead of accepting it for what it was. The Association has every right to toss her out.

And then?

She'll have to find other employment. Menial labor is the first thing that comes to mind. She's being unreasonable, but she can't stop herself from imagining a sweatshop where she sits, one among hundreds of other poorly paid women, hunched over a sewing machine, churning out endless pairs of pants. Eight, ten hours of stitching, not enough time to speak or think a single thought, a half hour for lunch, a ten minute bathroom break, and when she returns home, exhausted, she falls into bed, only to do it all over again the next day.

She realizes she's being melodramatic, but the problem is she can't imagine a future. Or rather, what she does imagine is bleak: a life empty of meaning because no one will ever hire her to do a translation again. She is not, unfortunately, a member of Moto's school of thought where meaning is there for the taking. She will be denied a meaningful life because she will forever be prohibited from doing what she loves. Because she is incompetent. Because she failed at her job. Kobayashi's charge hits her full force: *what you have done is wrong.*

Enough. She wills herself to stop this descent, for that's what it feels like—a free fall into self-flagellation. But isn't that what she deserves? She watches herself pick up the phone, aware that some part of her is trying to save herself. She dials her own phone number. Grasping at anything, she thinks, as she listens to the rings with a flutter of hope that there will be a message from a publisher. A new translation project waiting. The rings begin to sound like an alarm. After the twelfth ring, she hangs up. When was the last time she had this long of a break between projects? Maybe there's a letter for her waiting in her mailbox, but she doubts it. No one writes letters anymore.

She marvels at herself, to the level she will stoop as she dials Tomas; she's willing to bring him into her increasing dread. "I have to ask you for a favor." She wants him to check her e-mail. She has no computer here. Could he see if there is a message, anything about her translation of Kobayashi's novel? Or a translation project? Anything at all? Something from Claire Buttons?

"You're still in Japan?" he says.

She hears him tap his computer keys.

"Nothing, Mom. What's going on?"

She's too mortified to tell him: the accuracy of Kobayashi's claims. She can barely bring herself to think about it. There is a long silence. "How are my granddaughters?"

"Why are you still there?"

Her heart is pounding. She asks him to call her publisher.

She hangs up and waits. Out the window, everything is a blur. It seems hours go by when the phone finally rings.

"He pulled it. Kobayashi demanded it. Kobayashi is paying for a new translator to do it over."

In her mind, she's back in the cellar, Oma mad, her face a pale red. What did Hanne do this time? Spill a dot of milk on a clean floor? Track in a trace of mud? Ten years old, missing her mother too much, she wet the bed again, unable to untangle from the sheets in time to make it to the bathroom because in her dream she was holding on to her mother's wrists as her mother withered and pulled away. Incorrigible child. You do your own cleaning of the sheets. Scrub them twice and hang them outside on the line. Not Oma's job, she didn't make the mess. Then down to the cellar, blacker than black ink, blacker than the darkest night, with the rats scratching behind the walls and in the coal bin. Once a rat ran across her boot and she screamed "Mama!" Oma called down to her she'd have to stay another hour for making such a racket. So she put her back against the cold concrete wall and tried to will herself beyond the blackness by conjugating English verbs. *Scream, screamed, had screamed, screaming.*

"Mom?" says Tomas. "Are you there? What do you want me to do?"

She imagines Kobayashi racing home after their confrontation and calling the publisher. *I put my trust in Ms. Schubert, and she betrayed my story. She should be ashamed.* Hanne sees his face, full of anger and hurt. *You know nothing.* Dark sludge flows through her veins. Of course Claire hasn't called. Hanne is only as good as her reputation. And her reputation, now, is permanently stained. The world will forever turn its back on her. It wants nothing more from her.

She draws a deep breath. "I'll manage."

She calls the airlines. Though what she'll do upon her return, she hasn't a clue. A cheery Japanese woman says there's nothing available until Sunday—three days away, unless she wants to spend several thousands of dollars. It will have to be Sunday. Hanne hangs up and stares at the old apple tree. Its bare branches wave at her in the slight breeze. What is she going to do here for three long days? Whenever she's around Moto, she will be reminded of her failure, of what she has lost.

She makes herself put on her coat and set out for a walk. The dog stubbornly tags along. She takes a dirt path that crosses over a wooden bridge. On the other side, she passes by rows of Shinto shrines, miniature A-framed structures with one side left open, like a doll's house. A shrine to the wind god, the water god, air god, travel god, with fifty or more pairs of shoes dangling from the thick branches of a pine tree. She wonders if there is a god of misfortune to whom she can leave an offering.

When she returns to the house, Moto is sitting at the eating table. The stereo is playing something bluesy. When she comes over, she sees the table top is covered with puzzle pieces. He's putting together a puzzle. A picture of a bowl of red apples. Is this her future? Piddling away her time over a puzzle?

"I want to apologize for yesterday," she says. "You've been nothing but generous and accommodating and kind. I'm sorry I accused you of pulling a ruse."

His hair is a tangle, unruly. His eyelids are puffy and she can only describe his eyes as sad. Look at him, she tells herself. Give him your full and deliberate attention. Don't impose something on him that isn't there. This is a man who is resigned, beaten, defined by what he has lost.

"Apology accepted," he says in Japanese. It seems he has no energy to pull the English words out from his sluggish brain. Or maybe he's finished helping her.

He finds the corner piece of the puzzle. She looks at the cover of the box and sees that the puzzle has five thousand pieces. They seem a jumble, impossible to put together. He's completed less than a quarter of it. Hours and hours to go.

She'd like to go back to the cottage and crawl into bed, but it requires too much effort. The music fills the room. He searches the scattered pieces. She closes her eyes and rests her cheek on her fist. Minutes must pass by. "Thought I'd go to the pool," he says. "Try to shake off this stupor." He rubs his forehead. "If you want to come along."

She watches him closely, looking for signs that his offer is a polite pretense. He gives her a half smile that seems to say, haven't you at least figured out this? I'm not one for such nonsense.

"The translation. I made grave errors," she hears herself say. "I believe my career as a translator is officially over."

He sets down his puzzle piece and looks at her. "I'm sorry to hear that. Isn't there a way to fix things?"

"I don't think so."

"I thought everyone in America gets a second chance. Sometimes a third or fourth. Here we just commit hari kari and call it a day."

She thought he'd be more upset. But then again, she didn't ruin anything of his. "I thought you were far more resilient. But you haven't recovered from your wife's departure. And you have no interest in doing so. There is the type of person who glorifies his pain and suffering. Who wants to be defined by it. Who finds a kind of beauty in the pain."

She almost added, just like Brigitte.

He shakes his head, half smiling.

"What?"

"In your confession, or whatever you want to call it, you just insulted me again."

She feels her face redden. "I meant to plead guilty and explain my errors. It seems I must keep apologizing."

"But the way you phrased it," he says. "Why am I explaining this to you? You're the word master. It's clear that you put a lot of value on this idea of resilience, and you've decided I don't have an ounce of it. In your grade book, I get a big fat zero. Have you ever considered there are other values that might be important to someone besides resilience? Such as experiencing the full spectrum of human emotion? Guess what? I don't have a one-year or five-year plan. I'm here to experience life, and that includes being present for all of it, not just a small lousy corner of it labeled joy or mirth. Even going through the miserable pain of loss and down the long road of grief."

She sits up, knocking several puzzle pieces onto the floor. "But if you're stuck longing for your wife, how are you experiencing all of life? Life is going on right now and you're missing it because you're drowning in your longing for your wife. Haven't you chosen to confine yourself to a small lousy corner?" She hopes he hears the sincerity in her question because she means to be sincere.

"The most profound thing, the most real thing to me right now is the loss of my marriage and my wife. Besides, I'd say it takes a lot of resilience to go through this hell. Not deny it or try to forget it. Which I think is impossible anyway."

"But what about the rest of your life? As you said earlier, you've fallen off your stage."

He shrugs. "The stage is still there. I'm just not on it right now."

"What if this fallow period causes permanent damage? You will forever be off the stage if you don't put up more of a fight."

"A fight against what?"

"This malaise. This wallowing."

"Is that what you fear, Hanne? That you'll be thrown off your stage unless you kick and scream and demand to stay on it?"

She doesn't say anything.

"What do you think exists off your stage? Nothing? Let me tell you, there's life there too. It might be unfamiliar, but it's there. It emerges beyond your own will. And yes, there is something quite beautiful about it. Pain can pare things down to what's most important. A clarity comes. And here's another thing you don't understand about me. I told you before, but you didn't seem to hear it. I don't have a choice. I am buried in this right now." He looks directly at her. "You don't know what to make of me, do you?"

"Frankly, I don't. I don't understand why you can't make a decision to take charge. Discipline may be an archaic word these days, but it can be invoked to push through things."

"Well, we're different." He leans over, picks up the fallen pieces and studies his puzzle. It seems he's lost interest in this discussion. A minute seems to pass by before he notices she's still there. "That's all I can say right now."

At the indoor ocean, she sees he is, in fact, the one who charges back and forth beyond the waves, swimming expertly, flawlessly, lap after lap. Driven, a single-minded focus, a straight arrow slicing through the blue, each arm clearing the water in a perfect stroke. It looks as if someone wound him up, set him in the water—a swim machine—and said "Go!"

In this small way, he's like Jiro. Her Jiro, rather. A superficial detail that she happened to get right. A small triumph that gives her no satisfaction.

She considers changing into her suit, but the sun (heat lamp?) on her back feels good, and the rhythmic roar and retreat of the waves are soothing. She closes her eyes, letting the warmth penetrate. Like the waves, a question comes and goes: What will become of her?

Wasn't that the question that plagued her about Brigitte? What would become of Brigitte if Hanne didn't do something? After Hiro died, Hanne pleaded with Brigitte to go to school. To try harder. To keep up her grades. To imagine a better future. "I can't," said Brigitte. "I can't stop thinking about Dad. The world feels broken to me."

"Let's fix it," Hanne said to her. "We'll start a new project." Hanne suggested they learn Arabic together. Or maybe go on a trip. France. They hadn't been there for years. The Eiffel Tower, the Louvre, the croissants with the chocolate center, Brigitte loved it there. She wore a red beret everywhere.

No. She couldn't.

"Sure you can."

"No, I don't think you understand. I can't." Her eyes teary.

Someone had to be stalwart, a pillar. Someone had to remain steadfast and firm. Someone had to push, sometimes push hard. And wouldn't that rub off on Brigitte? Make it all feel less impossible? That's what Hanne told herself. But now she wonders, is that what Brigitte needed? How well did Hanne understand her role in Brigitte's life? If Brigitte's anything like Moto, Hanne's prodding wouldn't have done any good.

Moto swims to shore. Shaking his hair, spraying water everywhere. There's his lean, powerful body, his strong chest muscles and arms. Normally, she'd feel the stirrings of desire. Moto wipes his face, beginning at his forehead, pulling his hands down over his eyes, his chin, as if rubbing off a film and the real Moto—the one missing nothing—might emerge from underneath. But it's the same Moto, with shadowy circles below his eyes. He wraps a white towel around his waist and heads in his floating gait to the locker room.

She sits in the warm sand and waits for him outside the locker room.

His hand is on her shoulder. He's dressed in jeans, a T-shirt, and he sits beside her. "You didn't swim?"

"No. For some reason, I didn't feel like it."

He smiles his leonine smile. "Watch out, Hanne. You're going to become a good-for-nothing like me, wasting away your talent, the stage disappearing in front of you."

"That's what I'm afraid of."

Renzo announces he's going to have a dinner party tomorrow night. A farewell party for Hanne. Oh, dear god, no, she thinks. He'll invite his good friends. They'd love to meet her. He's at the eating table, surrounded by cookbooks, and he's riffling through pages of colorful fish dishes and soups.

"You needn't go to the trouble for me," says Hanne, taking a seat at the table. She's in no mood for parties, for anything festive. She is exhausted just thinking about meeting a group of new people. The cheery façade one must hide behind.

"No trouble at all." He puts on his glasses, then takes them off again. "Let me propose something. With your perfect Japanese, maybe you'll think of moving here? Many interesting people live around here." He pauses and smiles slyly at her. "And you seem interested in Moto."

It seems Moto has told him nothing about her translation, about Kobayashi's book. "You misunderstand."

"Moto is a good man. He's just in a slump right now."

"It's presumptuous of you to be arranging your brother's life."

199

The dog sits beside her and whines. She finds her coat. Renzo, it seems, is not done trying to persuade her; he's at the door in his coat and scarf, holding the leash.

Outside the air is cold. The trees seem taller, with their tips lost in the clouds.

"I've served as go-between for a number of very happily married couples," he goes on, pulling on gloves. "As you grow older, you need a good companion."

How exasperating! "I'm sure you don't mean—"

"Let me finish. I'm a good ten years older than you. I've crossed some of the territory you're about to enter. It's hard to grow old alone. Your friends die off or become ill and are no longer mobile. Your children are involved with their own lives, as they should be. I've learned to keep my loneliness in check with several female companions." He gives her a quick smile. "But an intelligent, cultured woman such as yourself requires much more from your relations than I."

In truth, she requires very little. Her handful of friends are just as busy as she is—or once was. After Hiro died, she had a fling with a visiting professor from Denmark. When he left, that was the end of it—though it was promised otherwise, they never wrote to each other, never called. And a two-week affair with the archeologist from Brazil. Oh, there was a certain pang for weeks afterward, and the circling of the question—what if he'd stayed? What might have been? But those questions eventually subsided. There is the relationship with her David, but really, if something more meaningful was going to come of that, it would have happened by now. It's become a matter of convenience.

They pass by the field of new cherry trees, branches with little green leaves. A crow flies by, calling out to the emptied sky. The dog stops and looks up, then begins to track the black bird.

"Besides, Midori is a diversion," he says. "She's not a suitable match for him at all."

Hanne shoves her cold hands deep into her pockets. "In whose opinion? I'm repeating myself, but it seems to me Moto has a say in the direction of his life."

"It's not good enough. And neither is this voice-over business."

"Maybe that's the life he wants right now."

Listen to her! Defending Moto, his right to wither and waste away.

He shakes his head vigorously. "I won't stand for it. He's an extremely talented Noh actor."

"He's a grown man. Listen, Renzo. If you keep at him like this, he might refuse your company." She was going to add "for years and years."

"He must use it, not only for the family's sake, but his. It's what he must do in this lifetime." He tears off a piece of grass, rolls it into a ball, throws it. "In another life, he can do something else."

So this is how fate is administered: This life can be circumscribed and made miserable because it's one of many lives. Freedom comes another time. "Let me guess. You didn't choose to be an antique dealer."

"No. Nor did I choose my wife, may her soul rest in peace. I grew to love her, but my real love was a young girl I knew in secondary school. Atsuko Tsukiyama. I can still picture her, her white school socks pulled above her knobby knees, her long black braids. Every time she rocked back on her heels, my stomach swooped. But she was promised to someone else and we went our separate ways."

"How sad."

"Not sad," he says, smiling, showing off his stained teeth. "The Japanese have a saying: 'The shade is part of light.'"

Before the guests have even been seated, Hanne is bored. By the fifth time she's been asked "What do you do for a living?" she has become crotchety. "Nothing. I do absolutely nothing. I'm just taking up space on this increasingly small planet." Which elicits nervous laughter.

Renzo sits at the head of the table with a woman his age, stroking her hand and cooing something in her ear. One of his many female companions? They seem enraptured with each other, sealed off from the dozen other guests. Hanne is drinking too much sake, suffering through a lecture by a store manager on the perils of perishable goods. She's watching the lecturer's cigarette wobble in his fingers, when Moto stumbles in halfway through dinner, unshaven, wearing a sloppy grin and an expensive navy blue suit, a white shirt, and a gray tie. His arm is draped around Midori's shoulder, as if he needs to be propped up.

Of all the places, Moto staggers to a spot right across from her. Next to him, Midori's lithe body folds like a fan.

This, too, feels like a scene from the book. She thinks about Kobayashi sitting here, trying to capture the mood, the details, the tension in the room. It feels overwhelming, nearly impossible. The task of a writer. A fresh wave of shame washes over her.

Moto waves at her.

"Looks like the party started a while ago for you," says Hanne. "Maybe yesterday."

Moto loosens his tie, then slowly pulls it off, slithering it along the back of his neck. He drops two ice cubes in a glass, then grabs the bottle of whiskey and with shaky hands pours it to the rim. Tipping it back, he keeps his free hand on Midori's shoulder, as if to claim her, or steady himself from falling over, then sets the glass down with a flourish. His birthmark is now a long streak of angry red. His eyes look glassy, faded, remote. "Rough day," he says in slurred Japanese.

"And you want to make it rougher?" says Hanne.

He gestures toward Midori. "This one? She's not looking out for me."

Midori laughs. Or rather giggles, putting her hand over her mouth.

"She's the one who got me drunk," he says. "Glass after glass. The wicked girl is trying to take advantage of me."

He puts one hand over his eyes to mask a glare, imagined or otherwise. The other hand clutches his sweating drink. Midori slaps him on the thigh. Midori gets the role of the bad girl; Hanne, mother. Hanne refuses to play along. Turning to the man on her right, she introduces herself.

Midori says she has to go to the powder room. She gets up and sways down the hall, balancing herself by extending both arms out to the side, her fingertips brushing the wall. The man sitting beside Hanne strokes his dark mustache and tells Hanne he sells rice. Owns a rice shop in town. "You eat rice? You should eat rice. Come by my shop and buy rice. It's very good, grown in the North."

She's leaving in two days. If she has time, she'll come by. How can she politely and forever leave the table?

Moto is staring at her, no longer smiling. Beseeching her—to do what? "Talk to me."

"About what?"

"Anything. Anything at all." He leans forward on his elbows. "You."

The full force of his dark gaze is on her. Wide awake now, his drunkenness vanishing like a disguise, he's filled with ferocious intention. "Tell me something. Tell me something I don't know about you."

How dizzying! One moment he's unreachable, lost in a haze of alcohol; the next, he's swooped in on her, and the rest of the room evaporates. Moto is waiting. "I'm used to being in many worlds at once." To her own surprise, she is complying, telling him something secret, something very much her own. "Not the real world," she says, gesturing her hand to the guests, "but I found solace in the world of language. In my mind, I used to glide from one language to another to another. It reminds me of the way you effortlessly glide around the room. To my ear, languages have always sounded like songs. I remember when I first heard someone speak English. A nanny of mine. Oh, how beautiful! I wanted to learn to sing like that—not to converse with her, though I was soon able, but to make those sounds. And when I heard French, Japanese, on and on, it was the same impulse. We all need to stand in awe of something, don't we? To feel that burst of astonishment. To become it, even if it's a moment."

He is regarding her, it seems, with piercing attention. Is that why she goes on? Flushing herself out?

"In Latin, translate comes from *translatus*, to carry over, to carry across. Something written in language A is carried over into language B. I always imagine a bridge in which language A is traveling over to meet B. Sometimes when I'm translating, the languages blend together in my mind, and when I hear this, what gets carried over isn't a grandiose idea. The songs merge together and what is brought forth is a new song. Such stunning and mysterious harmony. That probably sounds silly, but it's the closest I've come to believing in something more, something other than this, something of awe that humbles me. Not a god, but a sound."

It's what she used to keen her ear to, not one language or the other, but the melding of sound, a gestalt of sound.

"Can you sing?" He is hovering less than a meter from her.

"You mean really sing?" She laughs. "I need to be a lot drunker than I am now."

For a moment, he does nothing. Then with both hands on the table, he pushes himself to standing. He takes a deep breath, filling his lungs, his chest opening, his face expanding, and begins to sing in English an old Dean Martin song, "Under the Bridges of Paris."

His voice circles around her, sweeps her up, vibrating her teeth, her skull, and something deep inside relaxes, opens, and blossoms. His voice sounds like three voices at once—a deep baritone rumbling below a streaming tenor, and, rippling through it all, a high C tenor. She glances at Renzo, who is beaming, as is everyone at the table, radiantly beaming and they all look so beautiful.

But the song abruptly stops. "To flatten your belly in two weeks, try Pounds Off, the liquid diet," he says, in a completely different voice.

Midori, who must have come into the room during this performance, shrieks with laughter and applauds. Moto, sitting now, begins to sing, "London Bridge is falling down, falling down—"

Renzo frowns. The guests quickly return to their private conversations, as if nothing had just happened. As if just a moment ago, they had not been privy to an astonishing performance.

Moto, with a blank gaze, slurps his miso soup.

"You have a wonderful voice," says Hanne, "when you choose to use it."

He swallows. "Thanks for the backhanded compliment. I'll remember that." His tone is good-natured. If she didn't know better, she'd think he was happy, the loss of his wife behind him

205

and now ripe with good life, a beautiful woman, delicious food. But now she knows better.

"Tomorrow is your last full day here?" he says.

She nods.

"I've got a big day planned for us. We'll start early," he winks at her.

Midori murmurs something in Moto's ear. He waves his hand as if shooing away a pesky bug. He shovels in spoonfuls of rice, then together Moto and Midori rise. Midori gives Hanne a small wave, a quick, triumphant smile. Then they are gone.

Chapter Fourteen

It's Saturday morning and Moto is nowhere to be found. Renzo calls Midori. Yes, they left together. He dropped her off. He said he was going to see a friend, an old friend. Who? She doesn't know. Renzo makes more calls; no one has seen him.

"He was going to spend the day with you," says Renzo. "He told me so."

Given his inebriated state last night, Hanne doubts he remembers anything from then. By late Saturday afternoon, Renzo takes a deep breath and tries the hospital. No one has been checked in under that name or description. A dismal atmosphere falls over the house.

If Hanne harbored a grain of hope that she translated Moto correctly, it is now gone. Jiro—the Jiro she thought she knew—would never disappear for hours and hours on end. Even when he fantasized about picking up and escaping his life, the Jiro she translated bore the burdens of responsibilities to the very end, once a month dutifully visiting his wife in the institution.

Hanne has crossed over into unknown territory.

"I'm sure he's fine," she says. She pictures him asleep in the car, or worse, the car plunged on its side in a ditch. "We could drive around and look for him. Why don't we do that?"

Renzo sits hunched over, quiet.

"I'll make some calls. Give me a list."

When Brigitte left with the young man and didn't come home by evening, Hanne called all her friends. Had they seen her? What did they know about this young man? Some smoky character with a sly grin. No one would tell her anything, though she sensed they knew. For hours, Hanne drove up and down streets looking for Brigitte, through the Tenderloin, along Market Street, the Mission District, passing drug dealers and prostitutes and runaways, and Hanne's heart beat so fiercely, she feared it would burst. At home alone, she couldn't sleep. She sat at her big window and stared out at the cold city cloaked in darkness, her reflection silently staring back at her. When Brigitte finally came home the next day, with her two new tattoos, her glazed-over eyes, Hanne said "I've been up all night. Just who do you think you are?"

"No one you want to know."

"You're right," she snapped. "Not like this."

Brigitte looked at her, as if deciding whether Hanne really meant it. Then turned and went to her room and quietly shut the door. It seemed, after that, that a sheet of glass was forever between them. Brigitte firmly out of reach.

If she could take it back, if Hanne had taken Brigitte into her arms, told her she was frightened she'd lost her, frightened through the front door, bash into the Buddha, cause a ruckus, it won't matter because you're home.

Early Tuesday morning, she hears a car groan into the driveway. There's no grand entrance, a key in the front door and he stumbles into the foyer, as if he'd stepped out for milk.

"He's home!" says Renzo from his room upstairs.

Hanne is already at the front door. "You're here."

What she does not say: Where have you been? Do you know how worried I've been? She hunts for some sign of contrition.

Moto slips off his shoes and tosses them near the door.

He doesn't look well. Deep blue circles beneath his eyes, a heavy sag to his face and eyelids, and a crease—a new wrinkle?—cuts through his birthmark. It's back to the shape of Montana, but now it's sliced in half. His face looks too lived in, as if he's spent the last few days living out a thousand lives.

Renzo is all over Moto, a mix of joy, exhilaration, anger— "Where were you? Why didn't you call?"

"I'm so glad you're all right," says Hanne.

They stand in the foyer. Moto raises his eyebrows, as if to say: what's the fuss about? He went to a friend's house, he says. He fell asleep.

"For three days? You must have been drinking and blacked out. When is this going to stop? Lazy! That's what you are. Lazy and a drunk! I was worried sick! I thought you were dead. How could you make me worry like this? You are so selfish!"

Moto looks like he's about to say something, but then walks away.

"Where are you going now?" Renzo follows right on his heels.

Hanne tries to interject. "We're going to have breakfast—"

"A goddamn glass of water," says Moto, turning to confront his brother, who almost runs into him.

of receiving a nightmarish call that her daughter had been found in a ditch, a back alley, a dumpster. She couldn't lose one more thing.

Renzo clasps his hands together, almost as if he is about to pray.

The dog wants out. She stands on the back porch and watches Morsel run frantic laps around the yard. At some point Renzo comes over and stands beside her. The light makes the dew on the grass sparkle, and everything looks stunning except Renzo's face, with sunken cheeks, as if life has been chiseled out of him.

"Midori," he says, his voice wobbly. "A bad influence. Her lineage is farming."

Hanne doesn't reply. She's in no state to argue and neither is he. In the old apple tree, a group of birds bicker. Renzo frowns and for a long time says nothing. He hands her a list of phone numbers, then announces he's going to dig up the milkweed along the back fence. He can't just sit around anymore. Renzo marches to the fence and slams a hoe into the hard dirt.

She heads to the cottage and makes phone calls. No one knows anything. For a long time, she just sits, unable to do anything except listen to the steady beat of the hoe. Where is Moto? Would he have gone searching for his ex-wife? What does someone like Moto do? She thinks of Brigitte; how far did she run away? Her eyes wander over to her notes.

Months go by, Ono no Komachi can no longer afford the baths every day, and her silky black hair turns limp and oily, woven with strands of wiry, unruly gray. Whoever dares to sneak out of the imperial court to visit her doesn't do so to gaze upon her features, only to hear her poetry. But who would dare? Who would step outside the gates? No one. For whoever crosses over would return with the stench of her humiliation woven into his clothes.

And why was Ono no Komachi expelled in the first place? Hanne knows now how she'll write it in her play. A poem, maybe a series of poems that failed to please the court. Her mistakes cost her a way of life.

Hanne pushes her papers away. The dog starts barking and Renzo yells at it to shut up. Renzo is as irritable as she is. She needs to distract herself in order to calm down. She opens an anthology of Komachi's poems. *Iro miede utsurou mono wa yo no naka no hito no kokoro no hana ni zo arikeru.* She's drawn to the phrase in the center: *hito no kokoro no hana ni zo arikeru:* she translates it first as "the heart of man, like a fading flower." Then translates it again, "a flower that fades, like a man's heart." Or "a single flower fading, like the heart of a man."

What is a faded heart? One without passion? Without lust? Buried in grief? Is this what's happened to Moto? How does one revive such a heart?

Sunday morning, Moto still has not returned. Midori hasn't seen him. No one has. Renzo wanders through the house, his hand covering his mouth, up and down the stairs, as if Moto might magically appear in a room where he's already looked.

On his fourth time up and down the stairs, Hanne tries to quell her own panic. "Has this ever happened before?"

"No," he says sharply. "Something is wrong. Something bad."

There's nothing else to do but postpone her flight. Renzo is in no shape to drive and she must do something. They have been so gracious with her, she must return the favor. But it's more than that—she's surprised how much she cares about Moto, how worried she is about him. A worry that seems to trump all her other concerns. She drives Renzo around, stopping at Moto's usual spots—the restaurant along the canal, the pool, the library, the bars, the coffee shop, theater—no one has seen him.

Neither she nor Renzo feel like eating supper. Renzo fills a glass with whiskey. The dog seems to sense something is wrong and keeps tucking his tail between his legs and whining.

"Where else can we look?" she says.

Renzo shakes his head. "Nowhere."

"Might he have gone to Tokyo? Who does he know there?"

"Everyone. I don't know."

"His ex-wife?"

"No. That's over."

She says she's going to drive around again. Renzo doesn't do anything, just refills his glass.

The sky is a blanket of stars, and the air smells like cut hay. She drives to town, past the karaoke bars, searching for his shiny black Mercedes. What's next? Flyers posted to telephone poles, inside store windows, and in train stations, a grainy black and white photo of Moto, underneath in big bold letters, MISSING.

When she returns to the darkened house, it is past midnight. She traipses around the side of the house, through the dew-covered grass to the cottage so as not to wake Renzo. As she gets ready for bed, she realizes she's waiting for Morsel to scratch on the door, but the dog never arrives. It takes her hours to fall asleep. When she finally does, she has nightmares in which she is running through the fields, searching the tall grasses for a body.

Monday goes by. Renzo calls the hospital again. Nothing. He is convinced Moto has been in a terrible car accident. It won't be Moto who appears at the house, but police officers with bad news. Hanne can barely get down a piece of dry toast. She spends most of the night half awake, listening, feeling helpless. At some point, she stands at her window. The sky is filled with frozen stars. Come on, Moto. Gather yourself and drive yourself home. Come drunk

"Next time you can tell me where you're going," says Renzo, barely able to keep his voice level. "That's the least you can do."

"Why?"

"You don't want my help? Fine. You'll lose it all. Everything. See if I care. But you'll hear our parents and our ancestors crying out from their graves."

Moto rolls his eyes and heads to the kitchen.

Out on the patio, Renzo can't sit still. He paces back and forth, picks up clippers, sets them down. "What's wrong with him? Is he sick? On drugs?"

"It's a difficult time for him," she says, just talking, trying to fill the charged air with something else. "His wife, his employment. It's hard for him to stay engaged with the world, let alone carry on the day-to-day. You must go easy on him." She can hardly believe she's saying these words. In another life, she was Renzo shouting the exact same things.

Moto spends the entire day in his room. Renzo presses his ear to the door. A low rumbling of a snore. He's sleeping again! How can that be? Three days of sleep and he needs more? Renzo paces back and forth in the front dining area. Finally he says he's going out. He can't stand it. Did you see how he looked? An old man, he looks older than me, cries Renzo, picking up Morsel and cradling him like a baby. "Last night I had a nightmare that Moto went to sleep and never woke up."

After Renzo leaves, the silence is stifling. The house, as always, is freezing. She sits at the table and turns on the heater, waiting for Moto to wake, wondering: what worlds whirl under his eyelids?

When, an hour later, Moto is still asleep, she finds the keys to his car and drives in a downpour to the grocery store. The least she can do is stock the refrigerator. As she pushes the cart up and

213

down the aisles, her brain feels like mush, each thought straining through mud to make its way to the surface. What do they need? What's wrong with Moto? Seaweed, salmon, more rice, what else? Is he sick? He misses his wife so much he's making himself ill? Drinking himself into a comatose state? Fallen into depressing despair? She goes round and round the grocery store, as if hunting for something, though she has no idea what it is.

When she gets back, she hears dreary music with lyrics repeating, *Life is so boring, Life is so boring,* coming from Moto's room. She knocks lightly.

"Come in."

She pokes her head in. "How are you feeling?"

In the murky light, he's sitting up in bed, wearing a flimsy blue robe, his bare chest partly exposed. He squeezes his eyes shut, then opens them wide. His deep-set eyes look even deeper and his face is sweaty, pale. He makes a strange sound, like a swallowed breath.

She's not sure when Renzo is returning, she says, so she'll cook dinner tonight. "If you have any special requests, let me know."

She's never been inside his bedroom. It isn't the smell of sleep in the air or the rustle of his sheets that stir her as he adjusts himself on the bed. Lining his walls are more than two dozen masks. Red, blue, green demons with bulging eyes and horns, an old man with wrinkles, a gray beard, his hair tied up in a topknot; a man, his mouth partially opened, as if he's about to laugh or cry, another man with a white complexion, wide-eyed, who looks like he's seen a ghost or is a ghost; then a row of women—a young woman, with a broad forehead, high arched eyebrows and full cheeks, a middle-aged woman, her lips taut, her forehead wrinkled, and an old woman, her face lined, a quiet dignity.

Expressions of horror, despair, alarm, they seem alive, about to speak. As if they held the spark of life. How do you wake up to this and feel all is right with the world?

"You look like you should eat something now," she says.

He nods slowly.

She brings him a bowl of miso soup and brown rice crackers. With a trembling hand, he sips a couple of spoonfuls of soup, eats a cracker. "Just wanted to drown this sad old heart," he says.

"Have you tried speaking to your ex-wife?"

"In the early months. Every day. Then she told me to stop calling," he says, rubbing his eyelids. He is back to speaking English, which she takes as a good sign. At least he has the energy for that.

Hanne doesn't know what to say. "Moto," she says, her voice gentle, "you can't hold on to her forever."

He doesn't reply, but she can guess what he's thinking—he has no choice in the matter. She doesn't push him.

Evening falls and Moto shows no sign of emerging. She listens outside his door and hears him snoring. She has a bowl of soup, then lies on the tatami mat, listening to the rain hit the roof tiles, which eventually lulls her to sleep. The next thing she knows, it's morning and sunlight floods the room. She heads to the cottage, showers, dresses, and returns to the main house. She's greeted with the sound of the *Bossa Nova* spilling from Moto's room.

She taps on his door.

"Open."

She steps inside. His face is less puffy, and his eyes look more alert. He runs his hands over his face. "I've got to stop drinking."

"Good idea."

"Maybe next week. Or the week after."

Her gaze locks on to the masks, the faces glaring, shouting, screaming, wailing, laughing. He must see her fascination with them. Noh masks, he tells her. Made of cypress wood. Some are 250 years old.

What draws her over to the mask of a middle-aged woman? The mouth is a long gash, as if at the start of an expression of alarm, or sorrow, or a boisterous laugh.

"Have you been all these people?" she says.

"At one time or another. People think a mask covers up. But it's not true. It makes everything possible. You can put yourself into any state of being."

She takes the mask of the middle-aged woman off the wall and holds it out to him. For a moment, he does nothing. Then he reaches for it. The air seems to tremble as he slips it over his head. His center of gravity instantly sinks, and now he's gliding over to his desk, his head moving in a level line, one arm out in front of him, as if to prevent a collision or perhaps to touch something. Tipping back his head, the mouth of the mask appears to open, as if he's about to speak, and then he is speaking, not speaking, he's singing along with the record. It's a light sound, almost playful, tripping and skipping down the scales. A female voice.

Has he been waiting all this time? Waiting for someone to hand him a mask? His voice is frighteningly beautiful, as beautiful as the other night. And the ease with which he turned into this woman—this is where he belongs, she has no doubt.

But just as she decides this, he grips the back of the chair, his knuckles turn white, and he begins to moan, as if in horrible pain. She rushes over and grabs his shoulder, heat radiating through his thin robe. "Moto?" she whispers, afraid she might break something. A spell? But shouldn't it be broken? "Moto!" She's about to shake him, to call for help, when his entire body shudders and the cry of agony stops.

He turns toward her. She's staring into the face of a middle-aged woman. Is he in a trance? Acting out a play?

Before she can ask, he removes his mask, and there he is, his flushed face, his birthmark, small, shaped like a heart, and he's grinning madly, as if he might never stop.

"I can feel her," he says, his voice excited, bright. "My God! I can feel this woman's anguish!"

"Is that good?"

But she need not ask. He is glowing, as if lit up from within.

Chapter Fifteen

"*KANPAI*," A TOAST TO YOU, says Renzo, raising his wine glass.

Renzo has insisted on taking her to the restaurant in Kurashiki, ordering one dish after another to celebrate in lavish style the news. Moto is at rehearsal, as he has been for the past two days because he's been given a part in the upcoming Noh production.

"You're giving me far too much credit," says Hanne.

She doesn't pretend to understand what happened. The touch of a mask and—presto! his heart is beating vigorously, his engagement with life restored. Was that what happened? How is it possible to know or understand anyone?

But really, what does it matter? Moto has found his way back and Renzo is elated. Even the restaurant owner has come by the table to refill their sake glasses—on the house!—and say *"Omedeto gozaimasu,"* Congratulations!

Renzo is saying they'll probably perform in an elegant theater in Kyoto. Out the window the old men are gathered at the round stone tables, playing their last round of Go in the dying light.

"You must stay and see him perform. The real him," says Renzo.

"The real him?"

"On stage, that's where he's most alive. You'll see."

Renzo plans to go to the Buddhist temple tomorrow to make an offering and pray to his ancestors. "You're welcome to come along."

If she did believe in prayers and ancestors who haunted and cajoled, what would she say to the Germans on her mother's side, philosophers and priests brooding about whether reality existed or biding their time until they departed from this wretched world? Or to the Dutch scientists on her father's side, with their busy minds dissecting the world in order to explain it, understand it, turn it into a theory?

And why would her parents want to hear from her? Her mother's perpetual look of dissatisfaction would harden into something more severe—"My god, what's become of you? After everything I did for you, this is what you are?" And her father? She's not sure she'd even recognize him. A man in a brown suit. Let them have their peace. "Thank you," she says, "but I'm going to pass."

A breeze swirls the willow leaves, like green paper prayers at a Shinto shrine. A girl runs by the window, chasing loose notebook pages. Pages float into the canal and the girl stands on the bank and cries. A woman, presumably the girl's mother, runs over and tries to fish the papers out with a stick.

A familiar scene, thinks Hanne. Brigitte's kite stuck in the big oak tree, Brigitte weeping, Hanne first tried to release it with a stick, then kicked off her flats, put on her tennis shoes, and scaled the tree, carefully making her way to the third brittle branch, while Tomas stood below her, certain she was going to fall, calling out "Be careful, Mom!" Sitting on a branch, she reached high above her and, after many tries, rooted out the kite. Brigitte sprang up from the grass, shouting with delight. Afterwards, both children regaled her by telling the story over and over to Hiro, to their friends, to her. She became something of a hero to them. She thought it would be locked into their memories, a beau geste never to be forgotten. But eventually the story turned into something else, turned against her, evidence that she was stubborn, unwilling or unable to give in, to give up.

Now she is suddenly overwhelmed with sadness that almost makes her cry. How easily good intentions are seen as bad, a hero becomes a villain, competence becomes incompetence.

Ono no Komachi comes to mind, a possible scene unfolding: alone in her hut, she notices the shadow of someone standing in the doorway, someone who's come to taunt her, to ridicule the woman who has been tossed out of the official court. What does this shamed woman do? Hanne imagines several scenarios, but there's one she likes best. Komachi nods an acknowledgment and returns to her poem. She who has been stripped of nearly everything has come to peace with her fall. She has work to do; so please, let her get on with the making of poems.

Can she become like the poet? Forget everyone and everything and just proceed, as if nothing happened? Hanne gazes out the window. Fog smears the trees, making them vague. That's how she feels, vague, ghostly, as if she's been erased.

When she gets back from the restaurant, she calls Tomas.

After the usual chitchat, Tomas says "What are your plans?"

"Plans?"

"I mean job-wise. Are you going to come back and look for a job? Maybe get your old teaching position back?"

When was the last time she paid a bill? She doubts she'll be compensated for the translation of Kobayashi's book, minus perhaps a small kill fee, and she doesn't have an upcoming project. Plans? She feels the knot in her back tighten.

She tells him she'll stay for Moto's performance, she must see the real Moto, whatever that might mean. Then she's not sure what next. Maybe to Tokyo or travel up to Hokkaido to see the nesting grounds of the red crowned cranes. She and Hiro did that right after they were married. But then she'd feel compelled to visit his parents, which she'd rather not do. They didn't bother to conceal their disappointment that he'd married a woman who was not Japanese. Even with her perfect Japanese, she doubts she'd be acceptable now. "I guess I'm at loose ends."

She looks out the window. The sky is giving in to the dark. And now she recalls her dream from last night. Everywhere she turned, she kept bumping into a large gray cube, hard-edged, a dull, dark gray; it seemed to know exactly where she was going. For a while she thought she could walk right through it, if she persevered, if she willed herself not to stop; but after slamming her body into it enough times, her arms and legs badly bruised, she knew it was impossible. Attempting to go around it was also out of the question; it repositioned itself every time she changed her direction. What was this thing? How did it get here? When she tried again to charge through it, she hit herself against it so hard that it knocked her down, knocked the wind out of her, and she sat up in bed, wide awake, gasping for breath.

Tomas asks if she's checked in with her doctor. Tomorrow, she tells him she's going to call her doctor tomorrow, though she has no intention of doing so. She realizes she's resigned herself to speaking only Japanese. English, and all her other languages, they belong to a former life.

He begins talking about holiday plans—Christmas. Does she want to come to New York, or should they come to San Francisco? Or maybe they should meet on neutral territory.

Neutral territory? Are they at war? "It's only March." Is it March? She's not even sure what month it is.

"How about Colorado?"

She sighs. Removes her earrings and necklace and massages her sore toes. For some reason, her good shoes don't fit her any longer. "Fine. How are the girls? I miss them."

Then: "Brigitte called and needed money."

"Why?"

A pause.

"Christ." Then: "Don't worry, Mom. I took care of it."

"What's wrong? What's happened?"

"Forget it. I shouldn't have said anything. Colorado. Or we could head to Tahoe."

"Can I help? How much money?"

"No." He sighs. "She wouldn't accept help from you anyway."

Like a slap to the face. "Why not?"

"Do we have to go over this now? I've told you all this before." He waits for what seems like a long time. "She believes you kicked her out of your life at the very time she needed you most. You sent her off to boarding school when she was so traumatized—that's her word, not mine—about Dad's death."

She doesn't remember him saying it like that. She doesn't remember him saying the words "traumatized," or "needed you most." She thinks she'd remember that. That strong language. Those loaded words.

She repeats what she's told him before, what she's told everyone before—Brigitte was ruining her life. Something had to be done. To protect her. Save her.

He sighs again. "I know, Mom, I know. That's how you see it."

She tightens her grip on the phone cord. "What does that mean?"

"Look, you wanted to get into this, not me. She said she needed you and you turned your back. You sent her away. Abandoned her. And it doesn't matter what I believe. But I warned you not to. I told you she was too sensitive."

"I thought she'd eventually understand that it was in her best interest."

"What about when Maria moved away?" he snaps.

Brigitte's best friend from Russia. When Brigitte was eleven, Maria's parents separated, then divorced, and Maria's mother took her back to Russia. Hanne knew Brigitte would be upset, but it went beyond that. Brigitte refused to eat or do anything. One harsh or impatient word and tears spilled from her eyes.

At dinner one night, Brigitte pushed her food around on her plate with a fork and said she had to go to Russia. She missed Maria so much. Hiro said she was fortunate to have had such a good friend. But, Hanne interjected, they weren't going to yank her out of school for such a trip. She could wait until summer. They'd set up a list of chores for Brigitte to earn the money for the airfare. She could see by the way Hiro looked down at his plate that he disagreed. But he wouldn't challenge her in front of Brigitte. They'd have their disagreement behind closed doors.

"But I have to go," said Brigitte, shaking her head slowly, as if acknowledging some unspoken thought.

"You will. But not now."

Tomas chimed in with a long list of things he wanted, but didn't get, as if he was trying to console his sister. As he went on, Brigitte quietly pushed back her chair, went to her room, and shut her door. A moment later, she came out and announced that she'd just swallowed a bottleful of aspirin.

Now Hanne says: "She was eleven when that happened. When she went to boarding school, she was fourteen. She was a different girl by then, a very different girl. Once she was at boarding school, everything was fine. She made new friends, so many new friends."

"She hasn't spoken to you in six years. How is that fine?" She can hear the fury in his voice. Is it because he's been made responsible for Brigitte? Bearing the full burden of parenting? How many phone calls has he fielded from Brigitte asking for something, requesting guidance? "Did we live in the same house? With the same person? But I forget. This is what you do. Assign qualities to people so you can approve of them."

"What are you talking about?"

"Whatever you told yourself about Brigitte then so you could justify sending her to boarding school and believe she'd be fine."

"What a horrible thing to say."

He exhales loudly. "Christ, I'm under a lot of stress right now. Forget I said that. Forget the money. Forget everything." He says he'll buy her ticket to Colorado and he'll rent a condo. They'll have plenty of room. A week together for Christmas. And now he says he must go—a million things pressing.

She sets the receiver down in its cradle and watches the gingko trees flutter their heart-shaped leaves. A gray morning light saturates the room. She sees three small green buds nestled on the high branches of the apple tree. Soon the air will be scented with apple blossoms and summer with sweltering heat. A sign that things do not remain the same. And they haven't, have they? Things have gotten worse. Brigitte requires money. The word money clattered around in her head last night, along with a steady stream of thoughts—Brigitte needing money, and for what? Medical bills?

Car crash? Pregnancy? Money, and how will Hanne earn money if she has no job? But Brigitte won't take her money.

Still, she pulls out her checkbook and writes a check to Tomas for five hundred dollars. Hardly anything, she knows. *For Brigitte*, she writes on the memo line, her hand trembling.

Renzo's car is gone. She makes herself eat breakfast, then heads back to the cottage and stares at her play. What kind of story is it that ends with the main character's life just fizzling and fading away? Ono no Komachi is banished from the court—and then what? She dies a crazy old woman? She tries to think what this woman could have learned in this abandoned state. Loneliness? The ache of her heart? Or might someone or something come along and cause the poet's life to take another unexpected turn? She feels a flutter of excitement, but not enough to stop her from lying down on the bed and falling asleep again. Hours later, when she wakes, the dog is a small circle nestled on top of her feet.

Bleary-eyed, she gets up and wanders through the cold, empty house, with Morsel right on her heels. She does the few dishes in the sink, sweeps the kitchen floor. The wind picks up, blowing ghostly notes in the house made of paper walls. She makes herself go outside and sit in the back yard, hoping the fresh air will lift the dark mood that has settled over her shoulders like a shroud. Maybe she won't stay for the Noh production; she'll head back to San Francisco. But then what? She still can't speak any English.

For dinner, she has a bowl of miso soup. She finds a black-and-white TV in the upstairs study and watches the news, not paying much attention, but occasionally repeating random words out loud, as if to hear a voice, any voice—"purge," "roving," "stolen," "new zoo," "betrayal." When the drama shows come on, she still sits there, watching flickering images of women and men kissing, shouting, weeping into pillows.

In the morning with the house still empty, she takes the dog and heads out. She's getting a taste of how old age will be, she thinks, these long stretches of nothing and no one. No. Not old age. Her life now. She briskly walks past the tall grasses.

When her legs are weary, she registers very little except her exhaustion. This is what she hoped for. To wear herself out. Though along the way, a phrase has gotten stuck in her head: *I have been forsaken like a memory lost.* Over and over it plays; she can't remember who said it or if she's remembering it correctly. When she gets home, she and the dog collapse; the dog splays out on the floor, panting, its pink tongue lolling out of its mouth. She flops down on her bed, her legs throbbing. Good, she thinks, too tired to move. There's nothing she wants to do but lie here. She closes her eyes and sleeps until the sound of a car wakes her. She quickly brushes her hair and heads to the main house.

Midori steps out of a taxi. She hands some money to the driver and saunters up the front path. "I forgot some things," says Midori. "It's hard living so scattered. Some things here, some things at my apartment."

Midori smiles coyly at Hanne and slips off her pristine white high heels. Beside them are Hanne's walking shoes. How dirty they've become. A dark stain colors the toe of one shoe and both soles are worn thin. They were new when she arrived, and now they look as if she's trekked thousands of kilometers.

Midori heads to Moto's bedroom. Hanne puts on the tea kettle and sits at the table. A bowl of purple plums is in front of her. She picks one up. An astonishing purple. She rubs her thumb over its smooth, taut surface. Unexpectedly, the image of Moto's chest comes to mind. His robe spilling open, revealing his smooth, hairless chest.

The tea kettle whistles and Hanne brings out tea cups and the pot. Midori is waiting at the table.

"Renzo said you've enjoyed your stay here," says Midori, biting into a plum. "You know, you do look better. The worry lines have left your face."

Hanne lets pass the irritation of having a woman half her age assess her appearance. This woman, who in the past barely said a word to her, is now conversing. Perhaps without the male gaze flitting up and down her body, Midori no longer feels compelled to play the sex bomb.

"So Moto is back on stage," says Midori. "It was just bad karma being used up. Now the good can return."

Karma, from Sanskrit meaning action. This must be the kind of mystifying talk that has kept Brigitte spellbound over the years. Life assured and reassured, absolved of everything, it's nothing personal, this hardship, this pain. And the implicit guarantee that life will go on and on, the unfortunate or devastating only an incidental event. She can understand the appeal. Maybe if she'd been introduced to this spiritual mumbo-jumbo when she was Brigitte's age, she too would have signed up.

"He's something to behold."

"I'm sure," says Hanne.

Midori sets her cup down and leans forward. "Let me tell you a secret. Off stage, he's nothing like what you see on stage. Who could be that way all the time? I'm telling you this so you don't get the wrong idea about him. So many women fall for him and end up disappointed."

How much easier if this chapter of her life was about a love story. "And you, Midori? You're not disappointed?"

Midori shakes her head emphatically. She says she never knows when she'll see him again. He comes and goes as he pleases. "I accept him for who he is."

"And who is he?"

Midori laughs, covering her mouth with her hand.

"What's so funny?"

"I don't know. You make it sound so simple. As if you could just say who he is."

She thinks Midori is being evasive and coy. "Oh, come on. Try."

She stops laughing and looks directly at Hanne. "No, you try."

In the morning, when she opens the back door and enters the kitchen, Hanne hears light music trickling over her. Relieved, she knocks on his door.

"Come in." He's sitting cross-legged on the floor, sorting through his CDs. "I'm sorry if the music was too loud."

"Not at all." The silence has been stifling, she wants to say, as if I've been sentenced to solitary confinement. And also: it's awfully good to see you. She'd like to hug him. The simple act of human contact.

"I've got the day off." Before she can suggest that they do something together—a walk, breakfast, anything at all, he's says he's come to pick up some music to take back to his hotel room. He's in rehearsal from morning to dusk, he says, and he hasn't had one drink since his return. His face is full of color, his eyes bright, shining, his birthmark barely there. It seems his return to the theater has suited him. More than suited him.

"You look good," she says. "You've found your stage again." She sits at his desk. "So how is it? Does it feel as if you never left?"

He doesn't answer right away. "It's different. Better. It's like dying and coming back to life. Everything is vibrant, alive and incredibly beautiful, so beautiful you want to weep."

She pictures Charon carrying Moto across the River Styx and depositing him on the verdant shore of life, shaking his fist at Moto: "Now is not your time."

"I was walking down the street yesterday and stopped at a puddle," he says. "The sun was shining and the puddle was glimmering and sparkling. Cars were zooming by, people rushing behind me, but I couldn't tear my eyes away from it. It was holding light and dark, the road beneath it, the clouds and sky overhead. The longer I looked, the more I saw. Not just the road beneath, but the dirt and the rocks and the worms, and above, the birds and the stars, the entire galaxy. I haven't felt this alive since—I can't remember."

She remembers her ecstatic entrance into the world after the hospital—that was soon gone. She has to stop herself from saying that that feeling won't last.

He looks at her with concern. "Are you all right?"

She shakes her head. "It's nothing. I'm sorry."

The music is still playing. He waits, and it seems he will wait until she speaks.

"My daughter." Why is she telling him? There's nothing he can do, that anyone can do. This is her burden, her cross. "There seems so little I can do for her. I feel so helpless. I've made so many mistakes."

He comes over to her, folds himself around her.

Is this part of his coming back to life? Or hers?

"She'll find her way," she says, wanting to believe that, wanting to pull herself together.

He runs a finger from her throat to her breast bone, his touch full of appreciation. Wordlessly, they drift over to the bed into the tumble of blankets and sheets that fold around them like waves. His fingers spill all over her, unbuttoning her blouse, her skirt.

She hesitates only a moment before unzipping his trousers. He lifts her hair and kisses the back of her neck, her mouth, tentative, then more insistent. She's nearly forgotten the part that's alighting, heating her body. He's saying something, wiping the tears from her face.

Coming up out of it. Something along the way awakened and now swells inside her. An ache that catches in her throat. They lie in bed on the smooth white sheets, the smell of sex in the air. The shade is pulled down, the room dark, and the world feels like a vast emptiness, only the two of them left. He strokes the inside of her arm. She closes her eyes to stop them from watering.

"Here," he says, and hands her a tissue.

Not passion for him. She's overwhelmed by a deep, raw longing for Brigitte.

In the morning, the ache for Brigitte has lodged in her chest.

"Oh, Hanne, you look so beautiful and sad," says Moto.

At his urging they head to the pool. She swims in the ocean, which she's learned is always kept a steady 26.1 degrees Celsius. When she gets out of the water, she lies on her beach towel in the white sand and listens to the waves roll onto shore. As Moto predicted, she finds herself thinking the waves are real, as well as the ocean, the sand, the warm breeze ruffling her hair.

Moto comes out of the water and kisses her cheek. She feels a foolish happiness. She asks him to tell her again what it's like to come back from the dead. The words well up inside him and spill over to her. Him, wanting her to experience what he is experiencing, and her, listening greedily.

She closes her eyes and drifts. Her throat is dry. Her tongue sticks to the roof of her mouth. Where is her water bottle? She looks around, trying to get her bearings—she's at the beach,

Moto is swimming again, the waves are gently rolling in, palm trees waving in the breeze, and a girl is sitting beside her in the white sand.

The girl's knees are drawn up to her chest, and she's staring at Hanne. Her black hair is tied up in a ponytail, she smiles shyly. She must be ten or eleven, thin limbs, toenails painted seashell pink. Is this the sister of the boy who asked for a pen? She hands Hanne a paper origami crane and scampers away. On one of its blue wings, there is writing in English. *A pine tree pines for you.*

Another memorized line of English learned at grammar school? The girl has already vanished in the crowd. Probably hiding, watching Hanne's reaction, giggling. She reads the line again. Her head pounds, not like it did after the accident. The throbbing is in the back of her head, as if someone threw a ball from behind and smacked her. Was she struck by something as she dozed? Or last night, sleeping in Moto's arms, did she dream something hit her and as the fake beach has become real, so has her dream?

She puts the crane on her towel. Then picks up her book, Shakespeare's *Macbeth* in Japanese. She found the book in Renzo's library and tucked it into her bag, thinking she'd spend the day reading. But the book is so poorly translated that she finds it impossible to read without re-translating it. *Life's nothing but a dark shadow, a poor player fretting on stage. And then it's over.* She can remember the original sentence from secondary school: *Life's but a walking shadow, a poor player that struts and frets his hour upon the stage and then is heard no more.*

She picks up the girl's handwritten note again. "Pining," she says with immense effort. Her ear perks up. She says it again. The pursing of her lips, followed by a puff of air, a sound gliding upward to the front of her mouth, the tip of her tongue pressed to the roof of her mouth, her soft palate relaxing, letting the air pass through her nose.

"Pining," she whispers. "Pine. Pining. Pines."

She stands up and tries to get Moto's attention. He's charging back and forth in the water. She looks around to see if anyone heard her; if there is someone she might speak to. "Hello," she says to no one. The segment of her brain right beneath her forehead is pounding. "Hanne Schubert. My name is Hanne Schubert."

She is speaking English.

She walks to the water and swims out to him.

Is it all back? She recites memorized passages of *Macbeth* out loud. The words come slowly, but it seems that her entire cartload of English has returned, intact. How hard she worked to master this language. She remembers a teacher with chestnut hair writing an English word with white chalk on the blackboard— though she can't recall which classroom or what country—and she is at her scratched wood-top desk, hungrily copying it down. After the final bell, rushing home, not stopping at the candy shop, because she'd assigned herself more vocabulary, more exercises to do. The Germanic-based words came easily, so she concentrated on the elegant Latinate words. English soon became her preferred language. A language of action, of power, of agency, with its verb usually located at the beginning of the sentence, she used it all the time, instead of her German. Soon, English words came to her more quickly than German or Dutch. She hears herself explaining to her mother, "It's the first global lingua franca, which means the whole world is open to me. I can travel anywhere, live anywhere, become anything, and one day I'll move to America."

Moto sees her and swims toward her. When Hanne announced her intentions, her mother snapped: "You're no genius. If you want a chance at any of those possibilities, you better work harder than everyone else. You've got to prove yourself worthy."

Now a vision comes to Hanne, but not one of possibilities. She sees herself clearly—a woman living in San Francisco alone, in bed by nine, awake by six, a brisk walk, a purchase of a coffee, a hot bun, back to her silent apartment to work (what work?), a light supper of dark bread, prosciutto, brie, and a bowl of udon, in bed again by nine. So stark! So dull! So dull because she centered her life on the narrowest of perches; there she is, her former self in her king-size bed, a middle-aged woman fighting off a hot flash and the bed suddenly looks like a white raft, the anchor pulled up. She's adrift with the wreckage that is her life, floating out to sea.

But she's not there, she tells herself. She's here. And there are still possibilities. She need not settle for her old life.

"Good morning, Moto," she says in English. "So very nice to see you."

Chapter Sixteen

THE NOH THEATER IS A stately red-brick building, a former textile mill from the nineteenth century where silk was once woven into bolts of beautiful cloth for kimonos. The machines are long gone, replaced by tiered red velvet chairs nailed to the floor in a semicircular ring, their attention riveted on the stage. The stage is essentially empty. No curtain separates it from the audience, nothing is hidden—glassy wood floors, only a backdrop of a painting of an old gnarled pine tree. Over the main stage, four pillars support a roof, which looks like it once belonged on a Shinto shrine. It is Japan's version of beauty, everything stripped to its essence.

Renzo points to the bridge on the left that leads to the main stage. That's where Moto will enter, he says. "We watch as he moves from the real world to the stage. See the green curtain at the beginning of the bridge? Behind that curtain, there's a room where he looks at the mask until he can summon the spirit of the character."

Summons the spirit of the character? She feels the momentum of curiosity stir: How does he do that—and get it right?

Someone calls out to Renzo. He excuses himself and trots across the theater to a group of his friends. THE GREAT NOH ACTOR IS BACK, that was the headline in this morning's local newspaper, which Renzo cut out and proudly announced to her that his parents and ancestors were rejoicing in their graves. Renzo is shaking hands with a whole crowd of people, a big grin on his face. Moto is clearly the draw, the reason the theater is packed and buzzing with excitement. She watches Renzo, who is nodding and smiling. She has yet to tell him that her English has returned, though her other languages are still off in an anteroom of her brain. Does she think that if he knew, he'd have sent her back to San Francisco? Not permit her to see Moto perform? But if that's true, why does she feel a growing apprehension as the time approaches for the plays to begin?

She finds a seat near the front, on the aisle, and skims the program. *Moto, who has appeared in over 2000 productions, a Japanese treasure,* on and on. *A Noh play depicts one sweeping emotion that dominates the main character. As in life, words often fail to adequately express emotion, so Noh fuses music, dance, costume, song, and mask.* She glances through the texts of the plays; though most Japanese already know the plays, the text is provided for people like her, word-bound, because even native Japanese-speakers don't understand the words sung by the actors and chorus.

Before she can read the first play, the lights flick on and off. Renzo scurries over, takes the seat beside her, and squeezes her hand. "Here we go."

Four musicians shuffle onto the stage. The theater darkens and a flute fills the theater with a spectral sound. Minutes later, drums join in and a rhythm emerges, the flute flinging off light, airy notes, and the drums thudding low. But before the rhythm becomes predictable, the tempo changes, one drum beats faster, more insistent, demanding. She settles into it, but then it changes again—a beat goes missing, as if it found something better to do.

The music lulls like a habit, then disturbs. But given time, even the unexpected becomes predictable. This goes on for a while, a long while, and she listens, anticipating the disturbance, guessing when the music will change, guessing right nearly every time. Soon this game becomes tiresome. She looks around to see who's fallen asleep. On the other side of the aisle, a gray-haired man's chin is pressed to his chest; the slow steady rise and fall of his shoulders keeps its own beat. Someone two seats in front of him has assumed the same pose. She closes her eyes. She hears Renzo's raspy exhale. She listens to that. Then back to the music. Renzo's exhale, the music. Back and forth until she's sliding through memories, one after another, landing at her old desk, once her mother's, made from the sturdy boards of a German cargo ship. As she worked, Hanne used to rub her fingers against the grain, back and forth, the good years, thick and pronounced; the bad years, barely discernable to her fingertips. But her fingers knew and she heard the hum underneath her translation, a bad word choice, a good choice, a bad, a good, imprecise, perfect, horrid, perfect, dreadful, dreadful that diamond stud in Brigitte's left nostril that provoked and gleamed and dared, dared Hanne to say something, anything about it. "You're only fourteen," said Hanne, trying to use a level voice. "Get that thing out of your nose."

Brigitte stood in the doorway, expressionless. Hanne was so tired of the fighting, the sniping. Hanne looked at Brigitte's unwashed greasy hair, her dirty white T-shirt, her baggy sweat-pants. How had her daughter become so thin? So unkempt? To herself she quoted Keats, "Much have I traveled in the realms of gold, and many goodly states and kingdoms seen." Why must Brigitte forsake everything she's been given, that Hanne labored to give her? Out of love, mind you, to show you your wealth of possibilities.

Renzo bumps her elbow. Hanne opens her eyes. A whispered apology. No one new on stage, nothing has happened. She stares at the stage. Friends had often insisted she see a Noh produc-tion—you know the language, of all people, Hanne, you'd appreciate it. She doesn't understand a word. Why did she let Brigitte's physical appearance bother her so much? A faulty assumption that slovenliness meant laziness and the puncturing of her nostril meant disrespect. It all seems so mortifyingly trivial now. How small of her to care how Brigitte looked. How unkind, how unloving, because Brigitte—she's thinking of Moto's three-day stupor now—must have been trapped in grief over the loss of Hiro. And in need of Hanne. Not her firm hand or harsh rebukes. Or banishment across the country. That's how Brigitte saw it, according to Tomas. Hanne abandoned her in her time of need. And what did she need? Something far more generous, Hanne sees that now.

Hanne tries to concentrate. The music changes, the flute is gone. As she stares at a musician's shiny white shirt, her mind drifts again; then out of nowhere, the image of a white bowl of blueberries being rinsed under tap water. The tap water comes out orange brown. Rust in the pipes. What memory is this?

The flute rejoins the drums, like a wisp of a woman weeping.

Blueberries in a white bowl. How to translate that? In a white bowl, blueberries. Blueberries. In a white bowl. A bowl of blueberries. Her mind rearranges the words until finally she sees herself, seven or eight years old, sitting on the sun porch eating a bowl of blueberries, doing a crossword puzzle. Her father sat next to her smoking his pipe, the air filling with the scent of cloves, his lips kissing the pipe stem. The faucet ran in the kitchen, and from her parents' back bedroom a radio played something slow. Hanne put a spoonful of sweet berries in her mouth and bit each one separately, telling herself to remember this moment, sitting in the warm air, next to her father, her mother inside, humming something sweet in German, remember life could contain this extraordinary happiness, and that it would eventually disappear. Later, she looked back at herself and marveled at her clairvoyance. Soon after that bowl of blueberries, she and her parents moved again. She remembers weeping, "I don't want to go." Which was dismissed with silence. She was once again taken away from her few friends whom she had so patiently and carefully courted.

Compared to what has previously occurred, what follows on stage is a frenzy of activity: eight men file onto the main stage, carrying colorful fans, and sit with their legs tucked beneath them. Expressionless, their faces reveal nothing.

With a swish of silk, an actor finally steps onto the bridge in a black robe patterned with white squares. He wears the old man's mask, with a wrinkled, gray complexion, a topknot of gray. His white-socked feet skate along the floor, his upper trunk slightly ahead of his lower, as if there is an invisible force urging him along. It's Moto's manner of moving—is it him?

The old man on the bridge raises his arm and the chorus begins to chant. "Yo! Oh! Oh!" The voices fall at the end of each of the sounds in a monotonous cadence. And then more sounds, incomprehensible with the dragged vowels, the strange enunciation that resembles the chanting of an ancient Greek tragedy. She can't make sense of it, as if she's been sent to a foreign country and doesn't speak the language, and there is no hope of learning it.

The old man skates back and forth on the bridge, as if the air has currents that sweep and circle him. The chorus chants its gibberish and minutes go by, though it feels like hours. Finally, another actor emerges on the bridge in the mask of a young woman. The actor sings something in a low monotone voice. Except for the mask and costume, she's no different than the other actor. Her song, if it can be called that, is a shredding of words into their fundamental elements of sound and air. Hanne gropes for something, a word. It must be archaic Japanese. She steals a glance at Renzo. He's smiling, nodding, visibly enjoying the performance.

After some effort—that back-and-forth motion—the two actors finally make it to the stage. She peeks at her watch. An hour! Something should happen now. But the actors glide and whirl, waving their fans, the monotonous beat of the drums, the moaning vowels. There seems no point. It's akin to watching someone cook, fold laundry, read the newspaper, on and on, until the day dims and dies out and it's time for bed. There is no crescendo; nor, she suspects, will there be one. Closing her eyes, she wills herself to think of something pleasant.

Swimming, of all things, she finds herself in her mind swimming. The waves are choppy, the water ice green-blue. She's floating, drifting, staring at the cloudless blue sky. When she turns on her stomach, there's no sight of land, blue sky and ice green water—how did she float so far? Moto appears beside her. He nonchalantly nods hello.

How did we get out so far? she says, trying to keep fear from her voice.

He shakes his head. Don't know.

Which way is land?

He shrugs.

Which way are you going? she says.

This way.

Why? She hopes he says land, safety, she'll be safe if she follows him.

Current's going this way.

She must have dozed because when she opens her eyes again, new actors populate the stage, different costumes and masks, but it might as well be the same play. The same movement, the same dull droning of words. Is Moto on stage?

The play grinds on. During intermission, she's supposed to rave to Renzo about the stunning costumes, the captivating dances. Thankfully, Renzo is surrounded by friends who are doing just that. She overhears someone say Moto has yet to appear.

She steps outside, hoping the fresh air will ease her irritation and wake her up. Rain floats down, a soft misty rain. How little space between things, she thinks, growing more agitated and annoyed. Every single building abuts another building, and the sidewalks are so narrow that people must crowd, bump shoulders, jostle and almost collide, murmur apologies, and the alleyways are crammed with more shops, more signs, more carts and vending displays, more and more people.

She steps back inside and waits in the lobby. Before the lights turn off, she reads the title of the fourth play, *The Bridge to Nowhere*. It's a new play, not part of the traditional repertoire. Bare bones of a story: a woman's son runs away to the big city to seek his fortune, only to end up living on the street. She turns again to the front of the program. *Noh is the display of yugen or quiet beauty.* A nebulous, mysterious word, she thinks. "Yu," she knows, means dark, phantom-like, and "gen," subtle and profound.

When the lights flicker, she sighs and returns to her seat. An old man comes onto the bridge. Him again, she thinks, rolling her eyes. She looks around. The audience is Japanese, and they are, for the most part, alert now. Possibly even enjoying this. She couldn't feel more alien in this moment. Arrogant of her to profess that she understands the Japanese. One of their oldest art forms and she doesn't have a clue. Then she thinks she hears the word "depraved." She decides the old man is depraved and perhaps deranged because of the odd angle of his mouth, with its slackened lower jaw. He, too, moves in that strange way, which, by now, looks familiar, so familiar that she wonders if she began walking now, walking right out of here, she'd float along in the same manner.

More time passes before the second actor appears. Again it takes a while to make out a single word. "Beggar." He's the beggar. Then she hits gold; in quick succession, she hears "clouds," "mist," "obscure." A speck of satisfaction surges, and she tries to draw it out, savor it.

Now there's the haunting music to contend with. Again she's lost the lexicon. One of the drums sounds like raindrops hitting a steel roof. Is it supposed to signify rain? It probably means absolutely nothing.

Her only consolation: after this one, there's only one more play, then she can leave.

The air suddenly turns charged. The theater swells with the stillness of stunned absorption. She opens her eyes. The theater is silent except for the rustle of silk as someone moves on the bridge in the same stylized fashion as the other actors, but not like the others because he's barely moving at all, yet there's a force to his being, a magnetism that grabs and holds the eye, her eye.

She sits at the edge of her seat, her heart pounding. It's Moto, she has no doubt. Wearing a sumptuous robe of bright gold, embroidered with orange and red fans. His mask is smooth, with arched eyebrows, and his mouth slightly open, revealing white teeth. Black strands of hair fall in curls on his smooth forehead. She recognizes the mask, that of a beautiful young boy. He looks like the embodiment of purity, of inno-cence, of vulnerability.

"Look at him," whispers Renzo, a white shine to his voice. "Do you see him?"

Moto glides over to a post along the bridge and gazes at the actors on the main stage, his mouth at a palsied slant. He seems to be emoting longing. But how? He's wearing a mask. Raising his arms over his head, he opens his mouth, or so it seems, and out comes metal scraping against metal. Is he beseeching the beggar? The old man? What does he want?

Moto edges toward the main stage, but before he reaches it, he stops. Somehow the expression on his mask changes. He looks out toward the audience, his eyes seem to open wide, as if searching, and calls out—what? From the strain in the chant, it sounds like he's asking for help.

An anxious stillness grips the theater as everyone waits for an answer. It's as if a spell has been cast. She can't take her eyes off Moto, his mask is moving as if it's made of real skin. Pinpricks of perspiration seem to appear on the boy's upper lip and now tears run down his face.

She's glued to this moment, to Moto not as Moto but as a young boy. He raises the fan above his head, slowly opening it as if each newly unveiled fold contains the hidden meaning of everything. Hanne holds her breath. A brown fan with six white birds. Meaning? Meaning what? His voice is ringing out, vibrating the air molecules; it rings and rings, then slowly fades, dies out. There is no answer. The boy's face crumples. Hanne feels something lurch inside.

The beggar and the depraved man beckon to Moto to come over, promising to tend to his needs. Or maybe they don't. From the strange shrieks and silences, Hanne feels herself making up the words, a story, trying to hold on to something familiar. Moto glides onto the main stage, and the depraved man moves close, too close. Scrapes a long fingernail along his cheek. When the boy cringes and shrinks away, so does Hanne. A chill runs through her, then settles as a hard ball in her stomach. The old man and the beggar circle the boy, leering, running their hands over his pure gold robe. Run away, thinks Hanne. Go!

The frightened boy stands perfectly still, but at the same time motion sweeps over him, and now he's whirling around, then plummeting to the ground, whirling, plummeting, caught up in some sort of chaotic wind. She can't say how he's standing still, and at the same time generating a flurry of frenzied movement. The beggar and the old man back away, as if the boy has gone crazy and is giving off some horrible scent. The scent of fear and anguish, thinks Hanne.

"We are sundered," the chorus sings, "O sorrow: Nothing else remains."

When Moto finally sings along with the chorus, she falls into his voice, as if it's calling out to her, only her, falls all the way into the agony.

What follows is a blur. The final play—a demon with a red mask moving around, other characters, that's all she remembers. When it's over, Renzo murmurs something about a restaurant across the street. She hears herself tell him she wants to sit a moment longer. To gather herself, she thinks. But what needs gathering? What has been sundered?

The rest of the audience clears out and the theater is empty. She hears someone sweeping. The janitor, most likely. Slowly, she tries to stand, holding on to the back of the chair for support. Something is in her mouth. She touches it with her tongue. Inches it forward to her front teeth. A strand of hair, twisted around itself. She plucks it out. Black. About four centimeters long. It could be hers.

Chapter Seventeen

OUTSIDE, IT'S DARK. NIGHT HAS lowered itself onto Kyoto, bringing with it a chaos of cars, swarms of people, and bright blinking neon signs. Hanne heads through the soft rain, chin tucked down, passing plastic-covered fruit stands and shoe stores and camera shops, not knowing where, exactly, she's going. The rain comes down harder and she follows the crowd, until she veers off into the small lobby of a ryokan, enveloped in a hush. She wipes her wet face with her sleeve. From somewhere she hears gurgling water. In a small alcove behind the check-in desk, a single bare bamboo branch rises out of a white vase, like dark smoke. She pries off her soggy shoes and, through thin, damp socks, feels the tatami mat's polished strands.

An older woman dressed in a dark blue kimono and white obi appears at the front desk and bows slightly. With her powdered white face and her lips painted red, in another time in her life she might have been a geisha.

"May I help you?"

The transaction of securing a room is surprisingly easy, as is the encounter with Renzo, whom she finds with his gaggle of friends at the restaurant.

"I'll be staying in town to see the plays again," she says.

He nods and gives her a knowing smile, as if he understands; but how can he, because she does not. Why is she compelled to watch Moto again? And why is she trembling?

The older woman leads Hanne down a long narrow hallway, Hanne following the swish of the woman's narrow hem, the rustle of her underclothing. Her room is two adjacent rooms, with a sliding shoji door between them. In one, there is nothing: no television, no paintings on the wall, no phone, no table, no chairs, only a long stretch of tatami mats and wheat-colored walls. The connecting room holds a single black lacquered table, where, the older woman tells her, she'll be served her meals.

The woman opens the closet doors and pulls out pillows, blankets and a futon, and places them on the tatami mat. When the woman leaves and the door shuts, Hanne breaks into a cold sweat. Her stomach feels as if it is pressed against her heart. She slips out of her clothes and into the white bathrobe hanging behind the bathroom door and lies on the floor. The sliding glass door, which leads to a small enclosed garden, is open a crack, and a cool breeze moves underneath her robe. A board creaks, footsteps pitter-patter in the hallway. Then quiet.

Slowly her breathing deepens. She lies there a while longer, letting everything settle. Something tickles her hand and she remembers the game she and Brigitte used to play. Back and forth, tracing words on the back of each other's hand. Guessing the language, the word. When Brigitte guessed right, she'd squeal "Again, Mama, again!" "Okay, my love," Hanne said, laughing, "close your eyes." Over and over, Japanese, German, Spanish, French, Korean. And then when Brigitte learned Greek, "I'll teach you, Mama, if you want to know." And though Hanne already knew it, she said "I'd love that." Because it meant sitting beside her daughter, her body squirming with new knowledge.

Now Hanne rouses herself and heads for the bathroom. Sitting naked on the wooden stool, the water raining down on her, she scrubs herself with a rough cloth. Then meticulously shaves her legs, her underarms. She soaps her hair, which is no longer jet black but woven with wiry gray strands. She scours again every inch of her body. Then takes a pumice stone to sand her feet clean of calluses. She's not sure why she's washing herself with such care, but it feels necessary, as if something must be purged. She crosses from the shower to the round wooden tub of steaming hot water. Gingerly, she steps in, and a rush of heat scurries up her calf.

With her arms floating by her side, she wilts. Under the water, her legs look thinner, more sinewy than she remembered. Has she lost weight? Her troubles have pared her down? Sweat drips down the sides of her face, pooling at her jaw line, trickling down her neck, her breasts. Her breasts, though, look the same: sagging from nursing two children, and her pinkish brown areolas are now the size of quarters. She can't remember what they looked like before having children. That body is long gone.

Another memory: Brigitte must have been nine years old. A boy at school, something not quite right about him. "He has no friends, Mama," said Brigitte. "He sits on the edge of the blacktop at recess, tapping a stick." Brigitte befriended him. Baked him cookies and saved her money to buy him a baseball. Not just him. She was always spending her allowance on gifts for her friends.

Tears and more tears when he was sent to a school for special-needs children. "Who will be his friend?" pleaded Brigitte, who was worried that he would be lonely once again. So sensitive. Tomas's words come back to Hanne.

For a long time Hanne sits in the tub, as if bathing could take forever, canceling the need to do anything else. She's never believed in destiny; but watching Moto on stage, that's the word that came to mind. A perfect alignment: Moto and acting. He was superb, remarkable, spellbinding, otherworldly—she's fumbling for the right word. How to describe? She saw him whole, completely fitted to the world.

That must have been why he made her promise to come. To see him, dazzling.

If someone's destiny is to possess a talent, and the world embraces it, all is well. But when that talent is denied, what happens? When the soul, for whatever reason—even by one's own hand—is denied its destiny, what are the consequences?

The word "soul" stops her. Hiro used to talk about the soul descending from the heavens or bardo, crossing back into this world to be born again. The human form is precious, he'd say. It is earned after many lifetimes as other creatures, he'd tell Brigitte and Tomas. Hanne usually gave him a hard look when he spoke this way, but right now she can't find a more suitable word than soul. So be it. What happens, then, when the soul is assigned its purpose, but is neglected? Forgotten? Or worse, thwarted? When someone or something comes along and tells the soul that its reason for being here is not wanted? She stares at her pale toes underneath the water. She thinks of Moto on a drinking binge, a husk of himself. The soul can wither.

Without warning, Kobayashi comes to mind. Did his soul come with a vision of being a writer? To engage the world through his imagination and words? The Romantics said we arrive into the world "trailing clouds of glory." And what did Hanne do? Scatter Kobayashi's clouds of glory and turn them into something he refused to claim as his own.

She'd like to stop there, but there's another person to consider. What did Brigitte's soul want to live out? And how did Hanne deny it? Oppose it? For that's how she sees it now. She wasn't trying to guide, but alter Brigitte's purpose and fashion it into something else. Something she could love. But that's not true. She did love Brigitte. Loved her from the moment she saw her. So what was she doing?

A deliberate misreading of her daughter to bolster her, not just once but many times to cultivate something bold and resolute, something hearty and robust so the blows of the world would not break her like a cheap knickknack. Otherwise, what would come of such a life? What good? What extraordinary thing?

What any mother would do. But not a mother who didn't want to face years and years of silence.

By the time she climbs into bed, she is exhausted. She gives in to her weariness, the softness of the pillow, the coolness of the sheets. Before she falls asleep, she has one more thought—whatever the soul's destiny or purpose, it does not go away. Despite Moto's wanderings, he has found himself again on stage.

Chapter Eighteen

THE THEATER IS AS PACKED as it was yesterday. Next to her, a frail old man snores through the first play, and in his lap rest his bony hands, a little nest of sticks. Eventually Hanne dozes and dreams that she's seen the play so many times, she's lost count. The seasons wheel by, the leaves turn and turn again, and she's rooted there, like an old tree. Once she tries to leave, but upon reaching the exit she panics that someone might take her seat. Though the chair is nothing to covet; it's now threadbare and she can feel its broken seat springs. She hurries back and resumes her post. She is guarding something, or on the lookout—but for what? Tomas shows up. "What are you still doing here?" He's old now, his hair is gray and his shoulders slightly stooped. If he is old, she must be ancient. As he waits for an answer, he inspects her face, trying to decipher her. Lurking behind his look is the question "Have you gone dotty?"

"It's a world unto itself," she murmurs, keeping an eye on the play as she speaks. She knows the explanation means nothing to him—or her. What's happening, she wants to say, is not accessible through words.

Now she is startled awake by the electric charge in the air. And there is Moto dressed as the beautiful boy moving on the bridge, running luster in the air.

He glides to the side of the bridge, and the two men, the beggar and the depraved one, pounce on him, predators stalking prey. As soon as the boy crosses over to the main stage, the old man is right beside him. His puckered mouth seems to water. The beggar rifles through the boy's pockets. The lighting dims and Hanne imagines it is nighttime, and the street lights have yet to glow. In the pitch black, the buildings loom like giants and the hungry men grope. The boy's cheek muscle flinches. A tiny pucker of skin pops up in between the eyebrows. He looks frantically left, right, left, searching for an escape.

But there is no escape and the boy begins to cry. Hanne is barely breathing. She feels a knot in her chest, and the knot is expanding, wrapping around her, squeezing her. A bitter taste of fear floods Hanne's mouth. She is experiencing what the boy is experiencing and she can't seem to move, as if any wrong movement will cause the men to devour her.

"Mama," the boy calls out. His voice is faint, clamped down by fear.

Hanne grips the arms of her chair. This didn't happen yesterday. Or did it? The men cackle and shake their hairy heads. They have become monsters gnashing their long yellow teeth.

"Mama, please." A thread of a voice tossed out into the dark, like a flimsy lifeline. She feels the boy's deep desire: to nuzzle into his mother's warm body, to curl up in her warm lap, to drape around himself her warm voice that sounds like a lullaby telling him it's all right, everything's all right now, my child, the way good mothers do, even when it isn't true. Something Hanne never did, she realizes.

Hanne strains to hear a response. The moment stretches taut as it becomes seconds piled upon seconds that become minutes of silence. There's a sensation of something whooshing into her, something unfixing. The dreadful silence goes on and on. The theater erupts with the boy sobbing. Hanne presses her hands to her face.

The theater door opens, shuts. The building is emptying. Somewhere, someone is happily whistling. Hanne can't seem to move. The boy is still with her. As he has been for years.

She bought Brigitte a new blue dress for the plane ride to the boarding school. Slate blue, Brigitte's favorite color, but she refused to wear it. Instead, she put on ragged jeans and a white V-neck T-shirt. On the flight, Hanne again paged through the shiny brochure, showing Brigitte all the languages she could study, the photographs of her new teachers, the library, the living quarters. She could have her own room, if she wanted. But Brigitte refused to look, crying the entire flight, she didn't want to go, why did she have to go, why was she making her go? Her friends were in San Francisco, she promised to go to school, please, please, she'd be good, very good, just let her come back home. She wanted to go home. "Why can't I be with you?"

At one point, the flight attendant came over and asked in a concerned voice if there was anything she could do.

By the time the taxi pulled up in front of the school, Brigitte had spent her tears, but not her vocal cords. "Don't leave me!"

The headmistress strode outside, flanked by a hefty guard. "Come now."

Brigitte lunged at Hanne, maybe to clutch her coat, maybe to prevent Hanne's departure. Whatever the reason, her hand slapped Hanne squarely on the cheek. Hanne stood there, stunned, mortified, humiliated. The guard grabbed Brigitte, restrained her by pulling both arms behind her back.

"Mommy!"

Time stopped, ran backwards as Hanne heard the frightened voice of a young Brigitte. Two years old, four, six, her precious Brigitte. At that moment, Hanne almost declared it all a terrible mistake. She almost told the guard to take his god-awful hands off her daughter. Almost pulled Brigitte back into the taxi with her and took her back home. But the headmistress snapped at Hanne, "Go. You're making it worse. We'll take care of it. Just go."

It being her daughter. Hanne told herself, you will get through this. You are strong. Life is full of strife, but you will endure it. You bear your burdens quietly and move onward.

As she hurried to the taxi, she told herself, Brigitte, too, is strong. Because if Brigitte could march onward from this moment, Hanne could ignore the guilt at the center of her being. She knew what she was doing, and she did it anyway. Her daughter, the cry of a child needing to be held and rocked and comforted. Her daughter, who took everything to heart. In the past, she'd been tough with Brigitte to teach her resilience, to bolster her up. And now? Hanne was so tired. Each day was a sustained combat. And Hanne was losing. She couldn't do this anymore. Didn't want to do it anymore. Not strong, Hanne was not so strong after all. More than that, she gave up trying. She thought she had done all she could, that it would be for the best. But she was wrong. As the taxi pulled away, Hanne did not look back, but her eyes filled with tears, and her cheek burned brighter as she heard her daughter yell "Mommy!"

Now she sits in the darkened theater. In a daze, Hanne realizes she's made a noise, a sharp intake of air. It was a mistake, assigning resilience to Brigitte when there was none. And she made the same mistake with Jiro, because if Jiro longed for his wife, so might she long for Brigitte. And if he doubted his decision to send his beloved away, so might she. And if he felt the depth of his grief, so might she. And if he sunk into deep, immobilizing despair, so might she.

The lights flick off, throwing the theater into darkness, and a sliver of bluish light seeps from beneath the green curtain. Hanne heads to the front of the theater, unsure of what she's about to do until she's doing it. The floor of the bridge is surprisingly slick, like ice. Hanne takes a step, but the habit of walking is impossible. She shuffles across the bridge and slowly begins to glide. It seems as if she's no longer stuck to the ground, but floating on an air current. If such a thing as a soul exists, she thinks, it would feel like this, weightless, unhinged from gravity.

She moves aside the green curtain. He's still in costume, wearing the mask of the beautiful boy. He looks serene, self-contained, like a solid object, and yet porous, letting everything flow in and flow out. When he stands, he radiates his full presence. He reaches for her hand and kisses the back of it. She feels nothing sexual or passionate in the gesture. A blessing, it feels like a blessing.

A miracle that she finds her way to the ryokan. She soaks in the bath. A throbbing has infiltrated her body. When she gets out, the pain is still there. A deep ache in her core, perhaps her heart, has invaded every part of her.

The futon has been laid out for her and she lies in it. Almost immediately a sob rises up from her chest. A knock at her door interrupts the stream of self-recrimination.

"Hanne?"

Leave her alone. She welcomes the dissolution.

Moto says her name again.

He is standing at the door, his eyes shining and impenetrably dark. He still bears a relentless brilliance. The front clerk woman whisks in behind him, bowing low, bearing gifts of green tea, moshi, and a plate of sashimi.

He takes a seat at the black lacquered table. Hanne seems to be in an altered state, unsure of what to say or do. She imagines that her eyes are red-rimmed, her hair disheveled, and she's wearing a flimsy bathrobe. But she doesn't excuse herself because here is Moto and the memory of his mask and the boy's cry and Brigitte's and Moto's radiance pouring all over her.

What was Brigitte forced to face alone? What terror? What pleas went unanswered?

"That's why, isn't it?" she says. "You wanted me to stay. To hear the boy. To feel his fear, his need. That's why."

He reaches over and holds her hand. "I don't know. I don't plan like that, Hanne. You know that by now."

"You on stage. I felt every movement, every sound. Everything." She doesn't know if she is making any sense.

He doesn't say anything. No need for praise, she imagines him saying. It is what I do, what I am.

"You'll find your stage."

Probably not—not the stage she once knew so well. "I'm leaving in the morning." Her voice has only a slight shake to it.

255

He nods.

She can't stay here. She has the overwhelming urge to find her daughter. To demand her whereabouts from Tomas. To sit beside Brigitte and listen to her breathe.

They make the usual courteous platitudes to see each other again. He might someday come to San Francisco, and she'll return to Japan, someday. As they talk, she supposes it is likely she'll never see him again. Another chapter of her life is closing. Another person gone. He will rise, perhaps hug her one last time, kiss her cheek, and leave. The door will shut. She will grow older, as will he, and they'll either wither further or bloat; he'll likely be cremated in the Japanese way, with his bones placed in an urn, feet bones first, head bones last so he does not travel upside down in the afterlife. She would like to be cremated too. Perhaps Tomas will scatter her ashes in the sea.

"I'll fly over for your next show," she says suddenly. Why must she settle for an unacceptable future? She wants to make a plan.

He smiles at her, gives her his leonine smile.

His true essence, the secret of him, however indecipherable, is far too fine and subtle to go without. "You just tell me when it is," she says, "and I'll be there."

"All right," he says, "I believe you."

He stands. She comes over to him and takes him in her arms. "You should," she says. "I'm a woman of my word."

Chapter Nineteen

THE AIRPORT SHUTTLE ENTERS SAN Francisco via Highway 1. It's early morning, the pale dawn bleaching the blue sky. Jet lag doesn't account for the knot of queasiness in Hanne's stomach. She opens the window, hoping to ease her discomfort, but the air is pungent with wood smoke.

She shares the shuttle with three women who are talking about their recent European tour of cathedrals. Evidently, they attended a church service of some kind, because they are raving about a sermon. "The way the pastor told it," says one heavy-lidded woman, "everything makes sense."

What did he simplify? wonders Hanne. What did he leave out? because nothing seems simple anymore. Outside Hanne's window, there's the glimmering blue of the Pacific Ocean, stretching all the way to Japan.

When the driver deposits her in front of her apartment building, she pays him and hears herself say "Thank you," in English, with its rounded, drawn-out vowels. She murmurs it again to herself. This will be her primary language again.

A boy zooms by on a blue bike. Across the street, the red awning of the apartment building flaps in the cold wind, as if waving hello or good-bye. A pigeon struts around the sidewalk, looking for crumbs or bits of garbage, pecking at a piece of a hot dog bun, a gray glob of bubblegum. There's the bottlebrush tree, stripped of all its flowers. A malicious boy's hand has torn off the red blooms? Or maybe it's the wind's doing.

Her mailbox is full, mostly of bills. She watches herself stuff the stack into her handbag and step into the elevator, which rings its familiar high-pitched C note. She puts the key in the lock of her apartment and steps through the threshold. The air is stale, musty, dead still. A coat of dust dims the surfaces. She senses that her perceptions are being filtered through a haze of not quite being here, as if she is hovering above her body, her entire life, and reluctant to reenter.

In the front hallway, an oak table, a vase full of dead daisies, dried brown petals scattered on the tabletop, the floor, the water turned a thick, murky green. The apartment of someone in a hurry to depart, she thinks. A stench comes from somewhere else. As she heads down the hallway, the odor becomes more pungent, overpowering. She coughs and covers her nose with her turtleneck collar. It's coming from the bathroom—a toilet of old urine.

She opens all the windows and in pours the cold air heavy with the smell of sea and a torrent of city noises—horns, screeches, shouts, music—a dramatic play, everything in motion, and she stands at her window, watching the tiny people below carrying bright shopping bags and dull briefcases, the miniature cars racing down the street as if everything desirable is just around the corner. Across the street, where she once saw the couple running around naked, the gray curtains are drawn, no longer generous with their intimacy. A momentary vertigo. Still she stands there until she's no longer watching, but thinking, how disorienting all this is, to be here. The world, this world feels so far away.

She throws her dirty clothes in the hamper and surveys the bedroom, as if deciding whether to claim it. An entire wall of books. She's read them all, but by now most of them, because of the passage of time, are reduced to a sentence in her mind. That one, a man on a long journey; the book next to it, a woman going through a hellish divorce; the next, a day at the beach and a dinner party. Condensed and summarized, they sound trivial.

On her dresser are photographs of Tomas as a boy, of Tomas and Anne and her two granddaughters surrounded by palm trees and white sand. A holiday in Tahiti, if she remembers right; they asked her to go, but she declined. She can't take hot sun. Because his eyes are screwed up against the light, Tomas' smile looks half-hearted, even pained, but her granddaughters are in their bright pink bathing suits, smiling as if the world belonged to them. Hanne's gaze drifts to the empty space, which once held Brigitte's picture.

She takes it out. Hanne is hugging this wisp of a girl. Already at age seven, the outer edges to her potential were far beyond her peers, beyond what Hanne ever sensed for herself. How could she not become Hanne's receptacle for grandness? What's most striking to Hanne, something she's never seen before, is how dreamy and distant Brigitte looks. Her gaze is out beyond the camera—looking at what? Where did she transport herself? She was slipping from Hanne's clutches long before Hiro died. She failed her daughter so miserably that Brigitte had to retreat far into herself, or dream herself elsewhere, anywhere but near Hanne.

Or maybe not. How little she knows.

She puts the photo back in its place on the dresser. When she opens her closet door to hang up her coat, she sees Brigitte's four cardboard boxes stuffed in the corner. She opens one and looks inside. She remembers standing in that rundown lobby of the old monastery, with the dust-speckled murky light, one of Brigitte's boxes perched on the desk of that sinister woman who ran the spiritual group.

"I will see my daughter," Hanne said, her voice shaking. "I will see Brigitte."

The woman smiled a tight, condescending smile. "Nivedita is not seeing visitors."

Her final retreat from Hanne—relinquishing her birth name and running straight into the arms of this group.

She heads into her office. Her desk is swept clean of everything, a bare stretch of dark walnut oak stares ominously at her. She hesitates, hoping to prolong the sense of viewing her life from a distance. Of seeing it as someone else's life. But as she sits in her chair, her former life rushes at her, as if all along it was crouched in a corner, waiting for her to take her usual spot so it could pounce.

She calls Tomas's office.

"He's out of the country."

Hanne explains who she is. "What country?"

A pause. "I was told not to say."

"But I'm his mother."

The woman clears her throat. Another long pause. "I'm sorry."

He must have flown to see Brigitte. "When is he coming back?"

"Maybe three days, he can't say for sure."

She hangs up and looks around, stunned. She could call Anne, but can't stomach more evasion, denial. She suddenly doesn't want to be near her desk, or in her apartment or anywhere near her old life, which feels as alive as a pile of dead leaves. She grabs her coat, and, not bothering to wait for the elevator, runs down flight after flight of stairs. Winded, she steps out onto California Street and starts walking. The city is as she left it: people out with their panting dogs, children squealing in the playground, the old Russian men playing chess or checkers at their usual spot under the oak tree. There's the same doorman at the St. Francis, the same doorman at the Top of the Mark. Probably the blue-haired lady is on the treadmill walking to nowhere, gazing out with a bored expression. The city sails onward in its constant wind. Why is she surprised it's still here, nothing changed?

And now there is a familiar-looking man, a slight lope to his walk. David, dressed in pressed trousers, a brown suit coat and blue tie, his hair slightly damp from a recent shower, he must be on his way to the university, which is only a couple of blocks away. They used to walk together. She looks at her watch. If she'd waited fifteen minutes, she could have missed him. She pictures her old classroom—the rows of chipped wooden desks, the fluorescent light flickering, the chalk on her hands, her clothes, in the air, up her nose. She doesn't miss it.

"Hanne!" He embraces her, smiling. "You're back. How are you?"

She begins to feel the need to walk away. But where? "I just got back."

"And when did your English decide to return?"

An image comes to her: she is standing in a field, beckoning to the hills, trying to lure her English from its hideout. That's as strange as the story she tells him about the generous Japanese man

261

who spoke a steady stream of English, the fake beach, the bad translation of *Macbeth*, the note from a Japanese girl.

"The doctors will be puzzling over you for years," he says, smiling. "Do you feel like your old self again? Everything in its place?"

She gives him a simple pragmatic response, mostly because she wants to be on her way: her lifeline to the doorman, the postman, the grocer has been restored, she says. But there's something more that she doesn't try to convey. Nor can she, because it remains inchoate—it has to do with possibilities and the need for something richer, more meaningful.

He takes hold of her hand. "You look spectacular. Do you have time for a quick cup of coffee?" He gestures behind him to a café. She sees that look in his eye. Inside the café are big, comfortable chairs, only a few patrons, a fire burning in the hearth. She smells brewed coffee. She has all the time in the world, but she doesn't want to spend it with him, with anyone. Standing here, she is aware of the thinnest of threads running from him to her. He's a kind man, but how little she's survived on. Like thin gruel.

"Unfortunately, I've got to run," she says. "A possible job translating." Someone said—who was it?—that to say "no" to reality is one of the greatest ways to endure. So, she tells herself, she's enduring.

"Wonderful!" He looks disproportionately happy, as if he might hug her again.

"It's nothing grand, just a translation of some documents. Government documents. A big stack." She pauses. "And maybe a book of poems. Japanese love poems." Listen to her!

He kisses her on the cheek. "I'll call you. We can get together." He winks at her. "I've missed you terribly."

Of course there is no interview, no job waiting for her. Though mentioning it has stirred her up.

She calls Anne. After congratulating Hanne on the return of her English, Anne's voice becomes somber. "I've always hated this secrecy, this arrangement between Brigitte and Tomas," says Anne, but before Hanne's hope has a chance to flutter, she adds, "but it's not my role to dismantle it."

"You can at least tell me if he left in a hurry?"

"I'm not the one to do this. You'll have to talk to Tomas." Her voice is stern, as if she's admonishing a deviant child. Then she sighs. "Perhaps this time he'll break this awful code of silence."

"Do you have a phone number for him?"

A pause. "I'll have him call you when he gets home."

Sasha is suddenly on the line, telling Hanne that her mom has been reading to her about beetles. "The beetles camouflage themselves and you can't see them," says Sasha, her voice flush with excitement, pouncing on each word. "You have to look really hard and wait until they move. But I saw one in the back yard!"

Anne comes back on the phone. "We're heading out for the Hall of Science. Sasha wants to see the insect collection."

Or did you go on and on about the insects, subtly and craftily shaping Sasha's interest? Magically, Sasha thinks she's the sole originator of this desire, when it is you, Anne. Hanne can't restrain herself: "What if she grows up and despises science?"

Anne pauses. "I just want her to know that that world exists and she has choices."

Hanne recalls saying something similar about Brigitte and languages. She hangs up before she becomes a nag, a bad mother-in-law, though it's probably too late for that now.

Hanne must busy herself or she'll go mad. If she had a garden, she'd go out and put her hands into the dirt. Wasn't that her mother's refuge when Hanne became too much for her? When the world was too much? The fury with which she attended to her garden yielded an abundance of green beans, tomatoes, and lettuce.

There's her play to think about. It seems so long since she's looked at it because, truly, the project has come to depress her.

With a sigh, she pulls out her pages. There's Ono no Komachi, living out a steady drumbeat of days, one the same as the other. Another poem scratched out that no one bothers to read, stuffed in a box. By now, her small hut is packed with boxes of poems. Ono no Komachi writes one, flings it in the box—even she doesn't bother reading it, for she knows it falls far short of what she means to say. How come it's so difficult to write about things as they are?

But that's it. Hanne has reached the limits of her imagination. What's the ending? The one ending that seems most likely: a steady deterioration to her lonely death, her body crumpled over her latest poem. The world gets along just fine without her. Who would want to watch that?

How much easier to return the poet to her glory days, the glory of youth. She pulls out another sheet of paper. For a long time she sits there before thinking, What about a Noh play, but for a Western audience? Ono no Komachi in a mask, a mask covered with hundreds of words, random words. She finds inspiration for a poem by plucking from the mask a single word. "Water," and her mind alights, races off to write a poem. "Pine tree," another poem. "Betrayal," another. Day after day, a word chosen, a poem springs to life.

She is not alone in her hut. She's haunted by ghosts—the illustrious dead poets are with her, wearing white gowns and white masks empty of words. They are whispering in her ear. Is the poet writing to please the ghosts? Are the ghosts her audience? Not at all. Early on, they were welcome. But by now they are weary, meddling companions who she wishes would go away.

Why, then, put pen to paper? Why bother trying to fit words to the feeling of loneliness? Of love? Misunderstanding? Not for the ghosts, not for any readers waiting in the wings. There are none. Certainly she has other options. Hanne imagines marriage, children, grandchildren, friends. But Ono no Komachi does not choose this path, because it would be a betrayal. She can't disavow what feels like her heart's sole desire. She is here for one thing, not imposed by anyone but herself; she is, and always has been, circumscribed by herself. No choice in the matter; for, if a certain measure of happiness, a certain modicum of meaning is to be had in this world, it's through the arrangement of words into beautiful rhythms and sounds—the writing of poetry that no one cares about. It's as if she's in a small room making precise, detailed figurines out of crystal that no one wants, no one will ever buy. That is her life sentence, which she must live out to the very end.

Hanne pushes aside her notes and puts her head down on her desk. It has been so long since she's thoroughly immersed herself in the careful movement of words from one language to the other, weighing each word in her hand like a precious stone, the tone, the meaning, the context, then searching for its equivalent. At some point, she will have a sentence, melodic or anxious, liquid or jagged—whatever is required—and she'll run it through her mouth by saying it out loud.

She knows everything is made to perish, but why this? Why couldn't her work as a translator have waited until she could no longer hold pen in hand?

It has been so long. The passive voice, a passive verb, present perfect; she is not the agent, but the object of the sentence, the world acting upon her. She once chastised Moto and Brigitte for their lack of agency, but what about herself? Why has she denied herself this pleasure, when she has so few? Because she's been a coward, beaten down by a steady stream of self-castigations. But more than that: doubt—doubt that, if she tried again, she could do any better, so the only choice was to move forward.

She knows what sentence she will begin with even before she opens the desk drawer and pulls it out. Kobayashi wrote: *As his wife showered, the first time in a week, Jiro fled to the moon-filled garden. Each day his wife's health deteriorated, Jiro became more distant.*

How did she translate this? "Fled" became "went," to emphasize that Jiro had choices, and he chose to go. But how much choice did he really have? If Moto has taught her anything, it is how easily the mind's equanimity can be swallowed up by grief.

"Distant" became "despondent." Despondent, to give up, lose heart, resign. She wanted to be more precise, but it's more complicated than that, isn't it? A swarm of emotions—longing, anger, bewilderment, loneliness, guilt, humor—crowding into the gaping chasm between two people who love each other.

She saw that in Moto, his ever-changing emotional landscape. So much like Brigitte. How a mood could settle in, but then lift, by the seemingly most inconsequential thing. She remembers Brigitte spending an afternoon in a park collecting Japanese maple leaves. When they'd arrived, Brigitte was sulking about something, but two hours later, she didn't want to leave. Each leaf had its own display of colors—red, green, yellow, and brown. And that brought her infinite delight.

She turns to the beginning of the manuscript and pulls out a pen. Crosses out an unnecessary word. Step by step, she works slowly, methodically, and the hours tick by. She reads a sentence out loud, her ear tuned to the euphony or discord.

They wore the same gowns to the costume party, though hers showed off her shapely calves. She translated "same" to "identical." The four lively, bouncing syllables, i-den-ti-cal, to capture a joyful moment between Jiro and his wife before the calamity. A good decision, she thinks, feeling better about herself, but then she flips to another page: *His mouth tasted foul, his back stiff.*

After his stiff back, she inserted *They could do more for his wife than he. That's what he told himself.* Kobayashi placed these sentences later in the scene, but she moved them here to show his unwavering belief that he was doing the right thing for his wife. And she added *That's what he told himself, what he knew.* But maybe in that moment, he wouldn't be thinking so clearly; maybe he was in shock, so conflicted and torn apart, his reason could provide no comfort. He didn't know if he was doing the right thing. Maybe he even doubted he was doing the right thing. But he did it anyway, so weary of his wife and her need for constant tending. Hanne had set the wheels of a machine turning, and then there was the stern woman telling Hanne: "We'll take care of it. Just go."

It's late at night, the city quiet with only the occasional siren, and Hanne keeps following Jiro deeper into his sadness. He's at wits' end, watching his wife's decline, and the doctors say nothing is wrong with her, it's all in her head. Each day brings less of her, too weak to lift a fork, to comb her hair, brush her teeth, sometimes she can't even make it to the toilet. He's losing her. He doesn't recognize her, he doesn't recognize himself. This is not the life he wants! But what can he do?

Few of us get the lives we want, she murmurs to Jiro. She's surprised at her tone, not chastising or cold but gentle and soft and patient. That enticing illusion that everything is possible, how difficult it is to let it go. But it was never the case, we were never infinite possibilities. We were never wholly divine.

I can't sleep, says Jiro. *Her demons are becoming mine. There's nothing solid separating us. I don't recognize myself.*

Hanne looks up, startled. These words are not in the text. For the first time, she hears him speak. He is speaking to her. She has heard writers talk about how characters take on lives of their own. She has always written it off as a romanticized version of writing. Perhaps it is, but there is no denying that she is hearing Jiro speak to her. As if he's in the room, his head in his hands.

This stillness, this deadness inside. His voice wobbles and comes to Hanne as a moan. *When she looks at me, she doesn't really see me. I take her to the park and sit beside the river to feed the geese. But she sees none of it. Not the geese, not the water, not me. I am so tired.*

That's what the ache is, isn't it? she says back to him.

My heart is done with the human realm. I don't want daylight or the color of deep green. I despise a world that would take her from me. The world feels broken.

Hanne rests her cheek on the manuscript. She hears Brigitte speaking now, right after Hiro died. I'm broken, Mom. I feel broken inside. I don't want to fix it because I can't.

Sunder, everything is asunder, murmurs Hanne. You are losing your dearest one, Jiro. Your heart will feel broken for a long time, perhaps forever.

I no longer want a place here at the banquet. His voice is pleading, desperate. *I am lost without her. Her breath was mine.*

Nothing makes sense, she says. There's no understanding it.

She sits with him, tries to comfort him as he cries out *She's deserting me. How can she do this to me? I am lost without her.*

Chapter Twenty

THE PHONE RINGS. HANNE IS standing at her huge blackboard, considering the Japanese word "*ma.*" How to convey in English—a language with forceful directness and flat assertions like punches to the arm—a pause in a conversation pulsing with as much meaning as a spoken word? She is nearly finished re-translating Kobayashi's novel. The phone rings and rings until she can no longer ignore it.

"Hello," she hears herself say.

She is full of what she's plunged herself into—months of Jiro's depression and grief, his wanderings and circling back on himself with remorse and despair and doubt. He pops up for a day or so of fresh air, then returns to his deep grief. She looks at the window and is surprised to see it is dark and the windows are streaked with rain. At some point, she

269

remembers going to bed, then waking up, eating something, then back to her study.

"I just got back," says Tomas, his voice is tired.

If a moment ago Hanne was floating out of herself, absorbed in Jiro's story, she is now fully in her body. "What's happened?"

"Anne said your English is back." He takes a deep breath. "That's good news."

"Did you go see Brigitte? How is she?"

"You know the way it works. I can't—"

"No. I can't do this any longer. I can't stand it." Her voice is cracking. "She's my daughter, whether she wants to be or not."

"Oh, Mom."

"Please. You must do this for me." She's pleading now, desperate. "Won't you do this for me?"

"I don't think—"

"I have to see her."

Silence, only the sound of her refrigerator humming.

"Please, Tomas. Imagine if it was one of your daughters and you were denied."

Somehow, she's crossed into the living room and is standing by the window. It's raining and the lone tree across the street is a blur. Most likely, the last of the little red flowers have fallen to the sidewalk.

"I will see her." She speaks slowly, loudly. "I have to."

He doesn't say anything.

Her teeth chatter, as if she's suddenly been dunked in ice. "I've failed her miserably, I see that now. I was wrong to send her away. I must see her."

The wind rattles the windows and blows the tree across the street, and a couple passing below on the sidewalk pull their coats tighter, and still the rain falls. Most of the people living here came from somewhere else, she thinks. Including me. A city of transients. No one belongs here. Like dust balls rolling in on the wind and soon to roll out. Ashes to ashes, dust to dust. For dust thou art, and unto dust shalt thou return. Where is home?

Dear Brigitte, Hanne begins to compose in her head, I remember when we went to Sonora, Mexico. Just you and I. Tomas was off to college and your father was at another conference. Your spring break and we rented a convertible, you wanted that, and we drove for miles with the top down, our hair going wild, and everywhere, as far as the eye could see, there were marigolds. Valleys and hills of deep golden yellow. We entered the world of yellow. You were enchanted and insisted on a bouquet. We paid a small fee to enter a field, and the two men in cowboy hats and pointy boots laughed and said "Take as much as you want." They must have been sick of those flowers. We picked until our fingers turned bright yellow. And that smell for days after—musky and pungent and sharp.

One of those marigolds is pressed in your book, *Letters to a Young Poet*. It's in a box of your things, in the back of my closet. Four boxes of your things. I opened them the other day and looked inside.

Pages of your poetry are in those boxes. Do you remember: *The surface is still. The women slide off the muddy bank into the water that peels off warmth like a tight skirt, removing rings and bathing suit tops surnames and endless duties and turning them again into bodies of milk, blood and water, into luminescent bodies with green-blue tails and scales finely patterned.*

You wrote that after we swam at Bass Lake. A long hot hike, a jump in cool water. You dared me. "Go ahead, Mom. Jump!" Other things—a rock that sparkles gold, Fool's Gold, your blue ribbons from swimming and tennis, your beginning French book, your handwriting, careful, precise, handwriting of a six-year-old. You collected the world in small objects.

And a letter to your classmates, asking them in your nine-year-old handwriting to contribute money for the animal shelter. All those dogs and cats without homes. The animals need good food, you pleaded with your peers. Another of your fundraising efforts for the soup kitchen. When you were twelve, you volunteered there on Saturdays and served a hot meal to the homeless. I didn't approve, too worried about all those loose-ends men. People wanted to be near you. You drew them toward you, somehow. At least once a month you came home without something, a coat, a scarf, gloves, socks, you gave these things away. Are you listening? Or have you slipped away from me into a hidden seam I can't cross to? Don't turn away. I won't rave about you or tell you what you could have been. I won't say you are made of stars. I am brimming with memories, stored up, unknowingly, spilling out of me. I thought I'd forgotten them, but I haven't.

She stops. Gasps as she realizes what is happening. A life is passing before her eyes—Brigitte's life. As if Hanne will never see her again, and she is left with only memories. Hanne's eyes well up with tears. Faster now, she speaks faster to Brigitte, as if to keep her close. In those boxes is your version of Camus's story. You rewrote it, remember? You had the teacher go after the prisoner and guide him to freedom. It was his duty, you wrote. What he needed to do to remain human.

Yes, I have your objects, the things you said don't matter, that you'd rather live without. They belong to the life you renounced. But an object is a bridge to memory, and memory is a stored experience, something lived—the constitution of a life. Memories upon memories weave together into a fabric of a life. You are woven into me, me from whence you came. And I live inside it. Please. All I want is to sit beside you. You don't need to say a word to me.

She can hear Tomas breathing.

"She's at the end of the earth, Mom," says Tomas, his voice weary. "A remote village in India."

Chapter Twenty-One

MORE THAN THIRTY HOURS LATER, she stumbles off the plane and is bombarded by screeching tires, jackhammers, sirens, loud-speakers blasting music, shouts, rumbling engines, and hordes of people. It is Delhi and it's sunny and sticky hot and noisy and the air smells of diesel fumes and burning garbage. She has no interest in peering aghast at the poverty, no interest in anything but seeing her daughter, who has transported herself into the countryside. Hanne hails a taxi. She does not speak Hindi, Garhwali, Urdu, or Punjabi, but fortunately her young driver knows enough English.

He cranks up his radio, blasting American rock and roll, and heads into the hustle of traffic: cars, motorcycles, rickshaws, bikes, oxen, starving dogs, and emaciated cows wandering the sidewalks and streets. It is a collision of civilization—if it can be called that—and rural life.

When he stops at a traffic light and turns off the engine, a charge of alarm—this is not where she wants to be. He must see her panicked expression because he tells her it'll be a while, twenty minutes, maybe longer before the light changes, and he must save gas or he'll never make any money.

From her window, she watches a pack of scrawny boys dig through a ten-foot mountain of garbage. One boy wearing only a T-shirt and dirty underwear drags to the sidewalk an old bicycle tire. Another waves in the air a bent steel spoon, as if he's just won a magnificent trophy. Orphans fending for themselves? Or sent out to scrounge for scraps for their families? A boy retrieves a chair missing a leg, along with a torn blanket, a bit of frayed red carpet. When one of the boys finds a two-meter-long copper pipe, he holds it triumphantly above his head and dances in a circle. If one's standards drop, if one has no standards, anything, it seems, can be salvaged.

Before she left, she had packaged up her new translation of Kobayashi's novel and sent it to him with a letter. *Dear Kobayashi, I want to apologize. I see now how much I distorted your story, turning it into something it was not. You said I should be ashamed, and I am. In an attempt at recompense, I re-translated your novel. I don't expect you to use it, but I wanted you to know I believe I understand your story now. Jiro, his tortured heart, his immense loss that reverberates throughout, coloring everything. Again, my sincerest apology. Hanne Schubert.*

The light changes and the driver revs his engine and the music blares, joining the cacophony of noise, as they creep along to the outskirts of town, to the train station. After paying the driver, and with the heat pressing down, she elbows her way through the crowds waiting for the trains, sidestepping a large gathering of monkeys picking through a garbage can. She purchases her train ticket and, much later, collapses in a window seat, drowsily watching through the haze the farms speed by, the haystacks—or huts, she can't tell—the fields of sugar cane, and brown cows along the railroad track.

She's fifty-three years old, soon to be fifty-four in a matter of months, but she feels one hundred. She suspends her thoughts, her worry that Brigitte will refuse to see her. The point is to cross from A to B. It is one thing that is possible, one thing she can do, though it's taking nearly every ounce of her energy. She sees the shadow of her face in the window. She looks oddly serene. Perhaps because she is doing what she must do, she has no choice in the matter. Though she suspects it's because she is so tired.

Five hours later, when the train screeches and blows its whistle, she emerges bleary-eyed. Green tree-covered hills surround a green valley and she smells luscious water in the air. It's cooler here, at least, but not by much. The Ganges River flows through this city. Haridwar, she learned, is Hindi for Gateway to God.

Another taxi. This time the driver with glossy black hair and sparkling black eyes speaks only Urdu, and it takes a while to find another driver to translate her directions—please she'd like to be driven to what is called the Center for Higher Living and Thought.

The taxi driver nods, smiles, and says something. The other driver translates: "You are here for pilgrimage. Haridwar is one of the seven holy cities of Hindusim. Everyone comes for pilgrimage. You too?"

"Yes," she says. Of sorts.

"Foreigners come for the Ganges to wash away their sins and meditation and moksha." Moksha, says the translator, is nirvana.

Moksha, she is sure, is not for her in this lifetime.

As he drives, he chatters on in Urdu, and she slumps in the back, staring out the window. A spidery crack stretches across half the windshield, making it seem like she's looking at the world through a different lens. She's never wanted to come to India, never had a desire to explore the heart of the Hindu world. Too hot, too much suffering and despair. Naked, hungry children on the street. Dying children, abandoned children. Things that are unacceptable are eventually, resignedly accepted.

They pass by the green Ganges and men in rags along the roadside, pushing carts selling papayas and popcorn, and a stream of souvenir shops with colorful cloth lanterns, sandals, silk and cotton for saris and churidars. The perfect tourist destination for hungry souls, she thinks. Yoga and spiritual retreats are offered, like items on a menu. Her daughter is here, among the hungry souls.

She smells a hint of sewage, but the air is cleaner here than in Delhi. The taxi crosses over a bridge, with the Ganges calm and quiet below, then turns down a bumpy dirt road, with cows grazing in tall grasses.

To the ends of the earth, she thinks.

Up ahead must be the compound of Higher Living and Thought. A temple made of cracking white sandstone, the edges softened because large chunks have fallen off, along with many of the orange roof tiles. A cluster of small buildings surrounds the main temple in a U shape. In the center of the plaza is blood-red dirt. As the taxi pulls up, a plume of red dust rises up and surrounds it. Hanne steps out as if she's floated in on a blustery red cloud.

She hears the sound of children. She pays the driver and drags her one piece of luggage into a small building that has its door swung open wide. Fortunately, the frowning woman whom Hanne met long ago in France has been replaced by a young Indian girl in a white robe who smiles shyly at Hanne and places her palms together, bowing slightly. Hanne says she is here to see Brigitte. The girl looks at her, curiously, as if to say "Who?"

Has Brigitte gone? Did she know Hanne was coming and fled? Then it occurs to her: "Nivedita," says Hanne. "The woman named Nivedita."

The girl smiles brightly. "You're here for a blessing?"

A blessing? Hanne explains she is the mother of Nivedita.

The girl looks at her wide-eyed, as if it never occurred to her that Brigitte had such an earthly thing as a mother, and motions to a chair. "You have come so far. America, yes? Please sit. Rest your feet."

What a kind girl. Hanne moves away from the window and positions herself near the oscillating fan.

The girl, who introduces herself as Aruna, says "Welcome." She smiles shyly. "Nivedita taught me English."

"Wonderful," says Hanne.

She will bring Nivedita to Hanne.

While cooler than Delhi, the heat is still oppressive. She supposes one eventually acclimates, but she's soaked with sweat. The fan does little to alleviate the heat. She mops her forehead with her sleeve, slips off her shoes and presses her nylon-covered feet onto the cool tile floor. But that is not enough. She opens the top buttons of her blouse, leans over and strips off her nylons, letting her pale legs breathe. She drifts, observing the slow drip of her thoughts. She is here. She will or she will not see her daughter. Or rather, her daughter will or will not see her. She packed only a few things, unsure how long she'd be here—a day? A week? As Tomas cautioned, there is no predicting what Brigitte will do.

The air is a tangible presence, adhering to her skin, and the heat heavy with the smell of cows, hay, dirt, and sweat, her sweat. Sounds drift into the small room. Laughter, feet running by, the bleating of a sheep, the slosh of water in a bucket. Thirsty, she realizes she is thirsty, her throat parched.

A girl, maybe five, with big brown eyes, pokes her head through the open door and stares at Hanne, her mouth open. What does she see? An ugly old white woman with ghostly white legs? And what does Hanne see? A beautiful girl, drenched in youth, a whole life stretched out in front of her. Hanne smiles, which elicits a quick smile from the girl, who darts away.

She closes her eyes and listens to the hum and rhythm of the fan. All this way, what if her daughter refuses her? The rupture declared irreparable, Brigitte will not grant two minutes to acknowledge Hanne's presence.

"I can't guarantee anything," Tomas said.

"I didn't think you could," said Hanne.

"You'll be traveling for nearly two days, Mom. But I suppose that won't deter you."

Stubbornness had nothing to do with it. And she did not expect to show up and all to be forgiven. Nor did she assume a heart-warming reunion. She told Tomas she would cross all seven continents if given the chance to see Brigitte again.

Now minutes go by. I feel so old, Brigitte. You have every right to turn me away, to go about your life as you've seen fit. But I beg of you, please do not. Does this sound like a plea? I suppose it is.

A fly circles around Hanne's head. She tries to shoo it away, but it does no good. She looks out at the bright sun and sees a reddish brown cow eating hay, its tail twitching, flicking away black flies. A small starling lands on its head. For a moment she is deeply pleased by the sight and thinks of Moto. No five-year or ten-year plan, is that what he meant? A life made up of only these moments stitched together? Would that ever be enough for her? Not a translator, not anything, just a soul existing, living off a web of beauty and sorrow? If she is allowed to see Brigitte, will the sight of her be enough?

Finally Aruna appears and, with her head bowed and an expression of embarrassment, says Brigitte cannot see her right away. Unfortunately, she has a full schedule. Very busy. Hanne will have to wait until tomorrow morning. If Hanne would like to rest, she can show her to a vacant room. They are reserved for visitors.

Chapter Twenty-Two

THE ROOM'S SPARSENESS REMINDS HANNE of the ryokan. Or a monk's cell. Or a prison's. Only a twin-sized bed, a faded wood nightstand, a lamp, and one round window too high to look out of. With her head bowed, Aruna asks if she might need anything.

Don't feel ashamed, my dear girl. I am just relieved I wasn't sent away. "A glass of water would be wonderful," says Hanne.

Aruna quickly returns with a pitcher of water and a cup, along with slices of homemade bread and whipped butter. Hanne thanks her and empties the glass. A visitor only. She relinquished her status as mother when she sent her daughter away, and now she will be treated as someone visiting. To visit, to go to see, to avenge, to visit the sins of the father upon his children, to afflict, to reside as a guest. It is something. It is a beginning.

In the morning, Aruna appears, wearing a clean white robe. After she shows Hanne to the shower, she is to bring Hanne to the prayer hall. Hanne rushes through her bathing—an outdoor stall by the hay field—dresses and tells herself to accept whatever Brigitte has to give. Anger, frustration, rage, sorrow, self-pity, Hanne will nod and say she understands. She is here, that's what matters.

Hanne follows the girl outside to the large white sandstone building. Before entering, Aruna removes her shoes and points to Hanne's. "I'm sorry. Full of impurities," she says. Hanne takes them off, padding to the tile entrance in bare feet.

Inside, it is cavernous and dark. Thankfully, the air is cooler and it smells of incense and candle wax. Rows of pews fill most of the room. At the front, a window lets in a stream of sunlight. The girl bows and leaves. Is that Brigitte up at the front? If so, Hanne does not recognize her.

The woman does not come at once. She is lighting candles, one by one, about twenty or so, taking her time, as if she's never seen a flame before. As if it is the most astonishing thing. Hanne sits on a pew and watches the match touch the wick and burst into a flame. Two insignificant things coming together to create fire. Is that what is about to happen? Hanne and Brigitte meeting again, Brigitte igniting with fury?

Eventually the woman strides down the aisle toward Hanne. She wears a flowing white robe, but it does not conceal her skeletal frame. Nor does it does it hide her head, which is tan and bald.

Six years since they've seen each other. The world instantly stills. Brigitte stands in front of Hanne, erect, her hands clasped in front of her. Despite her thin body, her daughter feels sturdy and solid, as impermeable as a brick wall. Is this who she has become now? Or is she bracing herself? Hanne is transfixed. Her gaze bounces from Brigitte's hands, still held tight, to her shiny bald head. Has she become a monk, required to shave her head? Wear these robes? Gone, too, is her smooth, pale skin, which is now deeply tanned with a fan of faint lines at the corners of her pale green eyes and on her forehead. The backs of her hands are mottled with brown spots—too much sun?

There will be, it seems, no embrace. Brigitte's hands remain a circle unto themselves. "How are you?" says Hanne. A stupid thing to say. But what? Something catches in Hanne's throat. "Thank you for seeing me. I'm very grateful." She's about to say more, but she can't stand it any longer. She steps toward Brigitte and hugs her. She can feel Brigitte's bony ribs.

"Welcome," says Brigitte, gently pulling out of the embrace. She bows slightly, turns and heads to the front of the big hall. Hanne assumes she is to follow. When she reaches the front pew, Brigitte takes a seat. Hanne sits beside her, this woman who sits with perfect posture, who feels like a stone.

But that's not right. She is solid, as if what was once tumultuous and chaotic inside has settled into something hard. But not sharp, with dangerous angles. Water comes to mind. Can water be solid without turning into ice? It's what Hanne always wanted for Brigitte, to have the strength to weather life's hardships. And India is full of hardship. At least she's given Brigitte something worthwhile after all. "Have you been living here a while?" says Hanne, groping for something to say. She hadn't thought beyond this moment, beyond seeing Brigitte.

"Three years," she says. They first set up a school for the local children, she says, then an orphanage, a small outpatient clinic, a soup kitchen. The needs are so great, each year it seems a new service must be added and more funds raised. "We are here to serve, love, give, purify and meditate," says Brigitte. Her voice is formal and controlled, as if she's given this talk many times, perhaps to philanthropists and other visitors. A breeze comes through the window at the front of the room, bringing with it Brigitte's smell, something starchy and sharp and sour.

"I'll give you a tour," says Brigitte, standing.

Hanne almost weeps with relief. There will be no outbursts or vengeful words. She will not be sent home. A fact, frankly, she marvels at. Her daughter feels bigger than her personal history. She has surpassed her petty concerns, it seems, her resentments, her hatreds. As if she outgrew herself and now—Hanne despises invoking a cliché—Brigitte is full of love, enlightened. If moksha is to be had, it is for her daughter. Hanne will be given a tour.

Hanne follows obediently. Like Renzo's dog, she thinks. She will be like Morsel, pleased for any attention, waiting attentively by Brigitte's feet, tail wagging. And when Brigitte is preoccupied or uninterested, she will collapse on the floor or head outside and run madly in circles, as if chasing her tail. It will be enough.

Brigitte takes her to the one-room school, where thirty or more children, upon seeing Brigitte, stand and say "Good morning, Honorable Nivedita!" Smiling, Brigitte bows to them, and they proceed to sing a song in English.

It reminds Hanne of her years spent in Catholic school. Her parents were not religious, but they approved of the rigors of the school. When one of the crotchety old nuns poked her head into a classroom, if you did not politely call out "Good Morning!" in a sunshine voice, you were summarily whacked on the knuckles with a ruler and sent to the corner to stand and recite a thousand Hail Marys. Hanne didn't complain, convinced her parents would say that one must endure. Her mother one day saw Hanne's swollen knuckles and surprised Hanne by declaring that she would no longer attend such an abominable school. Hanne doubts that such disciplinary measures are invoked here, though. The politeness feels sweet, genuine.

The dormitory smells of bleach, and underneath that is the odor of urine. Neat little cots lined up in a row. About forty of them, their sheets pulled tight and tucked under thin mattresses. Orphans, Brigitte tells her. "I can't ever turn one away." Each cot has a small nightstand where the children keep small trinkets—bracelets, a blue bead, a miniature doll, a race car. A nest of private belongings. The kitchen is set up to make huge meals with big pots and pans, chopping areas, a colossal refrigerator that hums.

Brigitte's room is as bare as Hanne's. The only accessory is a bookshelf and a hotplate with a tarnished tea kettle.

"So much accomplished in three years," says Hanne as they head back to the prayer hall. "And your role here?"

Brigitte raises an eyebrow. "My role?" Her voice is full of wonder, as if she's baffled at the question. "I live here."

Hanne thinks she hears a rumble of anger. But maybe not. Maybe she's reading something into Brigitte's response that isn't there.

As they enter the dark prayer hall, Hanne rattles on about Tomas and Anne, and her two nieces. She refrains from saying Sasha reminds her of Brigitte when she was a girl, her aggressive curiosity, her intellect. She doesn't ask: Have you ever met them? She doesn't really care. Tomas, his family, her fall down the stairs, Japan, Moto, all of it feels like a previous life.

Brigitte walks to the front of the temple and lights incense. The place is empty. She returns to the pew and sits beside Hanne. Minutes of silence seem to tick by. Occasionally the silence is interrupted by the spit and sizzle of a candle, the scratch of a branch against the window.

Hanne draws a long breath. "I've come to apologize, Brigitte. I don't think I understood you. Who you were, what you truly needed and wanted. I made mistakes. So many of them, I've lost count. I've come to say I'm sorry."

"I've waited a long time to hear those words." Brigitte looks down at her hands. "Tossed into the wilderness and forgotten." Then, "I didn't mean to say that."

"Whatever you want to say." Hanne takes a deep breath. "If you'd had contact with me, told me where you were, I could have apologized long ago."

Brigitte raises an eyebrow. "It couldn't have happened earlier, because you didn't feel this way." Her tone is matter-of-fact. "It's not necessarily a bad thing, you know. If it weren't for you, I wouldn't be here. Wouldn't have found this." She looks directly at Hanne now. "You've gone through hardship, haven't you? Your voice. Your eyes. I'm sorry it's been so hard, but it's brought you here."

Silence. A long silence. Will Brigitte declare the meeting over? Good to see you, now I'm on my way? Hanne feels herself try to come up with something more to say. The distance between them feels like miles and miles. But then her daughter's breathing catches her attention. It's coming in short bursts. "Are you all right?"

Brigitte closes her eyes. "No. Unfortunately I'm not. I'm afraid I've made Tomas even more anxious."

In that instant, everything realigns—Brigitte's bald head, her frail body, her ribs.

"What?" says Hanne.

"Cancer."

"Cancer?"

Lymph nodes, now nearly everywhere. She's tried different treatments. "But I've had enough of that."

"You've had enough of that?" Hanne can't seem to do anything but repeat what her daughter has said. Her mind is spinning wildly, as if someone has snuck up behind her and hit her on the head. But no—that call from Tomas long ago. Brigitte is sick. And then nothing. Her heart hammers away, as she tries to think of something to say.

"No more experts or doctors," says Brigitte, her voice calm, steady. "I don't want to spend my days that way."

"But it seems you have a good life here," says Hanne, speaking rapidly, trying to find the right words. "Why not do more good work?"

Brigitte remains silent.

Hanne has her English back, her Japanese, and a handful of German, but none of it is of help. She has no words.

"This vessel may be dying," says Brigitte, running her hands down the front of her robe, "but my spirit is alive and strong and I can still be of service to others. I know you don't believe in God, but I do. God's ways are mysterious and profound and I don't pretend to understand why my time here is so short. But I do know more treatments mean more days in the hospital, more days feeling sick from the treatments. I want to spend my remaining time here. Here is my life's work. Here is where I am needed. This is my home."

Maybe Brigitte has fallen out of life as Moto fell off his stage. No longer able to feel, she is tired of going through the endless motions. Everything is used up, dried out, the meaning of life washed up. Not much difference between life and death, so why not throw herself into death's maw? "Assuming there is such a thing as a God," says Hanne, "why did he give us a mind that can figure out medicines and procedures to prolong life? Surely you feel you are doing good things here. That you've made a life that is valuable and meaningful to you. Why not continue?"

She goes on, money is no object, whatever needs to be done will be done, but as she babbles on, thinking she'll sell her apartment, her car, everything to raise money, she senses that she is losing. One of the candles burns out, and a spiral of smoke rises to the ceiling.

"We also have minds that know too well how to destroy and kill and demand more and more. It is never enough," says Brigitte. "The mind is never satisfied. Just because we can think of something does not give us license to act upon it. We're not God."

"But we are not talking about killing. We are discussing saving. Saving you."

"Yes, well, I think I've had enough of you trying to save me." Brigitte smiles patiently, but her voice has an edge to it. "I don't expect you to understand."

She was ready to accept it all, her daughter and her life, the years of silence. But this too? Hanne wants to cry. "Okay," she manages to say. "You're right. I'm sorry if I spoke out of turn." She wants to add: Please don't send me away.

Brigitte rubs her finger along her bottom lip. For a second, Brigitte is a child again who wanted Hanne to sit beside her on the couch while she read her book. And when Hanne didn't, when she was too busy, when she couldn't for whatever reason, she'd take a swatch of her hair and stroke the silkiness of it against her lip. A gesture to soothe herself. My poor child, she thinks, I'm failing you again, providing you no solace.

She's about to apologize again when forty or so children file into the prayer hall. Brigitte instantly reassembles her composure, her face now a mask of serenity. She climbs the four steps to the front stage, holding her head perfectly erect on her long neck, smiling. Her hands clasped in front of her, her two sandaled feet peeking out of the bottom of her robe, she looks like a pillar of strength. No one would guess she's sick, except for her excruciating thinness. But even that isn't much of an indicator, given the poverty here. The children are chattering excitedly, presumably because they have a visitor.

Brigitte raises her hands in the air and silence falls. Then she begins to speak. It's a language that Hanne does not know.

Hanne sits on the front pew, listening to her daughter say something, then the children's murmured response. Back and forth, Brigitte speaks, the children answer, an ebb and flow, a wave of sound washing up on shore. For a moment the waves are comforting. Whatever language they are speaking, it pulses with beautiful sounds and rhythms. Her daughter's face is rapt.

Hanne feels her face tighten, her heart clench. How can she bear it? But she must. Did Tomas know? Why didn't he tell her to prepare her? But how can a mother prepare for this? She must do more than bear it. She must accept it as her daughter has. Hiding her face in her hands, she finally lets herself weep.

After the service, when the prayer hall is quiet again, Brigitte stands on the stage, her face still serene, but her eyelids droop, her body sags. Worn out from the battle being waged inside, thinks Hanne, and everything else that must be done around here. Hanne quickly climbs the steps, takes Brigitte's elbow, and helps her down. She has the overwhelming desire to hold Brigitte in her arms, sing her a lullaby, rock her to sleep.

But there is no time for that.

"Lunch," announces Brigitte. "You are our honored guest."

In the dining hall, Hanne meets some of the other teachers and spiritual leaders. After their silent prayers, they turn out to be a happy group, full of smiles and laughter. Hanne is not hungry. Ever since she arrived, she's had an upset stomach. She sits on a hard bench, hunched over her plate of rice and something she can't identify, taking small bites. Brigitte is at the end of the table, laughing with one of the women. Nivedita, she learns, speaks Hindi, Urdu, Punjabi, and some of the local dialects. She is one of the top gurus, in part because she can communicate with the Indians, who come here to worship, and also the many foreigners.

So this is what she's done with her talent for language, thinks Hanne. How honorable. Certainly this lively group doesn't want to lose Brigitte. Are they pleading with her to try a new treatment? Gather herself and put up a fight? An older woman who speaks English sits next to Hanne and goes on and on about Nivedita, her dedication, her intelligence, her endless toil. "She is our ambassador to the world." The woman is from southern India and she wears colorful bangles on both arms. Nivedita, she tells Hanne, built the barn with the help of a local farmhand. She set up the school and the lesson plans. They are teaching the children how to speak English, French, Spanish. Of course there is math and science, poetry and literature. There are plans to refurbish the main temple. To enlarge the garden.

"Nivedita recently wrote a grant and received money for a new building."

A life of honorable labor and virtuous projects right up to the very end. Isn't that noble? Hanne interrupts. "You must know Brigitte is very ill."

The woman smiles and nods. "Yes, she faces death like a saint. She is an example for all of us. Nivedita never rests." The woman laughs. "She said she learned that from you. Do not rest until you are exhausted. It must be earned."

This is Hanne's inheritance to her daughter? If so, how pitiful.

The woman leans toward Hanne. "It must be difficult for you. But your daughter is not the one to console you."

The woman, of course, is right. The shock of it, Hanne must absorb it. She must not let herself fall to pieces.

By the time lunch is over, the room has turned hot and humid and Hanne can no longer keep her eyes open. She looks to the head of the table, where Brigitte, her voice gentle, is speaking in one of her new languages to a small girl. Hanne rises. It seems in an instant, Brigitte is there, taking her to the small cottage that houses visitors.

"I'm impressed with your new languages," says Hanne.

A faint knowing smile graces Brigitte's lips, as if she's thinking: of course such a thing would impress you. It reminds her of the many looks Moto gave her. "It's in service for others."

Her daughter's veiled rebuke. And she is quite right to do so, thinks Hanne. "Yes, of course."

She's glad that Brigitte doesn't linger. Because Hanne is still shaken. Because she doesn't know what else she might say that will offend her. Because everything she thinks of saying will surely offend. How long does she have? A year? Months? Weeks? For a long time, Hanne floats in and out of sleep because of the heat. It feels as if she's been dunked in a tub of hot water; all her clothes are wet and so is the bottom sheet. If she is to accept Brigitte's decision, she must learn to see it as Brigitte does.

And how does she see it?

Brigitte flew to Paris or Berlin or somewhere for treatments. Long days in the hospital, poked, prodded, chemicals poured into her body, and woken up at all hours of the night. She's suffered one doctor after another, and she's had enough. Yes, Hanne can do this, she can imagine what Brigitte has lived through. She's sick of that smell in hospital corridors, a stench of decaying flesh hidden by cleaners. Sick of feeling useless, used up. Feeling imprisoned. She wants life—even if it means ushering in death far too soon. Like Moto, Brigitte wants the full spectrum of being human. Including facing death. There will be no distractions, no attempt to thwart it. If so, thinks Hanne, how resolute, how courageous, how strong.

But it's her daughter.

Hanne watches the dance of shadows on the white wall. Eventually she falls asleep and dreams Brigitte is standing at the threshold of her door, but when Hanne beckons her to come in, she shakes her head, refusing to cross into the room. She has work to do. When Hanne finally wakes, she hears a bell clanging, the shuffle of feet, children laughing, murmuring. India. Northern India. At the foothills of the Himalayas. Another prayer service.

Hanne makes herself get out of bed. She throws cold water on her face and heads to the prayer hall. As she steps, little grasshoppers fly up from the tall grasses. Her stomach is a tight ball. The long road of grief. Moto's words. But this grief, she thinks, will never end. She sits for the hour of prayer, trying to lift the heavy weight off her heart by watching her daughter who is up on stage full of grace.

In the morning, before the heavy blanket of heat descends, Hanne walks to the end of the dirt driveway. The sun has yet to rise above the green hills. In the quiet while the world still sleeps, Hanne hears water flowing. The Ganges, most likely. It's beautiful here, the lush green, the birds, the astonishing moisture in the air. A good life, thinks Hanne, but then catches herself. A life that is ending far too soon.

When she heads back, the sun is up and already scorching. Hanne finds Brigitte and two others out in the field, trying to get the rusted tractor started. The hood is open and the three are peering at the engine. The air smells of gasoline and cut hay. Instantly, Hanne is drenched in sweat. Brigitte, in a big straw hat, looks cool.

"How come you aren't melting in this heat?" Hanne says.

Brigitte looks up from the manual. "You adapt, eventually."

One of the women picks up a frayed red wire. It seems these women have to figure out everything by themselves. Finally a wire is connected to another wire and the engine turns and the tractor exhales blue smoke. There is a chorus of cheers. Brigitte says she must see how lunch is coming along. They expect sixty or so people, not including the children. Hanne watches as Brigitte whisks away. Hanne wanders out to a big tree and sits for a while in the shade, but there is no relief from the heat. She heads to the kitchen, where she finds Aruna fixing a tray for Brigitte.

"Please let me," says Hanne.

Brigitte is in her room, stretched out on her bed, her eyes closed. A fan slowly churns the hot air. Hanne quietly sets down the tray of tea and sugar cubes and turns to leave.

Brigitte stirs, opens her eyes. Her face is pale, her eyes weary.

"Did I wake you?"

"Just resting."

Hanne pulls up a chair beside her bed. She sees the dark circles under Brigitte's eyes.

"I've been thinking," says Brigitte.

Hanne sits up. I'll take you wherever you want to go. Money is no object. The best care. Your hair will once again be long and

293

dark. We will take our time, get to know each other again, burn down the bad memories.

"Have you seen the way the dogs are treated? It breaks my heart."

Hanne barely holds her tongue.

Brigitte tells her the other day she saw a man hit a skinny old dog with a stick. Broke its leg. "I tried to catch it so we could take care of it, but it limped away so fast. Poor thing. Forever scared of humans."

"We can be a cruel lot."

Brigitte goes on, talking about how they could set up an animal shelter.

The light pours in through the open door.

Brigitte closes her eyes. "I can't keep my eyes open. I get these waves of tiredness."

Without thinking, Hanne reaches over and puts her hand on Brigitte's forehead. Brigitte opens her eyes. Sits up. "Do you know how many times I wished you'd been there to do that?" Her voice is strained, as if she's holding back a flood of emotions. "Your hand on my forehead. I was going to die without ever speaking to you again. Do you know that? I told myself it was because you meant nothing to me. The past is the past." She laughs bitterly. "That's something you'd say, and it isn't true. With you here, I feel everything I thought I'd put to rest. My anger and sadness and those long dark years of loneliness. I've worked so hard to forgive or at least forget, but right now it seems I've gotten nowhere." She wipes her eyes and shakes her head. "I wanted everything to be peaceful at the end."

"I'm so sorry, Brigitte. I've not been the person I wanted to be," says Hanne.

"Few of us are."

"I've always loved you, even if it didn't seem that way. You are my daughter."

Brigitte remains silent, but Hanne feels her listening closely. When a bell chimes, Brigitte rises. Hanne stands and finds she is trembling. It's time for school.

Hanne follows her into the classroom and takes a seat in the back. Brigitte is teaching the children basic French. Hanne tries to pay attention, but she keeps hearing Brigitte's words, *Those long dark years of loneliness.* Hanne's heart is tender, bruised, as if it's been dropped. When they break into small groups, a small girl with huge brown eyes comes over to Hanne.

"Please, can you read French?" She shows Hanne a book of fairy tales. Hanne nods, all the while watching her daughter speak French to a group of five children. The girl pulls a chair beside her. Hanne asks her to pick her favorite. The girl turns to *The Princess and the Pea* and Hanne begins to read.

It is night. Aruna finds Hanne in her room. Maybe Hanne would like to see the Ganges river worship ceremony? "Foreigners enjoy this," says Aruna.

"Is Brigitte all right?" says Hanne.

Aruna pauses. "She is so tired sometimes."

She hopes that's what it is, but worries it's something else: Brigitte needs a break from her, a permanent break. *I was going to die without ever speaking to you again.*

Aruna hands her a scarf to wear, as women must cover their heads for the ceremony. They head down the main road, and as they get closer to the river, Hanne hears the low roar of a crowd, along with bells and a loudspeaker playing Indian music, music in praise of Ganga Maiya and Shiva, says Aruna.

One big spiritual circus, thinks Hanne. Look at all the trinkets for sale—colorful powders and stones and necklaces and flower petals and candles. How could anyone find this otherworldly? A connection to anything other than the claustrophobic crush of flesh?

Hanne can't see the river, only the throngs of Indians clamoring along its banks. She follows Aruna, who weaves her way through the crowd. Finally they reach the water. Hundreds of little fires are floating down the river, as if all the stars have fallen out of the sky. The offerings are made from stitched-together banana leaves, says Aruna. Nestled in the cup of the leaf are red and pink flower petals, a small wick lamp.

"Maybe you make an offering?" says Aruna.

An offering. Latin, *offerre*, to present, bestow, a sacrifice given as part of worship. Worship of what? Who? To whomever, whatever, is cutting short her daughter's life?

"No, thank you," says Hanne.

Aruna pays her rupees and sets her boat into the water. They watch it float under a bridge, then it's gone.

Back in her room, Hanne sits on her bed. The children are asleep, the insects buzz and the cows and horses stir. She pulls out a notebook and a pen.

> *Dear Brigitte,*
>
> *I'm writing this letter in case my presence has disquieted your heart and you ask me to leave. I beg that you don't, but if you do, there are things I must say.*
>
> *I am in awe of your remarkable probity, the largess of your heart. You have your father's spirit, his gentleness, his big heart. Now that I look back on your life, I see how it was leading here, exactly to this point. An exquisite outpouring of generosity, service, empathy, and kindness. One of my greatest failings is that I didn't see it, you. But now I do. Your path of generosity is astonishingly beautiful.*

I always wished you'd have courage and resilience so that life's hardship would not leave debilitating scars. And here you are, overflowing with courage, tending to so many others, while facing your own death. But I should have seen this, too. Unlike me, you followed your grief when Dad died, allowing it take you wherever it must, even to the most desolate places.

I have many regrets, but my deepest regret is sending you away. You spoke of loneliness. I, too, have been terribly lonely for you. Those long years of silence when I missed out on your company, when I wasn't there to comfort you. I will never forgive myself, and that's just something I will have to live with.

I'll say this one more time and then won't speak of it again. I bitterly wish you had more time. It's a selfish desire—I wish to luxuriate in the presence of you. Just to take delight in your existence. Existence, I've come to learn, is an astonishing thing. If you were granted more time, I would put my hand on your forehead over and over to make up for those lost years.

Mom

Hanne reads it over. How inadequate, these words. She thinks of Noh and feels a new appreciation—its refusal to rest on words to convey emotion. If she's allowed to stay, she'll have many ways to show Brigitte how she feels. And if she's asked to leave? This will have to do.

At dawn, Hanne wanders around the compound, which is just stirring to life. She passes by the dormitories, the classroom, a two-room health clinic with five chairs in the waiting room.

The barn for the cows and goats. The compound is clean, neat, organized, but what Hanne mainly sees is the endless manual labor required to keep the place running, the labor her daughter must offer up every day. When she wanders into the kitchen, she finds Brigitte scrubbing dishes. On every counter, there are stacks of dishes from last night's dinner. The kitchen smells of curry and coconut.

Brigitte doesn't notice her right away. She has muscular arms and a fierce look of concentration on her face. A singular focus on the task at hand. Without hair, her face is rounder than Hanne remembered. Her thinness makes her cheekbones more pronounced, like two balls. She looks content, even happy doing the simple task of washing a dish.

"Good morning," says Hanne, forcing a cheery tone. She comes over beside Brigitte and picks up a sponge. "It's quite a place here." She feels like she keeps repeating herself.

Brigitte motions to the dirty dishes and says the dishwasher broke last night. "Another thing we must figure out how to fix."

"You seem pretty good at it."

"Practice. Lots of practice."

Hanne begins on the stack of plates. A mountain of mangoes waits to be peeled and sliced. There is a long silence between them, one that is relaxed, calm, peaceful. The morning air is cool and the birds are singing. Through the window above the sink, Hanne sees an ox harnessed to a plow. A young boy walks beside it, talking to it, whispering in its ear, perhaps urging it to pull the heavy contraption. He's trying to get it to go around a large tree.

"How does it feel to know you are dying?" Hanne is startled by her question. "If you don't want to talk about it—"

Brigitte stops scrubbing, lets the water run. "Some days everything is so vibrant, so precious. The slightest thing. The way the light flows through a leaf, the smell of dirt, the sound of rain on the roof. The other day, I spent the longest time watching a monkey crack open a walnut. I think, this is heaven. Everything is astonishingly beautiful. But other days, I'm scared. I'm scared because it's the unknown. I don't know what I'm crossing over into. Oh, I know what I've read about the afterlife, but I've never experienced it." She laughs at herself.

It's the most honest moment they've had so far.

"I couldn't do it," says Hanne. "What you're doing."

"We're different, that's all." Brigitte looks at Hanne, as if to make sure Hanne heard her.

"You're a saint," says Hanne, turning over the word in her mind. From Latin, *sanctus*, meaning "holy, consecrated." What she means to say is that her daughter is exemplary, extraordinary, far more evolved than most, including herself.

Brigitte smiles faintly. "No. Far from it."

The bell chimes. Prayer time again. Brigitte turns the water off and dries her hands. Hanne learned at lunch that Brigitte gives all the sermons, six a day.

Hanne skips the sermon and wanders out to the barn. The barn her daughter built with the help of a farmhand. It's a solid, sturdy post frame construction. A high roof, a loft and eight stalls. Hiro would be proud. He was always enthralled with architecture.

The woman who sat next to Hanne at lunch comes into the barn, bows to Hanne, and dips a bucket into the water barrel. She goes to each stall and refills the cows' bowls. When she is done, she comes over to Hanne, pulls a bandana from her pocket, and unwraps two biscuits. She hands one to Hanne.

"Your daughter has a strong spirit," she says. "So wise. That's what will help her. And a circle of people who love her dearly."

"Maybe that circle could help out more. Have her do less."

"They're doing what she wants. She wants to be part of life. You can understand that, can't you? Here, life requires a lot of work. She wants life until the very end." The woman tosses new hay around the barn, then comes over to Hanne. "Do you intend to stay? We could find you a job. Brigitte always said you were a hard worker. That you're a well-regarded translator."

"That was a lifetime ago."

"We've got plenty to do here. Work from dawn to dusk."

And what would she do? She knows none of the languages spoken here except English. Perhaps teach English or French or German. But that's not what the woman had in mind. She hands Hanne a bucket of soapy water. "If you want, you can scrub out the stalls."

Hanne spends the rest of the afternoon in the barn, on her knees, scrubbing cow shit from the walls. It's just as well. Brigitte, it seems, is busy the rest of the day. When the six stalls are clean, Hanne finds Aruna in the garden. After much pestering, Aruna agrees to let Hanne help. The soil is rich, heavily fertilized with manure. It seems every kind of grain is grown here, along with sugar cane and potatoes. Hanne points to a potato and Aruna tells her the word for it in Hindi and Urdu. We feed many of the villagers, she says, in addition to the schoolchildren, most of whom are orphans. In the field, she sees one of the women in white robes tickling a small boy. His laughter carries through the still air. A feeling of goodwill sweeps through Hanne.

Brigitte is not at dinner. "Receiving those who come for a blessing," someone tells Hanne.

Hanne goes to bed early, tired from the physical labor, but it's a welcome tiredness that sends her into a deep sleep. In the middle of the night, she's jarred awake by a vision of Brigitte cleaning, giving sermons, but her flesh is gone. Only her skeleton remains. Hanne grabs her bony wrist and tells her she must stop. Stop! Brigitte tersely shakes her head: "Go back to bed." Hanne looks around her white cell, breathing hard. What was most alarming about the dream, what most shook Hanne was that she complied—her shoulders stooped, she shuffled back to bed and fell asleep again.

In the morning, after the children have filed in, Hanne steps into the prayer hall and sits in the back. It seems the only way she's assured of seeing her daughter is by attending the services. She feels a dry pinch behind her eyes. She must have caught a cold, because her nose is runny. If she stayed on, how quickly could she learn these languages? And if she did, would these sermons mean something to her? Help her accept her daughter's slow demise? Can she watch as Brigitte becomes weaker and weaker and remain silent at her side? She looks at the thin points of her daughter's shoulders. Watches them rise and fall. Listens to the foreign language flowing from her dry lips.

Hanne closes her eyes and falls asleep. She wakes when she senses that someone is standing in front of her. It's Brigitte.

"I'm sorry," says Hanne. "The heat. I don't think I'm adapting."

"It doesn't happen that fast."

Brigitte waits while Hanne gathers herself, then tells her the schedule for the day. Breakfast next, classes to teach, prayers, more classes, prayers, lunch, class, prayers, and a walk to the Ganges, where they'll step into the river to cleanse and purify themselves.

The prayer hall is empty. In the cool darkness, Brigitte sits on the bench next to Hanne. When Hanne reaches over and rests her hand on her daughter's shoulder, she feels her daughter's body soften.

"I'd like to stay. Help out here," says Hanne, not swallowing her longing. "The garden. The barn. Anything. If you'll let me—"

Brigitte smiles. "I heard about the barn. I never thought I'd see the day."

Hanne laughs and Brigitte joins in. Something between them falls away. They sit for a while in the quiet. Hanne glances at Brigitte's hands and sees that her fingernails are chewed off, just as they were when she became frightened as a child. Whatever you want, I will do, thinks Hanne. There will be a point when you will be too weak to walk, to lift a cup of water to your lips. There will be no fight, only a slow, steady decline. If she is allowed to stay, this is what she must accept. What choice does she have?

"If only there was some way for your god to take me, not you," whispers Hanne.

"In the beginning, I did my fair share of bargaining, too."

When Brigitte rises, Hanne follows her up the stairs, onto the stage.

In the shadowy light, Brigitte gets down on her knees. "Will you pray with me?"

Hanne follows, huffing as she lowers herself onto one knee, then the other. Her joints ache. Everything aches. The prayer hall is silent, only the sound of children outside. She's on her knees because if she refuses, Brigitte might send her away, and if she asks to whom or what she should pray, to what cruel god who is curtailing her daughter's life too soon, Brigitte might send her away. If she pleads for Brigitte to save herself, she might send her away. So she blinks back her tears and says nothing. What choice does she really have?

The wind drops. The chatter is done. There is a moment of deep silence that seems to open up an enormous space around them, and Hanne looks at Brigitte without the haze of desire. This woman in front of her. The day's golden light pouring down on her clean white robe, her shiny bald head, her gentle eyes.

Brigitte takes both of Hanne's hands in hers. They are linked now, a bridge, her daughter's long, knobby fingers interlaced with her own. Brigitte's hands are calloused and strong, and they are gripping Hanne's. They are breathing in unison, breathing in the voices of the children, the rustle of the wind, the bloom of the fields.

When Brigitte begins to pray in her language, Hanne closes her eyes and listens closely, trying hard to understand.

Acknowledgments

I WOULD LIKE TO THANK THE following for their generous and invaluable help: my Japanese language sensei, Atsuko Sells, and also Hajime Ohno. I fear I will forget someone, but I'm very grateful to my readers, Ellen Sussman, Lalita Tademy, Elizabeth Stark, Rosemary Graham, Andreas Kriefall, Kate Brady, Michael Munson, Peter Allen, Lyn Motai, Izumi Motai, Tina Pohlman, Barbara Blasdel, and Gene Alexander. A special thanks to Marty Schuyler and Mollie Glick and Katie Hamblin. And in the end, no one deserves more thanks than Peter Seeger, my husband.

Several books were very important to me in my research: *After Babel: Aspects of Language & Translation*, by George Steiner, and *Performing Without A Stage: The Art of Literary Translation*, by

Robert Wechsler. Also important were *The Ink Dark Moon: Love Poems by Ono no Komachi and Izumi Shikibu, Women of the Ancient Court of Japan,* translated by Jane Hirshfield and Mariko Aratani, and *Japanese No Dramas,* edited and translated by Royall Tyler.